William Barrows, Making of America Project

The General

Twelve Nights in the Hunters' Camp

William Barrows, Making of America Project

The General
Twelve Nights in the Hunters' Camp

ISBN/EAN: 9783337053932

Printed in Europe, USA, Canada, Australia, Japan

Cover: Foto ©Raphael Reischuk / pixelio.de

More available books at **www.hansebooks.com**

THE HUNTERS' CAMP.   Fronti-piece.

THE GENERAL;

OR,

TWELVE NIGHTS

IN

THE HUNTERS' CAMP.

A NARRATIVE OF REAL LIFE.

ILLUSTRATED BY G. G. WHITE.

"To those who knew my BROTHER this book will doubtless bring back his image in many lights; for those who knew him not, I can only hope that it will make them wish that they had known him."

SCUDDER.

BOSTON:
LEE AND SHEPARD.
1869.

STEREOTYPED AT THE
BOSTON STEREOTYPE FOUNDRY,
19 Spring Lane.

EDITORIAL NOTE.

THIS volume is matter of fact, being the truthful records of the actual life of a real person. Knowing The General thoroughly, and the facts and incidents as here related while they were taking place, I persuaded him to write them out, and for this reason : There is a passion among the young for a kind of reading that is full of adventure and startling incidents. This desire has been gratified and unduly stimulated by overwrought fiction, and the manifestation of much low and unworthy character. As The General, in his eventful life, furnished rare and ample material for a truthful and useful book of adventures, it seemed a good thing to write it out for the young.

Here is a real case for their study, where one goes up from boyhood through difficulties and daring exploits and perils to a ripe manhood of intelligence, and usefulness, and honor. Much of his life was a real romance and heroism of the noblest kind, and the record of it must prove a healthful stimulus to every young reader, who has energy, and daring, and the fixed purpose to make his life noble. To such I dedicate the book.

The volume was planned on the shores of Swan Lake. The sketches of that excursion are true, and I was there mainly to prepare the way for what is now offered. I have taken a dramatic liberty in making The General tell there a nightly story. Volumes of stories were told around that memorable camp fire. He wrote out the twelve soon afterwards, substantially as here given.

It has been my conceit to vary his continuous narrative by sketches of each day, and experiences of my own at other times.

I trust I have not marred the picture in the framing. The frame, as the picture, is rustic, the style being of the wild and backwoods pattern.

I shall be happily content if my Preludes tempt any of my pale, Mondayish, clerical friends from the cloister, bookish life in which they are dying, to the grand hotels and promenades of tent and forest life for a season. For this we have good warrant. " Come ye yourselves apart into a desert place, and rest a while. . . . And they departed into a desert place privately."

In his discourse on the " Fulfilling of Prophecies," Peter du Molin well remarks, that when God was about to make any revelations or give any exalted notions to his prophets, he took them either into the desert and among mountains, or to the wild shores of seas and rivers, that he might have them alone, and in the most favorable condition for spiritual ends.

> " In such green palaces the first kings reigned,
> Slept in their shades, and angels entertained ;
> With such old counsellors they did advise,
> And by frequenting sacred groves grew wise."

And if any do incline to join us in " a desert place " and a forest life for vacations, let me suggest to them the puritanic advice of that good Pilgrim, Edward Winslow, in his letter to English friends, dated " Plimmouth in New-England, this 11 of December, 1621."

" Build your Cabbins as open as you can ; bring euery man a Musket or fowling Peece. Let your Peece be long in the barrell, and fear not the waight of it. Our Indian Corne, even the coursest, maketh as pleasant meat as Rice. . . . For hot waters Anni-seed water is the best, but vse it sparingly. . . . Let your shott be most for bigge Fowles, and bring store of Powder and shot. So I take my leaue, commending you to the LORD for a safe conduct vnto vs."

WILLIAM BARROWS

READING, MASS., January 5, 1869.

CONTENTS.

INTRODUCTORY.

FIRST NIGHT.

1

SECOND NIGHT.

THIRD NIGHT.

FOURTH NIGHT.

FIFTH NIGHT.

SIXTH NIGHT.

SEVENTH NIGHT.

EIGHTH NIGHT.

ELEVENTH NIGHT.

TWELFTH NIGHT.

INTRODUCTORY.

EIGHT tents in a semicircle. Seven of them are small, for two or three persons each, and the eighth, bearing conspicuously the government letters, U. S., is large enough to cover the hotel table of the encampment. The furniture of the small tents is a good carpeting of prairie hay, equivalent to mattress, feather bed, and lounge; then buffalo robes and bed quilts, overcoats, cavalry boots, and boots not cavalry, valises and shawls, cigar boxes, and chunky, battered chests, like an expressman's, marked Magazine, together with other articles, various and miscellaneous.

These all have that fancy arrangement common to camp life, and uncommon with good housekeepers; for every article had dropped into place, of its own accord, where last used.

In the corners of the tents, around the tent poles, or by tree and sapling within easy reach, lean securely light fowling-pieces of six and eight pounds; long and heavier ordnance of twelve and sixteen pounds, for geese and swan; and trim, snug-built rifles, for the wary deer and turkey. I put turkey last, for the watchful things, always on picket guard, are the last to be taken. Here and there, on peg and hook within, hang pouches, flasks, and hunters' belts, and game bags. Then some of these, and some other things, do not hang at all, but help to make the pleasing miscellany, the sportsman's whatnot, in the universal corner.

The U. S., the dining tent, towering with its snowy peak, covers provisions and groceries, flanking the long table, of appetizing variety and quieting abundance. Sacks and buckets, bags and boxes, tubs of butter, caddies of tea, hams, sardines, and coffee, cans of milk fresh from the nearest cabin, two miles away, flour, vegetables, and hard tack — these fortify our rear as we sit at the table. Between these and the table there is just room enough for standee seats, and extemporaneous chairs, so liable to fail an unsteady occupant.

These eight tents open inward on their semicircle, facing a long line of camp fire — a kind of burning diameter for the curving group. The extreme tents are a good gunshot asunder. Surrounding and overhanging the whole are majestic forest trees, oak, black walnut, hickory, and whitewood. Clear of undergrowth, and the trees themselves quite free of lower limbs, their majestic tops interlock and arch over the camp, as in some old Gothic church, where, arch springing from arch, nave, and choir, and wings seem struggling and bracing together to hold up the common roof.

The camp ground itself is a plateau, a kind of table. On one side is the low, level forest, where the vast native growth stretches away for miles, and on the other sleeps Swan Lake. Just our locality is a kind of shoulder hunched out towards the water. This is a beautiful sheet, six miles long — if it were stretched out, as fortunately it is not — by two or three wide. In places the bottom prairie comes down to its very shores to kiss the sandy beach, while on other sections the forest stands guard in thick ranks, and to the very water's edge.

If any one supposes that the view from this camp into the forest, or on the lake, whether by sunlight, moonlight, or starlight, was not enchanting, I would like to see the encampment again made, and then introduce my doubting reader to it. It would by no means be irksome to me to repeat the two weeks I spent there in the late autumn of 1863. If I could not convince my pavement and hotel friend of the beauties and glories of the scenery, I could console myself under defeat in enjoying them all over again.

The lake lies as nature made it and the red men left it. The shores are not marred by any traces of civilization, and the tall prairie grass comes boldly down and dips itself in the crystal waters; and the lofty old trees throw their long shadows over it in weird silence, the same as when the runners of Black Hawk beat up for warriors through all the region against General Atkinson, and Samoset, two centuries earlier, welcomed Englishmen to our eastern shores. The log cabin of our milkman, a herdsman, is the nearest evidence of the inexorable progress of the age, which is so fast using up and ruining this virgin country.

Even now, the most of us who covet the manly and invigorating sport must ride days and hundreds of miles to find a wolf, bear, deer, or wild turkey. It is sad to think of. For years I have seldom been able to find a quiet nook for rest in the wilderness free from settlers, neighbors, and travellers. Somebody would be there. Once I thought I was secure from intrusion, twenty miles into the woods from any settlement; but at ten o'clock one night two men entered our shanty, asking for supper and lodgings. We gave them venison stew and the front room, first floor. One of them has since been candidate for governor in the State of Maine. If elected ever, I shall claim of him a consideration for that mess of pottage. The truth is, this new country is already nearly spoiled by "settlements;" and, if not too late, Congress should reserve a square in our western interior, six hundred miles on a side, taking in a slope of the Rocky Mountains, and both banks of the Missouri, at the mouth of the Yellowstone, on which any improvements beyond tent pins should be forever prohibited.

But my feelings betray me into a wandering. I was speaking of Swan Lake, its grassy and wooded shores, its witching nooks and bays, and its long reaches of glassy surface. Here the wild fowl hold holidays, and the timid deer drinks once and looks up, and the glossy turkey picks up the myriads of little shells. Two miles of heavy, deep, original forest on the west, and you come to the Mississippi, over against the mouth of the Iowa. Below you is Sturgeon Bay, a large eddy of miles that the Mississippi has worn into the Illinois shore, and through which the overflow of Swan Lake runs direct to New Orleans.

This whole region, in which our temporary canvas village is located, is a saucer-like depression of the bottom lands on the Illinois shore, covering a diameter of ten miles or more. In this area are lakes and ponds, lagoons, creeks, and marshes, upland, lowland, and woodland, and grassland, all as wild as game or hunter can wish.

Who are we in such an out-of-the-way place? This is a very proper question for you to ask; and indeed, if you did not ask it, I could not well go on with my narrative. We are seventeen men strong, with a few rollicking boys thrown in. We stack twenty guns and more. We are the D—— Hunting Club; that is to say, we are the club regular on its annual excursion, with a number of guests regular. If you are curious to know who in particular we are, and whence we came, I must go back a little in my story, and up stream somewhat from our encampment.

At the levee, somewhere, — I cannot be exact, — lies a steamer, puffing, pulling, and paddling. Between her and Front Street are men in squads and single, going back and forth. They carry guns, and bundles, and boxes, overcoats, robes, and camp blankets. Store boys and draymen are loaded with groceries, vegetables, and ammunition chests. Here a lad holds a pointer in leash, and there go two or three setters over the gangway of the steamer. A couple of men carry on board a small, sharp-pointed boat, bow and stern alike, and lay it carefully on the guards; two more place a similar boat on the opposite guards; and a third and fourth boat is shipped, and so on, till seven of them are carefully bestowed and made fast. Also six hunting dogs are made fast on the asthmatic and uneasy craft.

Now the last things are put on board. There a runner goes for an extra gun, and another for the forgotten bags of shot, number eight for quail, and number four for mallard. The lastlies are shipped again, and we are about to cast off, when The General, by his inevitable memorandum, finds out that but one of the two tubs of butter has come down, and that Iulus has no buckskin gloves for a frosty morning hunt. Now the butter comes and the gloves, after much waiting and shouting, and miscellaneous talking. So we all go on board. Just as Jack is hauling in the plank, one of our men rushes back for his howling setter, tied to the wheat scales, thirty yards up the broad levee. Then our last-lies continue, like those of a long and poorly-arranged sermon. In a brief lull of them Jack gives the plank another and desperate pull, and we swing off into the stream, just when Mrs. —— sends down a cold roast of beef, for the first night in camp. The yawl secures the roast for us; and shouts and salvos follow us, till we are far down the majestic river, and beyond hearing.

Fairly afloat, all luggage properly stowed and made fast, the seven boats lashed, and the seven dogs tied, and we all beginning to feel quiet and at home on the craft that is to run us sixty miles down stream, it would be a good time for you, if still anxious to know who and what we all are, to walk about the boat, and make inquiries and observations, and notes, too, if you please.

All counted, you will find just a score of us, though the dogs are as worthy to be reckoned in, on the scale of importance, as many "persons," in taking the census, and on election days. The club proper is well represented by the honorable callings — merchants of dry goods, grocers, manufacturers, and real estate dealers, bankers, and gentlemen of leisure.

It would not be courteous in me, a guest, to be more personal and particular in speaking of the members themselves of this honorable association. Of the gentlemen invited to share in the luxuries and excitements of this annual excursion, there is a fur merchant from Detroit, with hunting boat and dog packed all the way; a banker and old Rocky Mountain trader from St. Louis; also a gentleman from the same city; an Eastern New Yorker, business unknown, but a good shot and camp fellow; two gentlemen from Georgetown, District of Columbia, far enough from the capital to be safe companions; a young Hungarian, said to be of noble blood, a noble hunter at least, which is often better; an Eastern pilgrim, with a title that would allow him to be converted into a chaplain for this Nimrod regiment, if occasion required; also a little Iulus of twelve years, following this pilgrim father.

It would not be patronizing to the rising race in our land, nor show well for The General of this campaign, if I should fail to call your attention to those two colored boys lounging about the steward's door, and among the firemen of the boat. They are Dock and Rube. When we are fortunate enough to pitch our camp, they are to serve as a pair of dark hyphens to connect the provisions above mentioned with the tent above mentioned, that is to serve as our dining hall. They are to be the sable gods of the camp fire, larder, and table, converting flesh, fish, and fowl into food, and hungry hunters into story-tellers and jolly idlers.

Dock is a veteran in this service. You will see at a glance that he is professional in his character, and a travelled gentleman. He takes the boat easily, and the

trip, and all on board. Nothing disturbs him, or sur-
prises him, or interests him. His time has not come to
assume the airs of office and responsibility. When he
comes to look after that part of the human system
where so many insurrections start and stop — the
stomach — he will rise up to due and dignified propor-
tions. He knows what a camp kettle is, and has almost
as many ways to serve up a fowl as Alexander's cook is
reported to have had — a new method for each day in
the year. For Dock has set the tent table for General
Harney on almost all the rivers and prairies between
the Mississippi and the Rocky Mountains. The savory
odors of broiled buffalo hump, and beaver-tail soup, of
the roasting ribs of the mountain sheep, and of elk, and
venison, and antelope steaks, have gone up from his
camp fires on many a river bank, and bleak prairie, and
mountain glen. The steam of his hissing kettles of tea
and coffee have made many an Indian camp follower
wish he was a white man in the American army, push-
ing civilization, with wages at eight dollars a month.
Smoke and sunshine, sleet and drizzle, never spoiled for
us, I will here say in advance, one of his good dinners.
Blessings be on that African for the broils and roasts,
the gravies and pastries, that he gave us hungry fellows in great abundance and at all hours. May his
shadow never be less, or his shade darker.

Of ebony Rube I cannot say so much. He does not
date back in his origin to the first family of anybody.
He has no reputation to sustain, his own or a master's.
He is a gentleman of ease, wishing to see the world,
and willing to work his own way in doing it. He
attached himself to our expedition because we show

signs of good living, good company, and a lively time. He takes naturally to gentlemen in easy circumstances, and to adventurous, out-of-the-way excursions. The portly bearing and the genial, hearty face of The General specially led him to offer his important services on this occasion.

Not to confuse my readers with too many characters, or be obliged, midway in the narrative, to dispose of any dramatically, after the manner of the sensational novelist, let me here, in advance of time, declare the end of poor Rube. When we came into camp he did not see the world as widely, or as fast, as he expected. Having an undue ambition to rise too rapidly, he could not see that keeping camp fires ablaze, and picking geese, teal, and snipe, was the true line for his success. Dock could not make the unlettered fellow realize that he was in the very best of society, enlarging his knowledge of men and things, and rising in the world, by scaling bass and pike, and skinning deer, catfish, and coons. The simple one did not know when he was well off, and so struck out into the cold world of the settlements again. Ambitious for city life, he left our select society, and started for the mixed multitude of New Boston.

Riding into camp, one afternoon, from the distant ridges of corn and wheat, The General and myself met Rube, with boots by his side, just after fording a creek. He was washing his ebony feet, to begin again his travels in search of society, sights, and adventures. So he was lost to fame — a sad warning to an excessive ambition that is impatient of the slow, sure steps of ng that come with being in the best society.

2

I have said that I cannot speak particularly of the members of this Hunting Club. An exception must be made of one, whom I have called The General, since he is the body and soul of this narrative. The president of the organization for this year, he is its animating centre. All the members are intelligent, active business men, and in civil, social, and religious affairs they expend their energies. They choose this mode of taking a few days' reprieve from the pressure of daily cares running through the year. Neighbors, and old friends of long and tried fellowship, they have now thrown off work, and put their hearts together for rest and enjoyment. The General has given himself, soul and body, to the excursion. Full of life and good humor, of which you can see his whole face is tell-tale, he is glad with everybody, and makes everybody glad. He has an eye, as chief, to the business in hand, and sees that luggage, stores, and guns are in safe packing and keeping. He knows the officers of the packet and the river interests, and talks with every one.

Follow him on deck and you will notice that he gives the history of every town we pass, for he has seen it start from its first rude cabins. He scans the shores of every island with the eye of an old acquaintance, for he meandered and plotted all of them for the government of the United States, from the mouth of Rock River to Quincy, when more canoes than steamers played around these shores and among these channels.

A stiff breeze up stream — almost a gale — compels us to struggle in a zigzag down stream. Now the wind shoots us into the woody shores, and now up and across. We weary of it. Let us go into the saloon.

The stories of The General make us forget head winds. Some reminiscence of California in 1850, the cane-brakes and bears of the Yazoo in 1836, interviews with Keokuk and Black Hawk, the keen joke, the cool, smooth repartee, and good-natured argument, fill the cabin with life, and all of us with good humor. The General leads us off because he cannot help it, and we do not care to. I may say here that we all call him The General, just as he has been called for years. He took the title, without a commission, from leading a company over the plains to California in 1850. The title was confirmed to him for heading expeditions to and from Montana and Idaho, by the common land route and by the Missouri. Little care we which way the wind blows, so merry a company are we. On deck or below no sorry face is seen.

And so, curious reader, your proper questions, who we are and whence we came, are answered.

The steamer lands us in the deep twilight. A house of one story and four rooms, fortunately empty, and rented for us by The General for the emergency, receives us. Stores, armament, cold provisions, a temporary stove, and the steam of hot coffee fill one room in twenty minutes. The dogs are made fast, each in a corner, in the rear rooms. Robes, blankets, and snoring hunters soon cover the floor of the remaining one. Energetic fleas, old enough, apparently, to have known La Salle and Marquette, and the howling dogs divided the hours for us between sleeping and waking. So passed the night, while we wished for the day, and our destination.

The day came in easier than we came into camp at

the close of it. The fleas, the howlings, and the darkness leave us in their own provokingly leisurely way.

> " Aurora, now, fair daughter of the dawn,
>   Sprinkles with rosy light the dewy lawn."

Only it should be said that in those two lines Homer
does not refer to New Boston, whose lawn is sand
ankle deep around our temporary abode.

We divide our forces in proceeding to the hunting-
grounds. A part of the boats are manned, and attempt
the passage through Sturgeon Bay, and up the outlet of
Swan Lake. The remainder of the company, with the
other boats and the freight, load two double teams, and
proceed to the same rendezvous by a ten miles' land
route. How the boats went the last few miles by land
up a dry creek, with mud bottom, and how the teams
went by water through muck and bog, over what in
Illinois they have a fashion of calling a road, I will not
delay the reader to tell. Each party wished they had
gone the other way, specially when midway they
seemed unable to go back or forward, and were in
grave doubts whether they belonged to the land or
water division.

In the sunny afternoon of that hazy October day we
all straggle in, muddy, jaded, and jolly, wondering
together whether that part of Illinois was listening
when it was said, " Let the waters be gathered together
unto one place, and let the dry land appear." But
Dock is ready for us with a cold lunch and hot coffee,
as we come on the ground, single and in squads, like a
regiment very recently from Bull Run.

We hang up a fair show of game, that we have

picked up in our rambling land-and-water journey, and fall readily to lounging in our freshly-spread tents. Evening creeps over forest and lake, while the rumbling of the returning wagons dies away in the distance. The fires give our white tents a beautiful setting against the dark background of night, and light up the tall old trees over us. The dogs, now well fed, crouch about the burning logs, and stretch themselves to sleep among our feet. The boys pile on the light wood, and the men smoke and gossip over the comic and serious incidents of our amphibious life for the day. The General issues the field orders for the morrow, to wit: Breakfast at sunrise, a miscellaneous hunt between sun and sun, each going where he pleases and bringing in what game he can, and dinner at the old conference-meeting time — " early candle lighting."

One by one we leave the cheerful brands for blanket and buffaloes; the fires grow paler, and the company thinner, till the last voice dies away and the last tent candle goes out. The drowsy blazes nod away into smoke, the coals creep in between the white sheets of feathery embers, and the very camp fire itself falls asleep.

THE GENERAL;

OR,

Twelve Nights in the Hunters' Camp.

FIRST NIGHT.

PERSONS familiar with wilderness life have noticed that morning follows night there with nearly
the same regularity as in old and settled regions,
where things have got into a kind of system. We
notice this in the first morning of our life at Swan
Lake. The dawn comes in on time, fresh and full
through the tree-tops, and mingles its golden flashes
with the silver ripples of the lake. The squirrels,
gray, and red, and fox, are chattering and running
from tree to tree over our heads, disturbed by the
novel entrance of our canvas village and camp fires;
the ducks are calling to each other across the lake and
down the creek, and the noisy geese are announcing
their departure for the grain fields, twenty miles away.
The delightful odors of Dock's cuisine come temptingly along our semicircular street, hurrying up our
brief toilet. But we pay fair attention to the outer
man.

(23)

Some semicivilized fisherman once gave me a good lesson on this, while boarding at a log shanty at the Middle Dam, on the Androscoggin. The rude fellows, with alder poles and cod-hooks, were essaying the noble art of trout-fishing. They slept in their day gear, and with the first blush and stir of morning rushed, unwashed and unkempt, to the choicest fishing localities. They went as hens from the roost, their undress being also full dress. Shade of St. Izaak the angler! that a man should presume to show an unwashed face at a mountain stream, or touch a trout with an unclean hand! Sportsmen should not soil wild nature with their untidiness.

Our toilet is finished, and we step out. The man who has not slept in a hunter's tent does not know what it means to wake up in the morning feeling all right. Languor, headache, an embittered mouth, and indifferent stomach belong to first-class hotels. It has been a problem, with naturalists and theologians, why the antediluvians lived to so great an age. Let the puzzled commentators spend a few vacations in camp, and dream under canvas, and the hard facts subjected to tent dreams will come clear. Those old men of immense age lived in tents all their days. Methuselah never heard of a French roof, Gothic cottage, or saw a frame house. As men began to forsake tents for houses, human life began to be shortened. We commend this fact to the careful consideration of the next editors of De Wette and Bleek, and Keil and Delitzsch, and Lange, Pustkuchew, and Stachelin.

While the sun is turning the first half hour on the dial we take our breakfast. Then come the rattling, and clicking, and snapping, and flashing of guns; the barking, and frolicking, and whining of dogs; the dipping of oars, and the tramping of hunters this way and that, as we start out for the day.

Of course my readers (always comfortably presuming that I have some) do not care to have me tell them in particular where we went, each, and all we did. My narrative would thus become as long as the Babylonian Talmud and Xenophon's Retreat of the Ten Thousand united. Let it suffice, then, that I start your fancy after us by mentioning deep forests, lake shores, bottom prairie, shrivelled creeks here and there, the delight of mallard and teal, ponds six miles off, oak openings, the resort of turkeys, and the banks of the Mississippi at two or three points. Your fancy may follow us over all this wild and wide region till high noon and the near nightfall; and you may follow our diverging and intersecting paths by our frequent reports echoing far and near.

The lengthening shadows of the declining sun turn us tent-ward, and from our many and wayward courses of the morning we all converge again, with the twilight, under the grand old trees. Flushed with the success of the first day's hunt, we look with no little satisfaction on the trophies brought in. Here it hangs in the light glare of the camp fires, weighing down many a lusty limb and sapling. The variety would do honor to Quincy Market.

And now begin the tales of the day's exploits. Each must tell what he did, and how, and what he failed to do, speak of the game that escaped him, and show what he bagged. Supper does not break off the cross-

ing and somewhat tangled threads of discourse. With
new vigor we start off again in our narratives on the
logs and camp chairs along the blazing pile.

> " 'Tis blithe at eve to tell the tale,
>   How we succeed, and how we fail."

By degrees other times and hunts come up in review, and each is left to declare his own wonderful
experiences in forest and frontier life. Buck, and bear,
and huge fish come into the foreground of story, with
now and then an antelope, or grizzly, or buffalo, brought
in by our Rocky Mountain member. The General has
some rare bits of personal adventure in Mississippi canebrakes, the North-West Territory, Indians on the Plains,
and California in its second summer, a bear's paw law-
suit in Central New York, and coons in the Old Bay
State thirty and forty years ago. An experience so
rich, and varied, and exciting, all agree should not remain untold. The General is, therefore, compelled to
promise a chapter of personal adventures for each night
in camp. Securing so much in promise, all become
earnest for a beginning on this first night of our first
hunt. The old pioneer, finding himself cornered, and
withal not unwilling to tell a good story, and fully able
to the task, glided off into his theme, as a birch canoe
into the current, and feeling equally at home in the
element.

THE ACORN.

"An old land surveyor, like me, must have a stake to start from in running his lines; and in chasing a deer, or fox, or prairie wolf, you must begin somewhere. I have no tact in beginning a story in the middle and spinning it out both ways. So, if you want to know how this old oak got its tough limbs and portly trunk, you must go back with me to the acorn. Another big armful of that light wood, Rube. My early days were bright and cheerful, and I cannot tell them over here in the dark. I want a cheerful camp fire to set them off well.

"Among the green hills of New England, not far from the eastern boundary of the old town of Monson, Mass., I was born. I do not distinctly recall the fact, but I am told it was on the 25th of September, 1806. My father was a native of Thompson, Conn., and my mother of Sudbury, Mass. By industry and perseverance they saved enough from the hard toil of their own hands to purchase a small farm there in Monson. This my father tilled for the support of his family, of which I was the third child.

"Of the early struggles of my parents for a living among the rocks and barrens of this portion of the state I have but little knowledge, and can judge only from my early impressions and the history of those youthful days, as told over by members of the family long afterwards. A part of the old farm where I was

born is now included in the grounds of the State
Almshouse. I hope the poor inmates get a better
living than the land would furnish. Somebody has
found a place to wedge in two very pretty lines of
poetry between those Yankee acres of rock : —

'But man's the nobler growth our realm supplies,
And souls are nurtured in these northern skies.'

"I cannot tell about the poetry. I found it a good
place to leave. By hard labor, prudence, and economy,
my parents made the farm porduce the necessaries of
life, and with these there came contentment and happiness. The week was spent in earnest, honest labor,
and every return of the Sabbath found them, with their
children, in their accustomed pew, in Dr. Ely's church,
about two miles away.

"The region was wild and picturesque, and in the
immediate vicinity of my home were barren and rocky
hills, or mountains, as the people there called them,
unfit for cultivation, and visited only by hunters. At
no great distance was the brook, where I learned to
catch the speckled trout, and in the deep glens, and
among the alders, I often started up the partridge and
rabbit from their secluded haunts. Here, in this retired and romantic spot, I received my first impressions
of the beauty and grandeur of mountains, and valleys,
and streams, and meadows.

"From an old coon-hunter by the name of Moulten
I first listened to the exciting stories of the chase, of a
winter evening, while every now and then he would stop
to replace the brands between the great andirons of his
kitchen fire. Although then quite young, I often went

with him in his hunting rambles over the mountains. So, early in life the fondness for hunting, and the love of wild scenes in nature, were impressed on my mind, and did much to shape my future course, as will be seen, if you do not weary of my stories, and turn in before I am done.

"It was here that I first took my seat in the public school-house, that nursery for youth everywhere in New England. This system of common education for all has led many a poor boy from the paths of ignorance and vice, to gather the laurels of statesmen, and heroes, and scholars.

"The pure moral and religious principles of my parents, and their exemplary life, laid the foundation very early for my future course, and they have been a guide and comfort to me in all the years since. When storm and tempest have overtaken me on the mountains, and hunger, and thirst, and weariness have brought me to an empty tent at night on the dreary plains, and I have lain down only to think of the morrow with sadness and anxiety, their teachings and example have kept me in good heart.

"But I must not tell the middle of my story at the beginning. The storm, and the desert, and hunger, and the Indian, and the wild beast will come in soon and often enough, unless you can enjoy them more than I did.

"I was a true son of New England, and I think I inherited in my very blood the earnest, searching, adventurous spirit that is so native to her children. Early trained to self-reliance and hardihood, and moved by the love of gain and adventure, they acquire habits of industry; and being fond of travel, research, and incidents, they are found in every clime, on the land and on the sea, speaking all languages, adopting the manners of all nations, and taking up the business of all peoples. Their indomitable courage and perseverance in the prosecution of any undertaking carry them through every enterprise, however difficult or hazardous. These are the characteristics of the children of that icy, rocky region, and these are the causes that make men out of her boys. My father was one of those self-made, self-reliant men, full of energy and ambition, with only the common-school education of a few weeks. He was kind, obliging, always ready to deny himself to do another a favor. The exhibition of his daily Christian character, his pure principles and instructions, were a constant restraint on any idleness or waywardness in his children. So it was with my mother. Her Christian character and usefulness were prominent, and though her arduous duties in a family finally of ten children pressed heavily on her, her faithfulness in properly bringing them up never wearied. They both lived to a good old age, and died in comfort and peace, 'like as a shock of corn cometh in in his season.' *

"My father purchased a farm in New Braintree, and removed and settled on it, when I was about ten years of age. Of course my recollections of the place of my birth can be of but little interest to any one of you. I

* The father died in Templeton, Mass., March 12, 1856, wanting but sixteen days of eighty-three years, and the mother at Foxboro', Mass., July 17, 1858, in her eighty-second year. — *Editor*.

had entered the district school, but tradition there tells
nothing wonderful about me, as it does about great
men.   I have noticed that when one does become re-
r owned, the memories of those who tried to beat dulness
cut of his little head are wonderfully quickened.

"My wandering propensities gave my mother no
little anxiety and watching.   At that early age I was
intent on discovering some new place or thing.   The
garden, that was enclosed by a stone wall, and full of
shrubbery, was, in my imagination, a place of beauty
and pleasure unsurpassed.   My conception of the Garden of Eden, as I had heard it described by my father
in his reading of the sacred volume, was exactly like ours
at the homestead.   When, later in life, I revisited the
place of my birth, after an absence of almost forty
years, I found the garden there still walled in, and in
all its primeval beauty.   There were still the stone
steps, and the stone curb to the well, with the 'old
oaken bucket;' and it seemed to me but as yesterday
when it hung there.   The roots of the old grape-vine,
that grew and ran in the corner of the orchard, were
still there.   I led the way, without a mistake, to some
of the apple-trees that bore choice fruit, and from which
I had gathered the same when only six years old.   I
also pointed out to those with me the very place in the
garden, where, in those young years, I went, early one
morning, in search of the tracks of the Lord, where I
supposed he must have 'walked in the garden, in the
cool of the day,' as I had heard my father read in
Holy Writ.

"But I think you have seen enough of the acorn.
Let us turn in for a good sleep against a rousing hunt

to-morrow. Those turkeys must not give you the
slip again."

This last remark The General made with a turn of
the head towards the chaplain, and so the company
broke up for the night.

I have called this the First Night, because the one
in the vacant house was not in camp, and the other
merely marked our arrival, with none of the incidents
and accompaniments proper of our excursion. Really
the stories of The General became our chronometer.
We dated our hunt from the beginning of his narrative, and, as will be seen, closed it and broke camp
when he was done.

Quiet settled over our grounds. Only the feeble
snapping of the dying fires could be heard near us. To
one who has never indulged the luxury I cannot give
a full idea of the comfort, the kind of sovereign easi-
ness and peace, with which a hunter falls asleep for
the night in his tent. No keys and bolts click, suggestive of robbery; no carriages clatter by, making
night hideous; no sounds of any farm-house or village.
Nature is not annoyed by any of these impertinences.
You may be sure the only noise, nigh or far, is made
by game of some kind. It may be the sharp bark of
the fox, or the half snarl and yelp of the prairie wolf,
or the flap and dash into the water of those geese returning late from the cornfields, or muskrat and otter
may be taking their nightly baths and frolics. But
you and wild nature are alone, and you glide off into
sleep as those who hear pleasantest music, or drop away
into the dream land of the lotos-eater.

SECOND NIGHT.

DOCK and Rube, the seven dogs, the young dawn, an awkward sprinkle of damp snow, and a dozen, more or less, of washing, combing, and dressing hunters were jumbled together about the morning fires. But plenty of wood at nothing a cord soon left the cooks masters of the situation, as the flames mounted higher and the beds of glowing coals spread themselves. Broils, roasts, and fries in due time smoked in the U. S., with the hissing and aroma of old Java and young Hyson. It has always been a mystery to me that a man in the woods could make such gravies so early in the morning. Our appetites came in the same mysterious way, and hot biscuit, halves of geese, whole teal, and crispy pike went in the same manner. Dock smiled aloud over empty plates to see that we appreciated his services. The dogs shared heartily in the carnival, while we girded on pouches and flasks, game belts and bags. Then how they frisked, and raced, and whined to be off!

Thus in motion and confusion, about to take our lines outward-bound for a long day, we were as goodly a sight to look upon as the French thought the company of Thomas à Becket to be, when, as ambassador of Henry II., he went from city to city, escorted by his hounds and falconers, with hawks on their wrists, and

3

a multitude of bowmen. If a chancellor, and about to
be archbishop, could do all that in a foreign land, why
not we, native sovereigns in our own wilds.

A gang of lordly turkeys had eluded me the day
before, the first I had ever attempted to stalk. The
impertinent spit of snow, therefore, that welcomed us
at our tent-fly that morning, pleased me, for I knew I
could strike their trail. Giving my purpose to no one,
I made a detour for the opposite shore of the lake, and
came warily to their old grounds. What was my
vexation then, as I hastened over a narrow tongue of
prairie, with oak opening on either side of me, to see a
stranger rifleman on my right, threading out their
tracks in the fast disappearing snow. In my warmth
I made a savage shot on a woodcock, and with turkey
shot, too, as it foolishly rose from the open grass.
While driving home my lead with a vexed energy, the
sharp crack of a rifle on my left brought my eye round,
and my gun into readiness. In a moment a turkey
under easy sail came bearing towards me. It was the
work of an instant, and the noble bird feel forty yards
away, with head and neck cut through and through.
It was my first turkey. No New York stallman ever
hung up a fowl so noble in my eye. The glossy, black
wings, the tail with dark bronze bands, and the royal
and rich neck plumage up to the very wattles! I
actually felt like a boy of ten with his first pheasant.
It graced the table of Madame M., at St. Louis, a few
days afterwards. More of the same flock came into our
dining tent before we quitted the encampment, and
their flavor is not yet forgotten.

But, patient reader, you will not care to follow fifteen

hunters all day over that saucer of bottom land ten miles across.   Let us suppose the day past, go back to camp, and simply make note of what they bring in.   If you are with me you will be saved some travel in the return, for I hail a boat from the shore opposite our rendezvous, and am spared a long tramp around an arm of the lake.   One by one they come in with the twilight shades, and throw down their game at the root of the monarch hickory.   Now a dog returns, running up familiarly to Rube for a lunch.   We know what man will report next, and soon the crackling limbs announce that dog's master.   Then you hear far out on the lake the dip of oars and the chuck in the rowlocks, and the little craft by and by glides easily up on the grassy shore, and we all go down to see what freight.   One or two linger longer than the twilight.   By and by two shots in quick succession tell that some poor fellow is studying our geography in the dark, and wants to know which way the camp lies.   We answer instantly by two shots, and a half hour brings him in. The best hunters come in last, for they bag game as long as they can see it, and think of camp afterwards.

But they are all in now : so, while supper goes on the table, let us count up the game.   Turkey leads to-night, and the chaplain is cheered for his maiden shot on the noblest feathered game that ranges in our western forests.   Geese follow, with brant close behind; then come mallards and teal, always together in pond or camp.   Sawbills and fish ducks we do not count, nor would we the crested wood duck, only that it is the

most beautiful of floating game in America. Two or
three pheasants, and as many woodcock — both rare
birds in that region, and the delight of sportsmen — and
partridges by the dozen — we call them quail in the
east. Jack snipe and a bunch of yellow legs, by one
man who went down the creek where our boats came
up by land through the mud. Five prairie chickens —
they had no rights in the low land, and were served as
wanderers deserved. Shall we count the squirrels and
that comic-looking coon? Yes; all that can be eaten
can be counted. We go well up to a hundred and
twenty pieces. Next we assort and hang them together.
How they grace the bending hickory and pawpaw, ash
and whitewood saplings! Just to look at the array,
now in the camp-fire light, and run your hand over
feathers and furs, is enough to put new life into every
tired bone of an overworked business man. Dyspeptic
are you? Let us go where you see those two darkies
carrying in dishes, and in twenty minutes you will
deny that you ever heard of dyspepsia, gastric juice, or
even a stomach.

It is a marvel that one a little dainty in his food,
liable to nightmare and horrid dreams, if he eats flesh,
fish, or fowl at home, within six hours of bedtime, can
stow away so much meat in camp, after all traces of
daylight are gone, draw a blanket over himself, and
hear nothing, know nothing, till Rube calls to a breakfast just like the supper, to be as voraciously devoured. It is not food, but business, care, and worry
that make so many dyspeptics, and supply water-cures
and the south of France with boarders. The Swan

Lake House, managed on the natural plan — that is, our plan — that gave us "dominion over the fish of the lake and over the fowl of the air," would upset the theories of Sylvester Graham and all the vegetarians.

But supper waits, first course, second course, third course, and then we wait around the blazing camp fire to hear once more The General.

BOYHOOD, AND THE BEAR'S PAW.

"I said that, when I was about ten years old, my father moved to a new home. In this I soon found much to excite and encourage my already ardent desire for research and discovery. Not far from the house there was an old hemlock swamp, almost impassable for man or beast. This dismal wild abounded with the partridge, hare, and rabbit. Here I soon learned to snare, and with the assistance of my brothers I added not a little to the supply of meat for the table. Fishing also I took up naturally; and there was no pond or trout brook in all the region with which I did not in a little time become familiar. In the summer I assisted on the farm, and in the winter attended the district school.

"An incident occurred about this time which showed that my financial abilities had not then been fully developed. A neighboring boy, who had been out hunting, called on me one day, having shot a red-headed woodpecker. The beauty of its plumage, and the pleasure of a close examination of a bird I had so often seen, but never handled, induced me at once to set about the purchase of it. After many trials with the boy to conclude a bargain, and having no money, and needing to give something in exchange, I offered him my fishing-line. This was a piece of boy's property that I had for a long time saved pennies to purchase. The offer was accepted, the exchange made, and the boy left for his home.

"This was a great thing for me. It was my first important bargain, and I marched into the house with my bird, prouder and happier by far than I ever have been since, when carrying home a wild goose or turkey, or standing over a deer, or the struggling buffalo of the plains.

"With much pride I exhibited the bird to my mother, showing its glossy plumage, with scarlet head and half-white wings. When my father saw it, he at once inquired how I came by it; for I was not yet permitted to use fire-arms. Learning that I had given my valuable fishing-line for a worthless and dead bird, he took occasion, as his custom was on questions of morals, and habits, and money, to speak freely, showing the perishable nature of the bird, its utter worthlessness, and the folly of purchasing bubbles that would soon burst. He then told the story to the children of Franklin's purchase of the whistle.

"I presume I looked ashamed. I hung my head, while I felt keenly both the reproof and the loss of my line. I saw very clearly that I had paid too dear for the woodpecker. It was a profitable purchase, however, taking a long life in view. That early investment in a dead bird has paid me good dividends annually ever since. But it was my father's moralizing that secured their payment. Ever after, while under the parental roof and about to make a trade, my father would remind me of paying too dear for a dead bird; and it was not till 1855, when I paid him my last visit, in his eighty-second year, that I heard from him the last of that unfortunate purchase, which, after all, turned out so well.

" The few years that I remained at home, and before leaving for the wide world, were spent in working the farm and attending school. But, like Walter Scott, I kept up my field sports. No fisher on the Tweed could spear a salmon more skilfully, and no hunter on the Yarrow was a better rider in the chase. In later days, when he was charming the world with his pen, he used it in the morning, and coursed hares in the afternoon. Many were the lessons taught me by my worthy parents, not of agriculture only, but of industry, prudence, caution, economy, and morality, in those younger days.

" I was like boys generally, not so fond of work as of play. Often my father would lay off my task for the day, that I might gain time to run wild among the little game and drown out the striped squirrel from his hole.

" It was on one of these occasions that my father left me a quart of beans to plant among the growing corn in a small field. Being in a great hurry to join a party of boys, who were going out for sport, I planted all the beans at once in a few hills. As I knew he would inquire whether I had planted them I thus prepared to reply that I had. When the beans came up, and we were hoeing the corn, we found them starting from the ground in large masses. An explanation was demanded, and, as usual, I frankly confessed the whole truth. He gave me a wholesome lecture on the matter, and enforced it in a manner more personal and pointed than agreeable, much as Gideon taught the men of Succoth. [Judges viii. 16. — *Editor*.]

" On another occasion my father had set me to plant

pumpkin seeds among the corn. This time, not wishing to have my works follow me so closely, I took the seed over the fence, and climbing a hollow, rotten stump of a tree some ten feet high, I poured the whole into it, and left. My father wondered why the seed did not come up. The mystery was explained one summer day, when, passing the old stump, he found it ornamented with pumpkin vines, that were hanging on all sides from the top in rich profusion.

"There was nothing, I think, malicious or wicked in these boyish tricks, yet I would not justify them; but at the time they seemed necessary for my enjoyment. I was impetuous, and sometimes resorted to rather extreme measures to gain my end. One day, when my playmates were gathered for sport, and were waiting for me, I found my shoes dried up hard and stiff, as boys' shoes will sometimes become, so that I could not put them on. Deeming the case a kind of military necessity, I dashed them into my mother's dish-water to soften them. About the same time something like a bomb exploded very near to one of my ears, and my shoes went suddenly out of doors without any feet in them.

"At the age of fifteen I was placed at the Worcester Academy, or High School, where I remained for three years. The pecuniary circumstances of my father did not permit me to draw any great amount of funds, and I often labored, as was the case with many New England boys at that time, to obtain means for the purchase of books. The first book I ever bought was the History of the United States. I purchased it of Messrs. Dorr & Howland, booksellers, and paid for it in sawing wood by night.

"From Worcester I went to live with an uncle in Pomfret, Conn., near to Putnam's wolf den. Here I remained a year or more. My uncle was an old fox-hunter, kept his hounds, and at the proper season of the year, indulged freely in this noble sport. I was a great favorite with my uncle, and on these occasions I was often permitted to attend him. When a chase was to take place, and a large number of hounds was needed, my cousin would take the hunter's horn — an old goat's horn — and give it a few blasts at the door, about daylight. The dogs of his uncle, a mile away, would take the call, and in a few minutes they would be heard on the way, sending their deep and prolonged notes among the hills, and through the stillness of the early, frosty morning.

"The chase often lasted all day, and if the fox was not taken, the hounds would sometimes follow up all night, and we renew the pursuit the next morning. These were pleasures well suited to my taste, and did much towards strengthening my passion for a frontier and hunter life.

"I spent one winter with a distant relative in Thompson, Conn., and in the spring went to Brimfield, Mass., where another uncle resided. Here I engaged at common labor on a farm with a Mr. M. L. C., at ten dollars a month. I was then about nineteen years of age. The winter following I spent at home in study and reading, and in the spring returned to B., and gave another season to farming for Mr. A. S.

"The associations formed during my stay in this beautiful and quiet village were of the most genial and happy character. There was a large circle of young people, and our amusements and enjoyments made us quite happy, and life very sunny. Those days were among the pleasantest of my early life. But I was still thinking of days to come, and something more than having a good time. I pressed on in my studies on every occasion that offered, and midnight often found me busy with my books in my secluded chamber. I felt keenly the want of such an education as would enable me to live by some employment less laborious than farming, and my ambition prompted me to look up, and fit myself for the position of an educated man.

"I did not ask charitable aid to do this thing, so freely granted in that day; but I resolutely determined to make and hew my own way, and gain the prize by my own exertions. Others, I knew, had done this with less advantages. I was full of energy, in good health, with an iron constitution, the world was open to my choice of a path to honor, and with industry, prudence, and good moral habits, I had a strong faith to believe I should succeed. This resolution, this fixed purpose, was to me of more value than money, or a popular and fashionable family name. It was a capital to me that was not likely to vanish and leave me bankrupt. I felt that I had the means, which have made more eminent men than all others combined — a determination to become a true man.

"In the fall of 1827 I became of age; and though for years I had been thrown very much on my own resources, I felt a new impulse in the fact that now I was alone in the world — that new plans must be formed and greater exertions made for the hastening future.

"At this time emigration had set in strongly for the

West. 'The Genesee country' and Western New York
was to many an enterprising mind ' a land flowing with
milk and honey,' and glowing accounts came back,
from friends who had settled there, of its beauty and
fertility. My father and my Brimfield uncle had a
debt there due them, from a man residing near Otisco
Lake, in Onondaga county. I thought this fact might
be made a good occasion for my visiting what was then
the Far West, while I collected the debt. I wrote my
father, and he turned the whole affair over to his
brother. By much importunity I gained his consent
and the necessary funds for the long journey. Late in
the fall of 1827 I set forth, in the old stage-coach, for
a region never yet reached — The West.

"Ten years afterwards I came nearer to reaching it,
when I crossed over the big river here side of us, and
walked over Black Hawk's old camping-grounds, with
the brands of his war councils scarcely done smoking.
General Scott's howitzers and canister had then but
recently scoured out the bottom lands and shores
around the mouths of Rock River, and the old warrior
ceded Iowa Territory to the United States, after his
bloody and limping flight across the Mississippi."

Here our sprinkling of boys around the camp fire,
now poking the brands and now each other, but all the
while catching every word of The General, interposed
. in the story to hear more about the Indians. They
were quieted by the assurance of the old pioneer settler, that they would hear enough about Indians before
the stories were all told and we broke camp. The
General continued : —

" Passing through Albany, I entered Utica on runners over deep snows, arrived in due time at my place
of destination, and for the first time in my life saw
log cabins.

" While here I visited the Oneida Indians at Onondaga Hollow, and attended a council and feast at their
council-house. I had never seen Indians before; but
these were the white man's Indians, and I shall not
stop to speak of them. By and by, when these boys
have done a few more and better days' works at hunting, I shall get along in my stories as far west as the
Platte and the Rocky Mountains, and then you shall
see Indians, big chiefs and young braves, squaws and
pappooses, and the scalp of many a venturesome settler hanging from their wigwam pole and horse's
mane.

" I also visited Syracuse and the Salina salt works —
small places then, though the salt manufacture was
creating considerable interest. Then I went to Camden, in Oneida county, to visit some cousins who had
settled there. I spent the most of the winter with
them, enjoying the novelties of a new country, catching trout through the ice, shooting the black squirrel,
and following up other game on snow-shoes, that often
gave me, at first, a dry bath and a white cravat, as I
awkwardly plunged into the soft snow.

" During my stay here a trial came off in a little village twelve miles away, for the theft of a bear caught
in a trap. The attorney for the plaintiff was a Camden
man, whose pleasant acquaintance I had formed, and
so he invited me to ride out with him to attend the
court. On arriving I was introduced, for a little quiet

humor, as a young man of the legal profession, seeking
a place to settle. The joke took a more serious turn
when the defendant in the case, whom we found to be
without a lawyer, asked me to take his interests in
hand, and free him from the claws of the bear and of
the law, that were just now giving him an uncomfortable hug. With a daring readiness, out among those
log cabin pioneers, I undertook the work. The bear, it
was alleged, was stolen by the defendant from the
plaintiff's trap, and the prosecution sought to prove the
fact by producing the paw found in the trap, and by
the circumstance that the defendant had the carcass of
a bear about that time, the acquisition of which he did
not choose to give an account of, and all the paws of
which he was not disposed to produce. With some
learned mention of law books I urged that all black
bears of North America of the same age have feet very
much alike, and that it belonged to the plaintiff to
prove that the paw in court, and taken from the trap
of the plaintiff, belonged to the body of the bear in the
cabin of the defendant. In this the prosecution failed,
and my client was cleared by the intelligent jury,
though I had no doubt of his guilt. The pleadings
were somewhat eloquent on both sides. I represented,
in the most touching manner of the profession, the
monstrous injustice of shutting up my client in the
loathsome prison, in dead of winter, away from his
almost distracted wife and hungry, half-naked little
ones, the cruelty of blasting his unsullied reputation
in the bloom of his manhood, and all on the unproved
supposition that he had taken a bear from his neighbor's
trap. The fact was, he had daringly hunted down and

captured another animal to appease the gnawings of hunger in his lonely cabin in the wilderness. The prisoner was discharged amid much out-door applause. Owing to the stringency in the money market I got no fees. I, however, took the paw, and carried it home with me to New England, the trophy of my first attempt to plead law.

"Here was my first experience in a free and easy backwoods gathering. Whiskey flowed abundantly, while target shooting for beef, pork, poultry, and other valuables was the pastime. The defendant was the lion of the day, after his acquittal, and the young attorney from the East was urged strongly to 'hang out his shingle,' as the Western phrase is.

"I received for the debt spoken of a horse in part payment, and making what was there called a 'jumper,' an extemporaneous sleigh, I started for home. Just as the snows of March were melting away on the rough hills of Worcester county I drove up at the old homestead. At that day a journey like this was regarded as quite an undertaking, even for experienced travellers. It was an important as well as interesting one for me. I improved it well, making many observations on frontier life, and keeping a journal of facts and incidents."

The youngsters wanted more bears' paws, snow-shoes, and jumpers, and the older hunters around the fire evidently wanted to see The General farther from home, and on the prairies, before they slept. But all things have an end, even good stories in the hunters' camp. Night had long since thrown her starry blanket over the sleeping lake; the owl in the deeper wood had repeatedly challenged us with his " Who, who: who, who?" as one of the night picket stationed at the head of Sturgeon Bay; and Rube, in his gathering of wood, found the fires as insatiable as Dock found our stomachs.

So one by one the candles glimmered in our tents; their fronts, thrown open during the day, dropped loosely together; robes and shawls were stretched and tucked in here and there; the lights disappeared; the voices died slowly away, the rollicking boys being the last to give up; and at length silence and sleep reigned over the encampment.

THIRD NIGHT.

OLD Hugh Latimer was right in that sermon. He preached it before the Sixth Edward, a lad of twelve years, and a king of two, on the 12th of April, 1549. Had the king obeyed the preaching, as hearers should when they hear so good a man as Master Latimer, I doubt whether he would have died of consumption at the early age of sixteen. Many a youth has died of consumption for not reading and practising that sermon. It is now more than a quarter of a century since I first read it. I practised the doctrine many years before, and more devoutly since he impressed it on me, and that he was sound in the faith in that sermon I have this evidence: For twenty-three years I have followed Latimer's instructions, as given before the young king, and have lost by sickness only two days of pulpit labor. This is his sound doctrine, and of the old martyr school of divines: —

"Men of England, in times past, when they would exercise themselues (for wee must needs have some recreation; our bodies cannot endure without some exercise), they were wont to goe abroad into the fieldes : shooting. . . . The game of shooting hath bin in times past much esteemed in this Realme. It is a gift hat God hath giuen us to excell all other Nations al. . . . A wondrous thing, that so excellent a

4

gift of God should be so little esteemed. I desire you, my Lordes, euen as yee loue the honour and glory of God, and intend to remoue his indignation, let there be sent forth some proclamation, some sharpe procla-mation to the Iustices of peace, that they may doe their dutie. For Iustices now be no Iustices. There be many good acts made for this matter alreadie. Charge them upon their allegiance that this singular benefite of God may be better practised, . . . for they be negli-gent in executing these lawes of shooting. In my time, my poore father was as diligent to teach mee to shoote, as to learne me any other thing. . . . I had my bowes bought mee, according to my age and strength, as I encreased in them; so my bowes were made bigger and bigger; for men shall never shoote well except they be brought up in it. It is a worthy game, a wholesome kinde of exercise, and much commended in Phisicke. . . . In the reuerence of God let it be continued."

That is practical preaching, and I should think it might be popular with many. More tents and less hotels in vacation would make our professional men more vig-orous; Moosehead and the Adirondacks are better re-cuperators than Saratoga, Cape May, and the Rhine; and fishing-rods and fowling-pieces are among the very best gymnastic apparatus for a college ; but they should be good time-keepers, and observers of good laws, and not allow a literary exercise to give way to a rural excur-sion. When I swam a river seven times one college half-holiday, for the sake of better fishing on the oppo-site shore, and not unfrequently cooked my own par-tridge, or trout, or squirrel on Pelham Hills for a lunch, I was enjoying "a wholesome kinde of exercise, and

much commended in Phisicke." Losing since that time
little sleep by night, or work by day, from sickness, and
no four meals in succession, I incline, from experience,
to a college gymnasium that embraces the most of
four townships, a wild, hilly range or two, some meadows, a river, and several brooks. The founder of the
celebrated Harrow School, John Lyon, had a good idea
of a gymnasium for boys. In his third rule for that
foundation, referring to parents, he says, "You shall
allow your child at all times bow, shafts, bow-strings,
and bracer, to exercise shooting." And that eminent
worthy, who wrote Holy Living and Dying, and enacted it too, the devout and scholarly Jeremy Taylor,
helps me to this view thus: "Nature's commons and
open fields, the shores of rivers, and the strand of the
sea, the unconfined air, and the wilderness that hath
no hedge, . . . in these every man may hunt, and
fowl, and fish respectively."

But I forget myself in my preaching and moralizing.
My last chapter left us all sleeping soundly in the
encampment at Swan Lake. The reader may think
me talking of these old authors in my sleep. Very
like. I have often hunted and fished with great success in Dreamland. The forests, rivers, and game there
are splendid.

Let the reader suppose, then, that we arose in due
time, ate a vast breakfast, had the usual success in our
diverging and miscellaneous hunt, helped Dock most
efficiently in clearing the supper table, and are now on
the logs, robes, and camp-stools around The General,
just where you left us a little less than twenty-four
hours ago. The audience are all in, with not one

straggler, and the sexton, old Nox, has closed the doors
of day on us.   Our dogs give us some trouble as
The General is about to begin his Third Story.   Two
of them, Shot and Grouse, have drawn rations after
dusk, from tent number eight, commissariat's headquarters, without the lawful amount of Rube's red tape.
As the two come within the camp circle to eat among
gentlemen of the same profession, the others file claims
for dividends on the draft, and so our meeting is
disturbed.   Having been all whipped out of camp,
the chaplain proposed the following, as a by-law for our
evening meetings, copied, he said, from the records of
his old Reading parish, under date of 1662: "Every
dog that comes to the meeting, after this present day,
or on lecture days, except it be their dogs that pay for
a dog-whipper, the owners of those dogs shall pay six-
pence for every such offence."   The Pilgrim by-law of
two centuries and a year old being accepted by accla-
mation, The General took up the thread of his narrative thus: —

In the Wilderness.

"In the month of November, 1828, I left the quiet
village of Brimfield to seek my fortune somewhere
away, I hardly guessed where. It was a day of sadness
to me when I left. I had long enjoyed the society of
esteemed friends there, whom I loved, and who, I
think, loved me. In the circle in which I moved, I
think I may say, few had warmer friends. I had never
known care and responsibility, and my even, lively
nature had kept me happy. Fond of society, jovial in
my disposition, the evening circle that I entered was
sure to have some animation. Others felt the separation, but I more; for I was launching my bark on the
sea of life without a guide or friendly adviser. But I
was full of hope, self-reliant, and fully determined, not
only to better my condition, but to attain to a higher
intellectual and moral standard, and more marked employment in life.

"With a small hand-trunk, containing all my effects,
and with a few dollars in money, I bade adieu to my
friends, and, taking the stage, went to Hartford, and
thence to New Haven, where I spent a few days in
visiting an old schoolmate. Then I took passage on
the first steamer I ever saw, for New York. The passage was delightful, and my happiness was marred only
as the thoughts of home and the separation from friends
came over me, and I felt that each hour hastened me
from them, and into a land of strangers. I visited

some of the more prominent objects of interest in New York, taking a few days for it, and then went on to Elizabethtown, N. J. At the hotel I noticed an advertisement for a school teacher, in a district three miles out. Procuring a horse, I went out to the place, engaged with the trustees to teach the school, and entered at once on the work.

"This calling soon introduced me to good society, and I was not long in finding that my location was among a people well noted for their hospitality and courtesy to strangers, and for their sterling integrity and moral and Christian worth. The most of them lived on lands inherited from their ancestors, many of whom were those old patriots who, in the Revolution, were first on the battle-fields of New Jersey.

"Here again I renewed my studies with double energy, and commenced others of a higher order, reciting in Latin, and geometry, and trigonometry to a private teacher, the Rev. Mr. Burroughs, who died a few years afterwards.

"The four years I spent here, in constant employment as a teacher, were eventful as well as very happy ones in my life. No one who has visited Elizabethtown and its vicinity can be ignorant of its unsurpassed beauty and loveliness, specially in the spring and summer. Here I mastered civil engineering and surveying, a profession I had chosen as adapted to favor the growing purpose of my heart — a settlement in the West.

"The society was of a solid, genial, intelligent character, and so made my residence in it both pleasant and profitable to me. During the first winter of my labors here, I boarded in one of those antiquated

cottage houses, where the stairs to the chamber commence in the room below, and have one step before the
door opens into the stairway. This convenient step
was often used as a kind of shelf for sundry articles.
On one occasion the boys had set a half-bushel measure on this step, in the dusk of the evening. In descending the stairs, I stepped into it, and sliding off,
fell at full length on the floor. On rising, I was introduced to a young lady, a cousin of the family, who had
incidentally called in. Four years afterwards, that
young lady became my wife, and has shared with me
the pleasures and privations of life for more than thirty
years. And though I was thus measured out to her at
first, she has never had reason to complain of scanty
weight or bulk."

Of course the camp had a laugh. It was useless to
try to do otherwise. That the portly dimensions of
The General, now quite an alderman in figure, should
ever have attempted to occupy a half-bushel, was too
ludicrous a thought, while the boys enlarged on his first
captivating approaches to the young lady. The pause
in the narration was used also to renew the fires, and
while Dock and Rube, who were picking ducks, drew
modestly nearer to join in the story and the laughing, The General proceeded:—

"In the autumn of 1832 I was married, and removed
to a small village in Sussex county, N. J., where I
spent two years as the principal of an academy. Then
I returned to Elizabethtown. The spring of 1835 I
spent in Norfolk, Va., in teaching. In the fall of the

4

same year I sailed for New Orleans, with a view of entering into some business there; but the yellow fever prevailed to an alarming extent, though it was as late as the 20th of October, and so I went up to Natchez, where I engaged for a time in teaching fancy painting (an art I had acquired while a teacher) to classes of young ladies and in seminaries. In this I was quite successful; but an opportunity offered where I could enter the business of land surveyor for the general government, and at the same time gratify my desires for wild life adventures and exploration.

"Cotton lands in the States of Mississippi and Louisiana, in fact throughout the whole South, had become valuable. Cotton was high, negroes commanded large prices, and speculation in the staples of that region was almost wild. As a consequence, the unsettled portions of those states were being explored for cotton lands, and plantations were fast opening wherever suitable soil could be found. I eagerly accepted proposals from the surveyor-general of that land district to explore and survey these new lands, and so prepare them for market, specially as such employment would gratify some of my ruling passions for frontier life.

"Having purchased a horse, compass, and other outfit, I set forth, about the first of January, 1836, going up the Yazoo River into the Pontotoc land district. At Chockchuma, on the Yallobusha River, in the Choctaw Purchase, as it was called, I obtained my maps, notes, and instructions from the land office there. Penetrating from Chockchuma far into the interior, I entered on my work in the depths of the dense forest, amid lakes and bayous, canebrakes and cypress swamps. In this exploring tour for selecting lands, I had but a single attendant, and camped beside the fallen log, or with the Mississippi raftman. The rivermen, runaway negroes, and fugitives from justice were then the only inhabitants of this wild country. It was in this desolate region that the notorious Morrill gang of desperadoes made their rendezvous, the dread and terror of the South, whose plot for a negro insurrection in the winter of 1835–6, at Natchez and vicinity, was discovered just in time to prevent a most horrible massacre.

"While on this expedition, I visited the old Eliot missionary station, on the Yallobusha River, planted there in 1818, among the Choctaw Indians. The mission had been abandoned, and the grounds turned into a cotton plantation. It was a beautiful location, on high and rolling lands, cleared from the native forests by the missionaries. The buildings were of logs, spacious, and had an air of neatness and comfort. In front of the mansion was a lawn, on which tame deer were feeding. A few scattered fruit trees remained, mementoes from the hands of those who, years before, had planted them in Indian soil, and had now gone to a brighter and better land.

"The whole scene, to a reflecting mind, was full of sadness. The remembrance of the labors and trials of those who, long years ago, had penetrated this dark wilderness to carry the news of salvation to the benighted Indian, and of those, too, who had gone home to their reward, flitted before my mind, as I wandered over the once consecrated grounds, and sought the places made sacred in teaching the sons of the

forest the way to eternal life. I roamed over the
fields, and traversed the old log buildings where the
schools were kept, and the morning and evening prayer
went up to the missionary's God, to endure unto good
fruit and the end.

"I blushed for our national government, when I considered how it unrighteously broke up all these good
beginnings among the Choctaws. By treaty, these
lands were reserved to this tribe forever, and the government favored and aided Christian missions here.
The Indians opened good farms, and introduced all the
simpler arts of civilization, and many of them had become wealthy. But Mississippi slaveholders wanted the
lands for cotton, and so the treaty with the Choctaws
was faithlessly broken, a sham treaty of sale was formed
with a few of the tribe, and the State of Mississippi
assumed jurisdiction over the Indian territory, the
great body of the Indians objecting to the whole thing.
A forced sale brought them but a trifle for their homes
and improvements, and they were forcibly removed to
the west of the Mississippi River, in the years 1831, '2,
and '3. Their number was about fifteen thousand. The
expenditure on these mission premises had been about
sixty thousand dollars by the Board of Missions; but,
under government appraisal and by sale, it returned to
the Board less than five thousand.

"I remained over night in the neighborhood, at a
little village near by, that had just begun its existence.
Learning that one of the missionaries, Father Smith,
still lived in the vicinty, I called on him at an early
hour the next morning. It was one of those clear,
beautiful mornings of a southern winter. The sun

began to shine through the thick forest.   As I reached the door of his rude cabin, I heard the voice of prayer. The pioneer Christian was praising God, in the stillness of the morning, that he had brought him through so many trials and dangers, and that he still 'dwelt under the shadow of his wing.'

"When the service was ended I entered and introduced myself. Mr. Smith had lost his first wife in the early part of his settlement there, and had married another from the tribe among whom he lived. A large family of children surrounded him, the most of whom could speak English with fluency. They were sprightly, and some of them quite handsome. The venerable patriarch, with clear recollections of the days of darkness and distress, related to me his trials and difficulties on their journey into the wilderness, and the misgivings and fears of their first settlement.

" They left the Mississippi River in flat-boats, and, in the heat of summer, ascended the Yazoo and its tributaries, into the unknown country. The men labored at the oars, and the women steered the boats. Sickness prevailed among them. One of their children died by the way, and they buried him in the deep, lone forest, and passed on to their labors of love and sacrifice. 'But,' said the good old man — and the tears rolled down his furrowed cheeks — 'I have never regretted my coming here. My wicked heart murmurs sometimes, but God sends comforts and blessings to us, as his missionaries, more than we deserve.'

" From Mr. Smith I learned much about the country, and particularly of the unexplored parts, a knowledge of which he had gained from the Indians. He also told me much of the bandit Morrill, and his gang, who had spread terror through that country.

"I travelled over the Black River country, which was at that time just beginning to be settled. In the early spring the river overflowed its banks, and the bridge on which I had crossed it was swept away. Not aware of the danger of the undertaking, I attempted to swim it with my horse, as it was near night-fall, and the last house passed was some distance back. When about half way over, some drift struck the horse, throwing me off, and so entangling him as to carry him down stream. Being a good swimmer, I freed the horse, and then seizing him by the tail, we landed on the same bank from which we started. Returning to the house, far behind, I remained there several days, till the river fell. I then returned to Natchez, made my report to the surveyor general, and in May arrived in New Jersey, well stored with observations and reflections on my first visit to the South, its people, soil, productions, and peculiar institutions."

And so, well housed, in the narrative, with his family, amid all the comforts of an old civilization, The General closed for the night. Better and better, the boys thought, as there were fewer houses, more Indians, and wild adventures in the forests. Still they begged for longer stories, and more bears thrown in; and they paddled up and down the Yazoo and Black River a long time, after their candle went out, before they tied up for the night in Sleepy Hollow Cove.

FOURTH NIGHT.

"HUNTING and fishing! What a recreation for civilized folks, men of business, professional men, and Christian ministers!" And then tender Miss Araminta exclaims again, "How cruel to torture the innocent fishes, and shoot the beautiful water fowl and timid deer! How can any one bear to kill anything for his own enjoyment!" And her silks rustle with a holy horror at the thought. Yes, maiden of the tender heart, but how many silk-worms were scalded to death that you "might have one dress fit to put on"? How many Andersons, and Spekes, and Livingstones almost, and poor Africans, lost their lives, as well as the frightened ostrich hers, that you might properly toss your head with its least bit of a hat and a splendid plume on it? Pitying the deer, is it? Sorry for poor dumb creatures, are you? See those sweating, jaded, and dying horses, toiling up the White Mountains with ladies' trunks too big to have gone into the ark through the door in the Primer picture.

I fear Miss Araminta would not have enjoyed, as a neighbor, Bernabo Visconti, whose tomb and equestrian statue may be seen at Milan. He kept five thousand hounds, quartered on his more wealthy subjects, and any dog became too fat or too lean at the peril of his keeper. What a glorious orchestra, to have them all

open at once on a slope of the Adirondacks, under "a
southerly wind and a cloudy sky," in an October morning! The famed and unfortunate hunt of Fitz James
around Loch Katrine and the steeps of Benledi and
Uam Var would be nothing to it. Tender Miss
Araminta must go out with us some morning. She
needs reconstructing. I fear me much she would now
be unwilling, the soft heart, to take the piece of money
from the mouth of St. Peter's fish.

Another cup, Dock, of that dark-brown Mocha.
Now a hot biscuit. They cool off very quickly in this
airy tent. One more partridge, rare and smoking.
Now for a wide range, a long day, and a heavy pack,
into camp again, not forgetting some rare duck's
plumage for Miss Araminta's love of a bonnet.

As I struck out to-day, wilder than usual, three, four,
seven miles, over low prairie, through heavy timber,
across marshes and around lagoons, I felt for a time
very happy without knowing why. At length the
thought from my deeper consciousness came to the
surface, that this hunting ground never can be settled.
Men cannot live here through the year. The annual
overflow will make it impossible. Then it is reserved
by a statute of nature for a hunting and fishing ground
forever! What a kind and wise provision of providence!

It was intended men should hunt and fish, and in the
final reconstruction of the world for man, just before
the days of Adam and Nimrod, large tracts were left in
a state impossible forever for human occupation. The
vast belt of bottom lands skirting the Mississippi — and
that the swelling river can cover when it will — keeps

men from encroaching on the domain of wild animal
life. The vast bayous around its mouth and in the
Gulf States, and its shores to its very sources, divide
the country between men and wild fowl and beasts.
So the Kankakee bottoms are providential game pre-
serves for Swan Lake settlers. Foolishly put in market
at ten cents an acre, their annual flooding laughs at
the Land Office at Washington and the stock board at
Chicago. The Winnebago Marsh, in Wisconsin — a
tract fifteen or twenty miles long, with half as much
breadth — was preëmpted by the Webfoots before the
days of Columbus, and will remain, by statute of Nature,
under their squatter sovereignty till the last gun is
fired.

It is not designed that the first settlers in a country
shall have the best time and exhaust the supplies;
some of the sporting is reserved. So large portions of
British America will remain as it is, all through the
millennium, a region for summer excursionists with
gun, angle, and camp, and the white bear can be
hunted around the north pole, till that distinguished
axle is worn out. The price of Alaska is cheap as an
addition to our national hunting-park, anticipating the
time when settlements and improvements, so called,
shall have ruined the rest of our habitable domain.
There are portions of the Rocky Mountains that
nothing but wild animals can occupy for any twelve-
month continuous, and streams that no steamer can
vex, or water-wheel use, and pay dividends. This is as
providential as the grain-fields of Iowa or the Nile.
So has Nature set up bars to irrepressible progress and
settlement and corner lots, that the goodly art of the

angle and the wholesome exercise of the chase may not be driven from the earth.

Possibly William the Conqueror carried the thing too far in destroying villages and towns to make forests for deer. When he had sixty-eight royal forests, he laid waste an immense tract in Hampshire to form another, called The New Forest, and the curses of the peasantry there came on him for it. And when his son Richard was gored to death in it by a stag, they called it the judgment of Heaven on him for so making that Forest. But, then, improvements, and progress, and settlements should not have been allowed to monopolize all the game regions of Merrie England. The English mistakes should be a warning to us in our new and splendid wilderness country.

I confess to an inward satisfaction when I hear that the population is falling off in some rural towns, and that others are too far from the track of the nineteenth century to be annoyed by the sound of the railroad. I own to some sympathy with Bryant's Indian at the burial-place of his fathers, now covered with the white man's thrift : —

> " I like it not; I would the plain
> Lay in its tall old groves again."

Yes, a portion of this world was set apart, primitively and organically, for hunting and fishing. Why, even the Holy Land had these reservations and human comforts. It had lakes and streams stocked with fish, and good fishermen were the very best of apostles, while its hill-sides, and ravines, and the great plain of Esdraelon, abounded in animals for the chase. There were the bear and panther, jackals and foxes, hyenas and wolves, the badger and lion, squirrels and hares, the wild goat, antelope, and fallow deer, and, in the best days of the Jewish commonwealth, the buffalo, or wild ox. This was the "goodly land," when promised, and in the earlier glories of the kingdom prophets and good men could chase "the wild gazelle on Judah's hills," or hunt the bulls of Bashan on the far side of the Dead Sea. David had good training in the chase for the army and the crown. "Thy servant slew both the lion and the bear," he says to Saul, pleadingly, when longing to meet him of Gath, who had defied the armies of Israel. Surely if David, the general and king, prophet, psalmist, and good man, could go on a bear hunt, "thy servant" might shoot wild geese at Swan Lake.

It is one of the discomforts now, in seeking a quiet little nook for summer rest, to find somebody there. "O for a lodge in some vast wilderness," where nobody could find a body! This has often been my wish, as it was of Walter Scott. "There is nothing I should like more," he once said to Irving, "than to be in the midst of one of your grand, wild, original forests, with the idea of hundreds of miles of unknown forest around me." I never have been able to find that lodge yet, though I have tried. Here at Swan Lake, we are disturbed by the deep, gruff, asthmatic cough of steamers two miles away.

Once three of us had depended on a little quiet on the head-waters of the Androscoggin, twenty-five miles comfortably from everybody; but two men broke our slumbers one night at ten o'clock. Again, thirty good miles from any house, on the Union River, in Maine,

5

an old college mate and myself were just dishing up, in the light of a camp fire, a venison stew, that at Parker's would cost a dollar a plate, with the amount of waiter there paid for, when two men walked in among our shadows and savory odors. We served them, of course, bountifully, and they paid us in pioneer stories, though it took us till midnight to settle the bill. One is obliged now to go a long and tedious way to be sure of meeting a deer or moose, or bear or wolf. The older parts of the country are nearly ruined, and the next generation would have poor prospects, but for these natural and providential reservations of bog, and wild mountain, and arctic patches a thousand miles square.

Now, after all this talking, I am quite sure that Miss Araminta is fully satisfied that hunting, fishing, and camping out are recreations perfectly proper for business men, scholars, and gentlemen, and that a kind providence has made parts of the world fit for game and uninhabitable for man, that we sportsmen might have ample grounds for tentage, angle, and gun.

A wide range and a long day, I said in the morning; and it has proved so. Night is closing in as I thread my path back to the encampment.

> " The shades of eve come slowly down,
> The woods are wrapped in deeper brown,
> The owl awakens from her dell,
> The fox is heard upon the fell;
> Enough remains of glimmering light
> To guide the wanderer's steps aright."

The bearings are familiar, and the cheerful fires and

camp lights soon make the tall old trees smile to their top branches, as I enter the ring again. The supper hour is past when I come in, but Dock has not forgotten the chaplain. The gravies and biscuit are hot, and the coffee steaming. Now the side of a brant, and now a coon's shoulder, renew me, and then comes a woodcock, while English snipe keep me busy a little longer, and The General is made to wait his fourth beginning. A dish of canned peaches brings the supper to a period and the story to an opening.

Not all Romance.

"In the autumn following, 1836, I again left New Jersey with men and outfit for a land surveyor, and returned South. Leaving my men in camp near Vicksburg, I went to Jackson, on Pearl River, about forty miles, and, for want of a public conveyance, on foot, to see the surveyor general, whose office was there, and get the contract and instructions for my first survey for government. The surveyor general for Mississippi at that time was General Henry S. Foot.

"My papers assigned me to the head waters of the Sunflower River, amid lakes, cypress swamps, and canebrakes, bears, snakes, and alligators. The region was unexplored, subject to overflow, and a part of the Choctaw Purchase. To reach the ground I had to ascend the Mississippi to a point nearly opposite the mouth of the Arkansas, and then pack my supplies to the field, across many small streams and bayous, that at times made the trip almost impossible.

"After reaching the Sunflower we found an old pirogue of about thirty feet in length, that enabled us to navigate the stream on which some of the work lay. This relieved the men of much labor, as in our situation no horse or mule could be used, and all transportation was made on our backs. These lands had been taken by the government from the Choctaw Indians, in the way I have mentioned. Though some of the land was worthless, its survey was necessary.

"The general face of the country was level, broken into ridges in places, with deep bayous, and all subject to an annual overflow from the Mississippi. In some portions there were extensive lakes and cypress swamps, while the more elevated parts were covered with heavy timber and almost impenetrable canebrakes. The country was uninhabited, except by raftsmen, who resorted there in winter months to cut cypress timber, and float it out on the spring·rise for a market down the river, and by criminals, who had fled from justice, and by runaway negroes.

"Reaching my work, thirty miles interior from the Mississippi, I found it anything but encouraging, and it would have been abandoned at once, and my party returned home, but that I was determined, and would not allow myself to abandon it because of difficulties. The company consisted of six men, the most of them of no experience in the rougher employments of life. Everything was new to them in this region and work and manner of living. They were therefore full of excitement, and ignorant of the future, and so entered into the enterprise with good feeling and alacrity.

"A month passed, and though the labor was extreme, cutting our lines through heavy cane, wading swamps and meandering lakes, yet all looked cheerful on our difficulties, and anticipated the day when we should be through, and return to civilization and our homes. But as the work progressed the labor increased, as the country became more low and marshy, so that often a day would be spent in water ten and fifteen inches deep.

"Besides this, often, in running meridian lines, our

work took us so far from camp during the day, that we could not return at night without great waste of time and travel. So at times we were obliged to carry with us, strapped to our backs, blankets and provision enough to last us several days, or while running round a township six miles square. Night often found us in water leg deep, away from any ridge, where a comfortable camp could be made. In such cases we had to cut trees of the water ash, form a scaffolding on crotches above the water, and start a blaze for our coffee and cold meats on one end. Here, on the poles softened up by brush, we would spend the night, and in the morning step off our bed and commence the wading for the day. During the coldest part of the winter, this was a rather cool proceeding, as the ice would sometimes form during the night, and lie on the overflow till ten o'clock in the day. Generally the weather was cool, frequently frosty, with heavy rain storms.

"Game became scarce, excepting bears, and these it was hard to kill in the canebrake."

When The General mentioned bears, the boys shouted, "Good!" "There they are!" "Now bring on your bears!" and the like. The General quietly remarked, "There are two kinds of black bears in America, boys: one is the bear in a story, and the other is the bear out doors." He continued : —

"There were some opossums on the ridges and among the persimmon trees, the fruit of which they like much. The wild fowl were abundant, but the immense spread of water made the field too large for

hunting them.   The dependence of the party for supplies was, therefore, almost wholly on the settlements
on the Mississippi, thirty miles distant.

"The winter of 1836-7 was noted for an unusual overflow of the Lower Mississippi, in the month of February.
This was occasioned by the open winter at the North,
the early melting of the snows, and heavy rains. As a
result, many suffered from it extremely, who were not
prepared for it; and we were among them.   The
pirogue had been snagged, her bows staved in beyond
repair, and so abandoned.   Provisions grew scanty, little game could be killed, and our camp was fast coming to short rations.

"Indeed, a crisis soon came, and something must be
done.   We put ourselves on short allowance, and eked
out, as best we could, our famished larder with opossums and other small game, with now and then a catfish.   But we could not run the risk of such uncertain
supplies.   They must be packed in from the river. I
could not trust any of my men to thread a way to the
nearest post, and find the path back again. I must go
myself. I realized the personal peril in this, the already
half starving condition of my men, endangered much
more by being left probably two weeks while I went
for supplies.

"It had become warm and sultry on the morning I
started, and by ten o'clock thick, heavy clouds began
to darken the sky. To one accustomed to the rainy
season in the South, all the premonitory symptoms of
a thunder-storm appeared. It was not long before it
burst with deep rolling thunder over the solitary and
endless waste of that desolate country. Never had I

seen such vivid flashes, as it were currents of lightning, or heard such awful peals of thunder. In the dense forest, with patches of impenetrable canebrake and thicket, it was dark at noonday. I sought shelter in a hollow tree till the strength of the storm should be spent.

"Real night was drawing on, when, after wandering on in some confusion, I judged it best to retrace my steps for camp. But all was changed. In the darkness of the storm I had become bewildered, and could not recognize a single object; and there is a terrible sameness to a southern forest. Not one known point could I make to steer by. I was lost! I thought of a fire, and my matches, and even pistol, were soaked, like myself. As the darkness deepened, I sought shelter under a fallen tree that rested on its limbs, two feet from the ground. Here, amid the crash of falling trees, whose trunks were decayed, and that after heavy rains are apt to fall, without a fire, in the thick darkness, and made more sensible and gloomy by the hooting of owls, I ate my moist lunch, and then tried to while away the tedious hours of the night.

"There was the hut of a raftsman about half way on my route to the river, that I had intended to enjoy on my first night out. I had a sorry camp instead. As soon as daylight appeared I was in search again of my trail, or some lines of my previous surveys, that I might know my location and take my bearings; but all was strange to me. About noon, however, I came across a line of my survey, cut through a canebrake in the early part of my work. I followed this for some time, but when the sun came out I found I was going in the wrong direction. I then doubled on my track, and went in the opposite course till I struck the Sunflower River, and soon found familiar points and bearings on my old survey. With light steps and a lighter heart I set forward with renewed vigor for the camp of the raftsman, which I reached a little after nightfall.

"I have told you before that these camps were almost the only place of human habitation in this wilderness, and that these were often the abode also of the freebooter. The escaped criminal, the negrostealer, and the fugitive slave himself, were often found in these cabins; and woe to the officer of justice, the master, or any one else, who attempted an arrest in such a den of desperadoes.

"I had been at this hut before, on my first entrance into the forest, and had seen men there who pretended to be choppers and raftsmen, whose whole appearance indicated another business. On entering at this time I found a head man, and a good supply of game, meat, and corn meal. There were piles of plunder in different parts of the house, which seemed to have been built at different times, and as occasion required. Logs, bark, and cane were used indifferently as material.

"It was very evident that labor was not the intention of the dwellers in this den. There were no evidences of it in the vicinity, and I soon had more than suspicions that I was in a rendezvous of bandits. As I sat by the fire, awaiting the preparation of the supper by a negro, my assurance of the character of the house was confirmed by a study of the faces of the men, and by the vile and profane language they used. They were evidently a gang who infested that country, plundering traders in flat-boats, merchants, travellers, and planters; being negro stealers, cutthroats, and murderers. I was in a den of outlaws, and beyond the pale of civilized life.

"The keeper knew me and my profession, and when this was explained to the gang, the restraint imposed by a stranger's presence was thrown off in a measure, and they talked with more freedom. But I felt secure even among such a horde of villains. I knew that the amount of money I might be supposed to have would not tempt them to injure me, or pay the risk they would incur in doing it.

"A blanket was given me, and I lay down in one corner of the cabin for the night. During the late hours there was a fresh arrival of two white men and a negro. Whether they came from the settlement on the river, or from similar camps in the forest, I knew not; but the whites seemed acquainted with the head man.

"It is a characteristic of camp life, not only in Mississippi, but all through the new settlements and wilds of the West, that travellers and strangers are always welcome to the cabin of the hunter or of the raftsman. If one in hunting or exploring pass a camp from which the occupants are gone for the time, he is expected to help himself of what the house affords to the supply of his wants, and also to so much as he may need to carry him to his next point of destination. These are courtesies well understood by all backwoodsmen. The Rocky Mountain trapper has, on such occasions, no luxuries too choice to be brought out for his stranger-guest. The fattest ribs of the mountain sheep, the best steak of the antelope, the juicy hump of the buffalo, or the rich tail of the beaver, is set forth, and the wanderer to that cabin is made welcome and glad.

"Years afterwards, in those far western wilds I proved this. The courtesy of Roderick Dhu to James Fitz James was a fair type of our frontier hunters and trappers, when

> 'He gave him of his highland cheer
> The hardened flesh of mountain deer.'

"I resumed my weary journey in the morning, not without much difficulty, owing to the rise in the river and the wide overflow; but I reached the settlement. Several days were consumed in the purchase of provisions, and in arranging to get them in to my men, since I had to do all this at St. Francis, on the opposite side of the river. I hired a woodcutter's cart to haul my stores as far as possible towards my camp. The wheels of this cart were made by sawing off two sections from the end of a log three feet in diameter, and placing a rude frame on their axle. Such affairs . were used then to carry wood to the river's bank for steamboats. On one of these primitive vehicles I placed my provisions, bacon, corn meal, flour, coffee, and sugar, with a few articles of clothing.

"Thus prepared, with one man as driver, I commenced my anxious return to camp. I avoided the den of the bandits by another though longer route. It also led me over higher ground, by which I hoped to reach the upper waters of the Sunflower with the team. I had ordered my men to remove our camp to

the banks of this river, where, in the early part of our
work, we had what we called Cane Camp; and to this
point I hoped to raft my supplies after discharging the
team. But the second day brought us to the banks of
a deep bayou. Here was a dilemma, formidable and
trying. We traversed it for some distance up and
down, but found no indications of its coming to an
end. In fact there was a current in it, caused by the
overflow, which was still on the increase. These bayous are not, in general, very wide, but deep, having
been cut through the alluvial soil by the annual over-
flows. A tree was soon felled across, and a portion of
the provisions taken over. Night came on; the camp
fire was lighted, the oxen made secure, and we slept
after the fatigues of the day.

"It was decided, the next morning, that we should
load ourselves with as much provision as we could
carry, and attempt so to reach the Sunflower. There
the teamster was to aid me in making the raft, and then
return to his cattle, pack up the remaining provisions,
and go home, while I was to float what we had carried
to the river down to my famishing men, and bring
them all in to the settlement. We started at an early
hour, each of us carrying about one hundred pounds
of bacon and flour. At the distance of about three
miles we crossed a second bayou on a fallen log, where
a false step would have sent us into ten feet of water.

"The journey was tedious both for want of path and
from the weight of our packs. On reaching the river
we found it so wide from the overflow as to be almost
unable to define its channel. It was impossible to make
a raft on the overflow, and run it into the channel, on

account of the trees and undergrowth. We spent much time in exploring for a place where we could build and launch a raft, and then abandoned this project from necessity. Anxious and excited for the condition of my men, and as a last resort, I cached a portion of the provisions on a ridge near by, and taking the balance on my back, I started down stream almost in despair, leaving the teamster to return home.

"I well knew that to follow that stream would bring me to the camp of my suffering men, and also knew, that from the condition of the country in the present high stage of water, I must meet many streams and bayous putting in, that it would be exceedingly difficult to pass. But I pressed on as rapidly as my burden would allow, sometimes wading deep ravines, and at others forcing my way through thickets of cane and prickly ash. At length night overtook me, and I found refuge in the hollow of a cypress tree. The hollow would not allow me to lie down, but in a reclining posture, with a fire in front, I passed the night, sleeping but little, and in anxiety and alarm for my men.

"The next day I had travelled but a few hours when a broad sheet of water presented itself like a lake, concealing the river in its vast expanse. Here again were trouble and delay, though not unexpected. My purpose was formed at once. Wading in as far as I could, I procured a drift log afloat. Separating it from the jam, I got astride of it, with my pack on my back, and thus for half a mile worked my way with a pole through the drift, till I came to land on the opposite side. So I urged my way on again by land till night overtook

me. I slept in a thick clump of cane, and was early on
my way the next morning.

"About ten o'clock I came where some of my surveys
struck the river; then I knew where I was, and how
far from my men. With renewed energy I now pressed
on, heeding no obstacles, my thoughts wild with emotion, and the condition of my poor men constantly prey-
ing on my feelings. The circuitous channel of the river
had greatly increased the distance, and night again
found me afar from them. I laid myself down weary
and almost discouraged. In any other circumstances,
although my powers of endurance were great, I should
have sank by the way; but my whole soul was wrought
up to a kind of frenzy. I knew that my men could not
escape, that they had long been without provisions,
that all game had fled the country, that starvation was
before them, and that relief could come only from me.
I knew that I was within a few miles of Cane Camp,
where I had appointed to meet them. But, two weeks
had elapsed since I left them. Would I find them all
there, and alive? These were my thoughts that night
and the next morning, as I dragged my weary limbs
along down the banks of the Sunflower.

"Suddenly I came upon the camp! My men were
lying around in a listless, dejected state of mind. If
they showed any animation, it was in watching the large
camp kettle that hung over the fire, as if containing
something most valuable. Taken all in all, they had a
wretched, forlorn appearance. I stood looking at them
but a moment, when my strength gave way, and, with
emotions of gratitude for their preservation, I fell

in among them, and we all wept together like children.

"One of the men had just caught a catfish, and they were boiling it without salt or pepper, and watching with eagerness the slow process of its cooking. They had caught one three days before, and eaten it, but the high water had prevented their getting a supply. Game of every kind, except the opossum, had fled from the country, as if by instinct, to escape the overflow. This animal, being slow in motion, had escaped to the ridges, and there lived on the persimmon. Of these animals the men had killed a scanty supply, and sustained life, roasting and eating them without any seasoning, except the white ashes of the hickory bark that served as a kind of substitute for pepper and salt. They had also gathered the persimmon, and eaten it, cooked and raw. So they lingered in life and hope, awaiting my return, knowing the cause of my delay, but believing, too, that I would come.

" The overflow had now begun to subside, and not having much provision to rely on, we abandoned the survey, and took up our march for the settlement. Near the head of the Sunflower we found a canoe adrift. Into this we put our luggage, and after floating it as far as the stream would allow, we fitted poles, like yokes, to the bows by a rope, and then, by two and two, like Dr. Kane's men, we drew it across to the Mississippi, a distance of nine miles, and launched it on its waters. Here the party broke up. Some went to St. Francis, some returned North, while my assistant, H., and myself went down to Vicksburg in the canoe. I thence went out to Jackson, made my report to the Land Office, and then H. and myself took steamer for St. Louis."

Many questions were put, and thrilling incidents elicited in reply, and it was the honest hour of twelve before the camp fire of Swan Lake dozed that night.

FIFTH NIGHT.

"To sit on rocks, to muse o'er flood and fell,
　To slowly trace the forest's shady scene,
　Where things that own not man's dominion dwell,
　And mortal foot hath ne'er or rarely been;
　To climb the trackless mountain all unseen,
　With the wild flock that never needs a fold;
　Alone o'er steeps and foaming falls to lean, —
　This is not solitude; 'tis but to hold
Converse with Nature's charms, and view her stores unrolled."

　　　　　　　　　　　　　CHILDE HAROLD.

NEVER spent a night in a sportman's camp? How old are you? "Well, over twenty-five." You have lost a great deal, but it is not too late to recover something from your mistakes and losses. You have never yet enjoyed a night for what it is in itself, or, as the moralists say, a night *per se*. To be beyond the sight of any midnight lamp of neighbors; beyond the sound of lowing cattle; beyond the noise of any carriage, mill, or other human activity; beyond the bark of any "cur of low degree," — I mean a common watch and farm dog, or any dog except a hunter's — to know that solid, splendid miles of unsettled country lie in a state of pure nature between your blanket pillow and the nearest clearing or dwelling; to feel this frontier, uncivilized darkness wrapping you about in its deep black folds — that is to enjoy a night *per se*. If, fortu-

6

nately, you are alone, you exult in a monopoly of the whole thing; you control the market without a competitor, like a Rothschild on 'change. If you have camp fellows, you may use the luxury of your partial solitude by talking about it. Still there will be the loss of real value by human interruptions and encroachments. The darkness, the starry expanse, or awful storm, the wide reach of silence, you must divide up into shares, and part with the control and comforts of some of them; your meditations will be interrupted, and the deep, silent flow of thought diverted.

You sometimes speak of a morning as "beautiful," "charming," and all that the boarding-school girls say of it. Allow me to ask whether you ever had a whole morning all to yourself. I mean all out doors at that hour of the day, as far as the eye can reach, or the ear; as extensive a morning, I mean, as would cover twelve hours' foot-travel in all directions. Perhaps you have taken a part in a morning from the balcony of the Ocean House, or the Tip-top House, or from a crest of the Alleghanies, in old stage times. Well, that is better than no morning at all. City people, who are seldom off the pavement, and out of coal smoke and the odor of garbage, often say to me, "What a delightful morning!" and they speak so sincerely and joyfully, just as if they know the article when they see it, and the varieties in it, and had, right there on those flag stones and brick walls, and through that dingy window on a back alley with a grape vine, a number one specimen of mornings.

Come, now, let us see a morning in camp. We are on the St. Croix — two of us — between Great

Lake and Grand Lake. Our tent crowns a bit of a mound overlooking the river. Back of us, on the east, goes up a hill, as the hill of Bashan, and over it the gray dawn is just coming. Throw open the tent-fly, and step out, and stand still, and keep silence, for half an hour. You catch at once the outline of the hills against the blushing eastern sky. Leaving you standing in twilight, the rays pass over your tent, and gild the western mountains, that stretch right and left. The birds open their anthem of Morn Among The Mountains, and a full orchestra renders the chorus. The light deepens, fills the valley on the south, and comes flooding up the channel, where the river, on rocks, and in gorges, and over falls, has been sending up its rich bass all the night, and ever since the night of chaos, when the waters began their circuit to keep their place. Look north, and how the new light gives the lake a morning kiss! Far up, farther, and still beyond, see with your field-glass the golden sheet of a real morning. Fleecy, misty patches of clouds now go up, as blankets, from the bed of the lake, to be aired. The trees — and you never saw trees so green before — flutter their welcome to the young day, and, as sunrise falls at your feet, the wild flowers lift up their dewy heads.

That is a clean, full, original morning, and all ours. A beautiful morning in a city! What a delusive thought! We sportsmen have the first chance at Nature, and get all the best specimens.

Now for a breakfast. One kindles the camp fire, and the other throws a well-selected fly where the river makes a deep eddy. In twenty minutes three land-locked salmon lie very close to the coals, and the breakfast is as good as that morning of June 4, 1864, when we ate it.

A storm is nowhere so thoroughly natural and terrible as in a deep forest, where it has always had its way. It was in September, 1854, when we were lying by in the logmen's cabin, on the head-waters of Union River, Maine, where we dished our venison stew to those strangers, that I first felt the grandeur and glory of a forest storm. We were well housed when night closed in with a little rain and stiff wind, and clouds running from the south-east. On rising ground, and in a clearing, with a massive old log cabin, we had nothing to fear, and so only to enjoy the elements in a rage. There was never a darker night, and I think it never rained harder. It came slopping, splashing, as if spilled over from some wandering cistern in the sky. The wind rose from breeze to gale. It rushed and howled as if it were a personal fury. A low marsh, or lagoon, in front of us, exposed our cabin to all the force of the tempest. The forest groaned and roared, as the storm swept into it. Old trees, decayed and dry, were saturated with the pelting rain; and then, partly from their own weight, and partly from the violence of the storm, they would go crashing and thundering to the ground. All through the first part of the night, at intervals, we could hear these falling trees near by. They had endured for ages, and been passed by the woodman as unsound, and this was their last night. Many a green and strong one also went with them. I never knew so wild a night. The location, twenty long miles from any human habitation, the darkness, the rain, the wind, the roaring forest, and the crash of trees, made the

scene fairly sublime. It needed only the lightning and
thunder in proportion to make it terrible. I would
sooner shut from my memory and mind's eye a score
of the best paintings I ever saw than the impressions
of that night. The warm sun came with the morning,
and for a still hunt among the deer the day was delightful. I would Bierstadt had been with us that night:
in what a frenzy of inspiration would he the next day
have dashed off After The Storm !

You err hugely in supposing we sportsmen follow
the wilderness mainly for the joy of so many pieces of
game shot or angled. So we have our morning and
evening meal of our labor, we are filled with success,
and all the rest is the higher enjoyment of studying the
pictures of Nature in her own studio. You should read
what good Wynkyn de Worde says in The Treatyse
of Fysshynge wyth an Angle — a small folio of 1496.
Yet, to be exact, I must add, that Wynkyn only re-
published this valuable work. The author was my lady
Iulyans Berners, prioress of the nunnery of Sopwell,
near St. Albans ; and she printed ten years before, with
Caxton's letter, this Treatyse. And it is a great infeli-
city that "Mary Powell," in her Household of Sir
Thomas More, makes that rare and exact scholar quote
the work to Erasmus as Wynkyn's. Sir Thomas would
not so blunder. This is what Lady Juliana Barnes
says : —

"Also ye shall not use this forsayd crafty dysporte,
for no couetysense, to the encreasynge and sparynge
of your money oonly ; but pryncypally for your solace,
and to cause the helthe of your body, and specyally of
your soule. For whanne ye purpoos to goo on your

dysportes in fysshynge, ye woll not desyre gretly many persons wyth you, whyche myghte lette you of your game. And thenne ye may serue God denowtly, in sayenge affectuously your custumable prayer; and, thus doynge, ye shall eschewe and voyde many vices."

It is thus enjoying Nature in her undisturbed simplicity, before any blemish of man has marred the naturalness in all her varied phases, and moods, and times, that makes the wilderness pastime so fascinating. Let me illustrate by showing you a picture I took, in memory, about the middle of July, 1861. For if you go back to camp now, in the middle of the afternoon, you will not find The General there, or any hunters, not even a dog, but only Dock and Rube among the kettles.

With salmon-rod, reels and lines, choice flies and gaff, and some smaller "harnays," as the prioress calls it, for the smaller members of the Salmo family, I ran through Bangor to Old Town by rail. Thence the ancient stage took me by the Matawamkeag and Holton to Presque Isle. A one-horse power worked me along to Fort Fairfax, of bloodless memory, and the Falls of the Aroostook, four miles above its entrance into the St. John's. No steamer runs to those falls, or railroad, or stage — a blissful region. Nothing runs there but game and the river. The few scattered inhabitants walk about, just a little. No hotel, no boarding-house, and, what is better still, nobody inquiring for one. I found a tent on the beach, just under the falls, occupied by one man — a Scotch Presbyterian, from Tobique — who was netting salmon. I at once rented one half the establishment, and paid him in news from The States, and all about the war just opened. I found my Tent

On The Beach quite equal to Whittier's, the only difference being that I cannot give mine as good a poetic
setting for the public eye.

Here is a river of good volume for one hundred and
twenty miles, hunting for an outlet to the sea. Near
the St. John's, that it has scented from afar, it meets a
mountain range and barrier a mile and more in depth.
Through this it has sapped and mined, worried and
worn and forced its way for ages no doubt, making its
channel. As if still vexed for long delay, it rushes madly
down this gorge. The chasm is not more than two
bow-shots wide, and at points not one. Vast masses
of rock lie along in the channel confusedly, as if an
earthquake should topple and tumble all the blocks on
both sides of Broadway into that New York thoroughfare. The walls are ragged cliffs, forty, sixty, a hundred and fifty feet high in places, and often perpendicular. With the greatest care one can, here and
there, get down to the water's edge. But it is an angry
torrent, boiling, thundering, and foaming. Now it lets
itself roughly over a precipice of five or ten feet, and
now a clean shoot and unbroken plunge of twenty. It
gouges into the sides of the mountain, grinding with
the loose stone it keeps whirling there, vast smooth
caldrons forty feet in diameter. In these great eddies
the salmon rest as they try to work their way up. The
noise drowns all other sounds, and conversation at
many points along the channel is impossible. Fortunately for me, I had it all to myself.

I lay about on the edges of the cliffs, and on projecting rocks, and wherever I could reach a bracket on the
bald walls, for hours each day. I was never weary or

satisfied in looking. Beauty, strength, terror, security, combined in the picture. Each new position gave a new view, and the old one was never twice alike. It was a great addition to my solitary enjoyment of the scene, that at the time I was there a rise in the river of twenty inches took place, and made it possible to work off a jam of logs, that had lodged at the upper entrance of the falls. A gang of red shirts were working these loose, and so one by one they were running the gantlet of the rocky pass. Some of these sticks of timber squared three feet and more on a side, and were forty and fifty long. They were all squared. The mad river tilted them against projecting rocks, and into curved banks, with a concussion that could be felt far from the shore, and be heard for a mile. Sometimes they would be pitched over the rapid shoots end for end, and rise and fall on the water or rocks, or each other, in a terrific manner.

At the foot of these rapids, and where the stream is most tumultuous, it dashes itself furiously against a high rock as huge as a large church, standing midway in the channel. The waters leap far up the front of this barrier, as if in a last effort of strength, and then fall off madly right and left, and about equally, into a basin of fifty acres or more — a kind of Titan's wash-bowl. Here they seethe, and boil, and foam in a frolic of good-natured riot. In this basin, up to the very plunge around that huge dividing rock, I lay long hours dancing, as in an egg shell, in my fragile birch, tempting the salmon with my fly. The lusty fellows would occasionally throw themselves out of water with a lazy majesty, but were very shy of my attentions. I took only smaller ones — the grilse. The freshet, that gave me the grand river views, almost spoiled my fly-fishing for salmon, by filling the water with drift and refuse.

But evening steals on with my long stories, and we are on the wrong side of the Union. Let us telegraph ourselves from the Aroostook Falls to Swan Lake, or we shall lose the opening of The General's fifth story. But as we scud along over the wires, will you not concede that we sportsmen get the very best views of Nature — author's proofs, so to speak?

Over the Mississippi.

"When I closed last night I had escaped from the canebrakes and cutthroats of the Mississippi swamps, and was directing my course towards St. Louis. This was in the spring of 1837. At this time there was much excitement about Wisconsin Territory and the Black Hawk Purchase lying on the Upper Mississippi. A treaty had been made with the Sac and Fox Indians, and that territory purchased and laid open to settlement. Immigration had already commenced. The surveys of the country had been ordered, and the beauty and fertility of it made public.

"Therefore my friend H. and myself, now returning home from the South, determined to visit that region. We planned to go up the river as far as the Dubuque lead mines, thence across to Chicago, and down the lakes by Niagara Falls to New Jersey.

"At that time the Territory of Wisconsin comprised not only what is now that large and beautiful state, but all the present State of Iowa, and a portion of Minnesota, then little known except to the hunter and trapper.

"On board the steamer from St. Louis I became acquainted with Colonel George L. Davenport, of Rock Island, murdered in 1845, and D. C. Eldridge, postmaster at Davenport — a little town then just starting on the Iowa side of the river, and opposite to Rock Island. These gentlemen, learning my profession, urged me very much to stop at Davenport, and examine the country with a view to settlement.

"We had left St. Louis in a little steamer — the Olive Branch — of small dimension, as the water on the rapids was too low for a large boat, and were five days in making the trip to Rock Island. We lay by at Keokuk one day — a place then of a few log shanties and whiskey shops. Here were gathered Keokuk's band of Sacs and Foxes, spending a few days at the old trading-post of the American Fur Company. Black Hawk and his family were encamped a short distance above the village. It was here that I first saw those two celebrated chiefs — Black Hawk and Keokuk. Keokuk, the gifted orator, one of Nature's own noblemen, was in a most beastly state of intoxication. They were on their way to Rock Island to attend a council, called to reply to an invitation of the President of the United States, Martin Van Buren, to visit Washington by a delegation.

"The passage was somewhat tedious, but passed pleasantly amid new scenes constantly coming in view. The marked difference in the scenery between the Lower and the Upper Mississippi, from the monotonous, dead level of the South to the beautiful and varied sloping bluffs of the North, at once excited emotions of pleasure. The newly-built cabin of the immigrant, the virgin soil for the first time opened to receive the seed of the husbandman, were scenes of interest to all, and we could see that the darkness of barbarism was giving way to civilization and improvements. On that trip I for the first time set my eyes on Sturgeon Bay, and surveyed the margins of this beautiful hunting-ground, now made forever famous by the grand encampment of this Club on Swan Lake."

When this was said, with all the gravity that the august circumstances required, the entire company, led off by the boys, sent out three cheers into the darkness, that I make no doubt could be heard to the shore of the big river. The General continued:—

"It was about the middle of April, 1837, when we landed at Rock Island. After the delay of an hour or two we ran across to Davenport. Of this beautiful spot, and to be, as it proved, my future home, I will speak more fully another night.

"At the time of which I now speak, the interior of Iowa was but little known. In a few days I was mounted with three others, having my old and faithful canebrake compass by my side, to explore the strange land. We struck out where the only path was the Indian trail. Now, for the first time, I saw a prairie — one of those great western seas of living green. To me it was not only a new but a noble sight. Gently rolling, it looked like the waves of the ocean, stayed in their course by Him who stilleth the tempest, and now covered over with the grass and flowers of an early spring. Here and there stood small clusters of trees, but the whole country looked like a deserted land — a land where man once dwelt, but where by some desolating blast all had been swept away — houses, fences, all traces of settlement. The stillness of the scene, as we galloped along over the bed of flowers, cast a tinge of melancholy over my feelings. For the thoughts would

arise of a once prosperous people, who may have lived
here, and of the causes of their desolation and extinc-
tion.

"At night we came to a small grove — one of those
little islands of trees in the great sea of grass — and
here we encamped. It was near the first of May, and
in the stillness of the region nothing could be heard
but the cooing of the prairie fowl, and the noisy gabble
of the ducks and wild geese in some distant lake.

"We proceeded on our way with the morning, sometimes frightening the deer from his bed in the tall
grass, and sometimes the prairie wolf from his retreat
in the hazel clump. And so on and on, till we came to
the timber that skirted the banks of the Cedar. We
went up that stream for many days, examining the
country, admiring its beauty, and exulting in the prospect of its settlement into the stir and progress of civil
society. The streams and branches that we found were
swift and clear, and though timber was scarce, except
near the watercourses, no land seemed better adapted
to the wants of man.

"The unrivalled beauty of this section of the West,
not only of Rock Island and its immediate surroundings, but of its rich interior, its tempting soil fruitful in
so many of the staples of life, and its noble river and
banks, nowhere in its long course nobler than here,
induced me at once to fix on it as the place of my
future home. I had travelled over the rugged hills of
New England, and tarried on the pleasant plains of
New Jersey; I had seen, too, the rich cotton lands
of the sunny South; but nowhere had I beheld such
climate, fertility, and beauty combined.

"After our return from this excursion for exploring the interior, I had leisure for more particular observations on the location, beauties, and history of Rock Island, and the wild region about, and for an acquaintance with the Indian, his habits of life, virtues and vices, prejudices and preferences. This was just after the Black Hawk war closed. The Indians had sold their possessions to the United States, but a portion of the tribe, being dissatisfied, were unwilling to remove from the scenes of their childhood and the graves of their fathers.

"The great war chief Black Hawk, five years before, had been basely treated by the civil chief of the tribe, Keokuk, by a treaty sale of the territory, in which he was not consulted, and to which he never gave his consent or signature. Following this, his wigwams had been burned by the whites, his cornfields ploughed up, and his people driven off to seek asylum in other tribes.

"These cruelties, imposed on him by the grasping avarice of the white man, rendered him desperate; so, gathering around him a few faithful warriors, he commenced hostilities against the whites, with all the bitterness of Indian cruelty and revenge. With the tomahawk and scalping-knife he crept through the little settlements of the Rock River country in Illinois, spreading terror, and burning, and death in his track; but armed forces of the government, with volunteers, were soon on his trail.

"Black Hawk had been made a brave for some daring act at the early age of sixteen, and was celebrated in his nation and among the surrounding tribes as a great warrior. He had served the English in the war of 1812, and was the intimate and devoted friend of Tecumseh. He succeeded his father in the chieftainship, and had but rarely known defeat in battle. He was a proud, imperious man, feared by his enemies, and venerated by his own people. Keokuk was his rival, but had no hereditary claim to lead the tribe. He rose from obscurity by the mere force of native talent, and earned his name, which means Watchful Fox. He was a Sac in blood, and disposing of the lands of his tribe in the way I have mentioned, brought about a bitter strife between him and Black Hawk. He was an intimate friend of the whites, and was influenced by them in the matter of the treaty that dispossessed Black Hawk's band of their homes without their knowledge.

"In his bloody march up the Rock River valley, Black Hawk expected aid from his old allies, the Winnebagoes. But when he reached their villages, he found that the tribe would not assist him. He had been to Canada, before entering on this war-path, visiting various tribes there, and obtaining from them a promise of aid in his present campaign. These also now disappointed him, and he was left to fight his battles alone.

"General Atkinson was at the head of our forces in pursuit, and came up with Black Hawk at Sycamore Creek, on Rock River, when a skirmish took place, and the whites were forced to fall back. Black Hawk then fled across the country, towards the Wisconsin River, with our forces in close pursuit. He reached a point on the Mississippi about one hundred miles above Prairie du Chien, called Bad Axe, where he was forced to abandon the field before superior numbers. He was eye-witness to the destruction of his little band while swimming the river, and he himself was captured through the treachery of two Winnebago chiefs.

" When carried, as a prisoner of war, down the river past Rock Island, the grand theatre of his life, and where were the graves of his fathers, with the ashes of his wigwams, he is said to have wept like a child. A sight of so many familiar and hallowed spots, with the memories connected, harrowed up the soul. This was his last look, and it was manliness to weep. And then came out the great truth that there is feeling in the heart of the Indian. It was nobleness in the aged warrior, going, as he was, to the prison of the white man, robbed of his earthly possessions, and bowed down with wrongs, to weep over his fallen greatness, when it was so ignominiously trodden under foot. In full view of all that was good of earth, the home of his fathers for nearly two centuries, the endearing spot of his childhood, and with his children and tribe driven about and slain like the deer of his native wilds, why should he not be in bitterness? The stoical nature of the Indian is proverbial, but oppression and cruel wrong, long continued, can bring him to grief like a woman's.

" About the middle of May of this year, an Indian council was held at the trading-post and fort on Rock Island, by the Sacs and Foxes. It was the one I have already mentioned, to answer the invitation of Mr. Van Buren. There were also, at this time, about five hundred Potawatamies encamped on the west bank of the river, who were invited to be present. These were on their way to new homes on the Missouri River, having been removed by government from the Rock River country.   By the courtesy of Colonel Davenport, the Indian agent, I had the pleasure of sitting in the council.

"The council was opened by passing around the calumet, of which all took a few puffs. This pipe belongs to the tribe, and is requisite on all public occasions when business of importance is to be transacted. The bowl is made from the red pipe-stone, obtained near Spirit Lake, Minnesota, and will hold about half a pint of what they smoke — kinnikinnic — being a mixture of tobacco with a native weed.   The stem of the pipe is about six feet in length, made from an ash sapling, with the pith driven out.   The whole is highly ornamented with the feathers of various birds, and beads, and bells.   The pipe having been smoked, silence was observed for a short time, when a chief arose, and addressed the assembly, dwelling principally on the condition of the tribe, and how they had passed the winter.   Then another brave harangued the council on matters of a more popular nature; when the agent, through the interpreter, Mr. Le Claire, read to them the invitation of the president.   Much satisfaction was visible on the countenances of the dusky assembly.

"When the agent asked what answer he should send back to their great father, Keokuk slowly rose, letting fall his scarlet blanket from his shoulders, displaying a gaudy calico shirt, ruffled after the fashion of his people.   From his scalp-lock hung the feathers of the bald eagle, the hawk, and the raven, while around his neck, in bold relief, drooped a necklace of the claws of the grizzly bear, mounted on wampum of

7

beads and porcupine quills. His noble features were
painted in the most fantastic colors, and his bosom was
thrown open, exposing the broad chest and full muscle.

"With slow and measured tread, the little bells on
his leggings tinkling at every step, he shook hands first
with the whites, and then with his own people. Taking
his position in front of the agent, he began his speech
by expressing the pleasure he felt in seeing his friends,
the white men, around him, and his braves, who had
always stood by him, and fought the Sioux so nobly.
He then spoke of the invitation sent them by his great
father at Washington, and complimented him on his
good sense in sending for him and his chiefs. He said
his father was a great chief, and the white people a great
nation ; that the fires of their wigwams always burned
brightly, and their hearts were very large; and that he
should go to see his great father. He then branched off,
much like a congressman, into a powerful speech, intended to present his own greatness as well as that of
his people.

"His utterance was rapid, clear, and distinct. Often,
in the excitement of his subject, particularly when referring to the aggressions of his enemies — the Sioux —
his interpreter had to stop him, and have the glowing
passages repeated. His position at times was very
commanding. He would draw himself up, and fling
back his noble head, with one foot advanced, and long,
sinewy arm extended, while every muscle was strained
to its utmost tension, and his keen, piercing eye rested
on the agent, in almost exact imitation of Clay or
Webster.

"He was nature's own orator, the best among all the

tribes of the North-West. He was frequently cheered by his warriors with the characteristic Indian Ugh! Ugh! and How! How! reminding one of the gruff Englishman's Hear! Hear!

" The Potawatamie chiefs were invited to speak, and did so; when the council broke up with presents of pipes, tobacco, and pails of sweetened water. Then commenced a game of ball by the young men, while others went to their wigwams on the grassy slopes of the river bank. Here the ceremony of giving presents to their friends — the Potawatamies — took place. The ceremony consisted in placing blankets on the ground, in front of the wigwams, when a Potawatamie brave would step forward, set up a stick four or five feet long, and place on it a rag or tuft of grass, to represent the enemy to be killed. He would return to the wigwam, and in a few moments be seen stealthily approaching the object, then spring with a fierce bound and piercing yell on the enemy, and tomahawk and scalp him, amid the shouts of the whole encampment. He then stands by the blankets, and while he harangues the crowd, detailing the circumstances of the exploit just represented, his friends make donations in flour, meal, meat, coffee, and blankets, depositing all in a pile before him. This being done, another goes through a similar ceremony, and so on till the entertainment is completed.

" Rock Island and its vicinity had been the camping-ground of the Indians from time immemorial. Marquette and Joliet found a large village on the west bank of the river, where Davenport now stands; and the tradition of the Indians, still extant, is, that tribe fought tribe for the possession of this beautiful land, conquering, and in turn being conquered. The discoverers of The Great River, which they called Conception, reaching it on the 17th of June, 1763, found the tribes of the Illini here. The tradition of the Sacs and Foxes is, that they came from the Gitche Gumee (Big Sea Water) — Lake Superior; and Indians yet living say that the home of their fathers was at Sac Creek, emptying into Lake Superior.

"The Sac and Fox Indians were originally two distinct tribes; but war, pestilence, and famine reduced them, till they united as one people, and have become one band. They had possession of the country at the time of its purchase by the United States, and though they had been paid, and surrendered their titles on both sides of the Mississippi, they lingered around the haunts of their early days, and at the time of which I now speak, they were encamped on the island and its immediate vicinity. By nature fond of ease and idleness, so much like the pale faces, they hung around the frontier towns, exchanging their few furs and peltries for whiskey, tobacco, and trinkets, eking out a scanty living and contracting the vices of the whites, who would buy their last blanket with fire-water. Thus situated, they would be often embroiled in quarrels, not only with the white man, but with each other.

" On one occasion, soon after I arrived there, a dispute arose between two young Indians in a drunken frolic, when one struck the other — an indignity that an Indian seldom submits to, as it places him in the position of a dog. The matter remained until morning, when both were sober. They then repaired to a little island off the lower part of Davenport, armed, one with a rifle and the other with a shot-gun, to settle the difficulty in an 'honorable' way, after the white man's fashion. The friends of both parties were present, but left the two to make their own arrangements. When it was determined that they should shoot at each other, the hero of the shot-gun marched off for the agreed distance; but, before he could turn and fire, he of the rifle shot him through the head, and then fled like a deer. He was a Winnebago, and lived on Rock River, at Shab-be-na's Grove. His friends were in deep distress, for they well knew his doom, in accordance with Indian law.

"The relatives of the deceased clamored for blood. He was sent for by his friends, his own sister going after him. He was found in his wigwam, with blackened face, brooding in silence over his doom, well knowing that the Great Spirit was angry with him, and that no sacrifice was too great to appease his wrath.

"He returned to Rock Island with that sister, whom he tenderly loved, and who urged him, for the honor of his family and tribe, to submit to his fate. One bright morning in June, about a month after the murder, the quiet camp of the Indians on the island was startled by the doleful chant of the death-song. A few canoes, with a white flag in the bows of the foremost, which was paddled by an Indian girl of some twenty summers, came gliding around the lower point of the island. In the forward part of the canoe, wrapped in his blanket, with his face blackened, sat the murderer, singing his last song, this side the good hunting-grounds.

"The long, protracted howl of the wigwam crier soon put in motion the camps on both sides of the river. From every nook and eddy along the river there soon shot forth canoes filled with excited savages, eager to participate in the bloody scene at hand. Grave old men were there, the mothers of many a young warrior, and maidens who had often played on the green earth where they now stood. All looked on with stoical indifference, while the wailing and lamentation of the culprit's sister were enough to pierce a heart of stone.

"The prisoner was led up the bank from the canoe by his sister, bowed with grief; but no muscle of his moved, nor any tear came to his eye. He chanted his death-song as he moved slowly to the place of execution. This was a large, open green, with a stone for his seat. The spot was surrounded by hundreds of Indians, but no sound could be heard as they marched into the circle, except the smothered grief of the sister and relatives. After being seated, his blanket was taken from his shoulders, and the black wampum of Pagunk (death) was put into his hands by one of the 'medicine men.'

"The nearest relative of the murdered man then approached from behind him, with a tomahawk, and commenced the death-song in a dance. Soon others joined who were next of kin, until all the relatives were in the circle, armed with knives and tomahawks, and dancing around the prisoner. This ceremony was kept up for some time, when other braves entered, and the yell became deafening.

"At a given signal from the first that entered, all

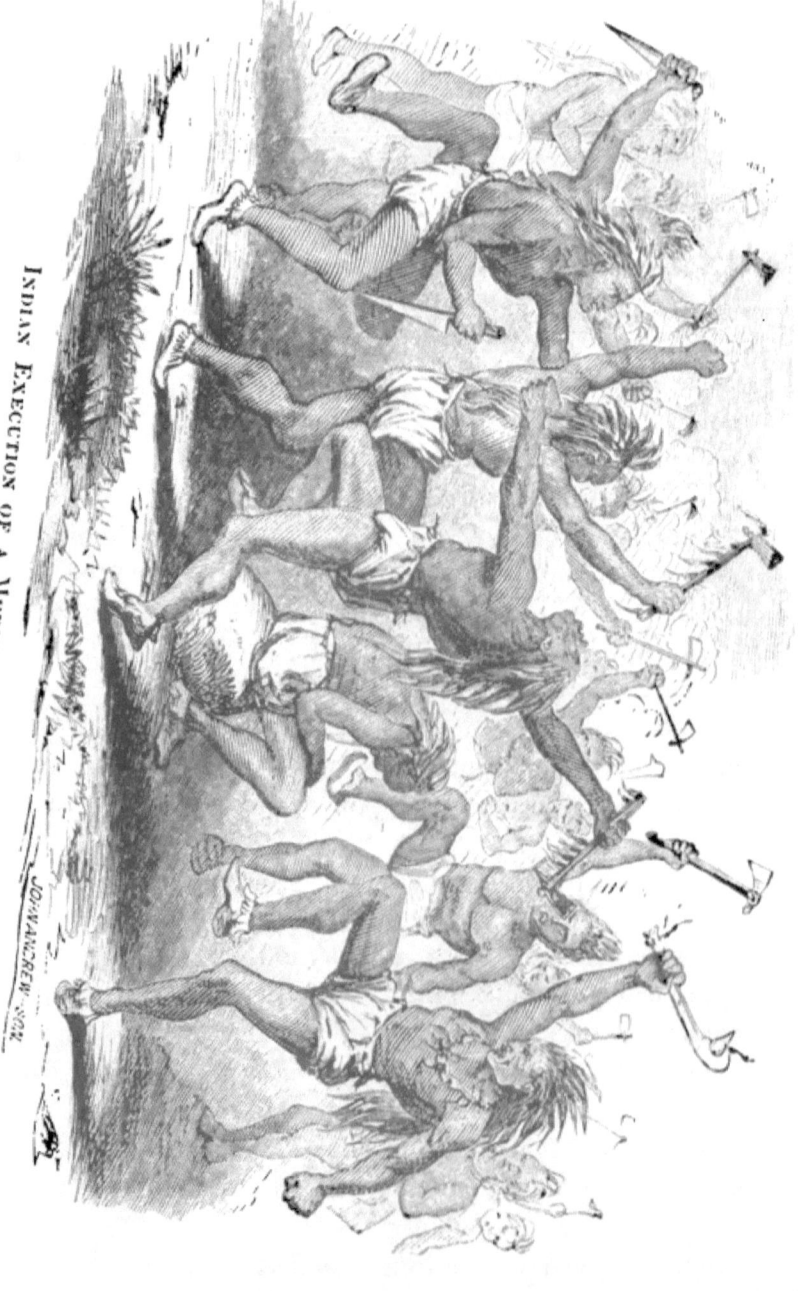

INDIAN EXECUTION OF A MURDERER. Page 102.

sprang at the victim with the most horrid outburst that human voices could make, and in a few moments all that was left of the prisoner was a clotted mass of flesh and blood."

After The General closed this fearful story scarcely a word was spoken, and we glided away silently to our tents.

SIXTH NIGHT.

THERE must be, of course, a sameness in the routine of each day in our camp life, and yet, after all, a pleasing and often exciting variety. No two meals are alike; the weather is constantly changing; the parties are made up differently every morning for the hunt; our success varies, and our kinds of game. Now a package of wild fowl is starting off for dear ones at home, with letters and mementoes safely stowed in; and now a backwoods mail comes in over no post route laid down here, or known at Washington. Occasionally a visitor is piloted to the encampment in polished boots, broadcloth, and pure white linen. We are sorry, and so is he, at the mistake in coming, and there is a mutual gladness when he goes. The man who visits a sportsman's camp, expecting a front room on the second floor, finger-bowls at dinner, and a night police to keep the owls from hooting at him, has mistaken his calling; at least, he is not master of the situation. Before a man joins a company of hunters, he should read what Master Izaak Walton says of fishing, and think the same to be true of hunting:—

"Doubt not, sir, but that Angling is an art, and an art worth your learning. The question is rather, whether you be capable of learning it. For Angling is somewhat like Poetry: men are to be born so."

In his later years Palmerston was distinguished for his expert use of the horse and the gun in field sports; but this was the crowning of his youthful habits. The first in the chase, in Parliament, and in the nation — those excellences go well together. Many have wondered at the juvenile vitality of the old man. His gun could speak on that subject.

To-day our ordinary list of game, as we swing it up about the camp grounds, was varied, and graced by two splendid swans. They cost the two gentlemen who bagged them a night's bivouac on a marsh, six miles away; but that was all right. They left camp with that expectation yesterday morning, and shouted their trophies home to-night, as they came gliding down the lake. This is the most intelligent and wary, as well as most weighty and royal, of our American water fowl. Flocks of them will pass to and fro in the clear sky, almost out of sight, so high are they, and peal out their trumpet and bugle notes for miles in every direction. When looking for a night's rest and feeding-grounds, they come nearer and nearer to some lake or lagoon, and circle up and down and around it, coming lower and lower in the dusk of the twilight, till, assured against danger, they plough into the water. This is the time for the hunter, under cover, to take them as they sweep by on their broad wings. So these two were taken. They were pure white, excepting black bill and legs, and a tinge of russet about the head and upper portion of the neck. They were so large that in lifting them from the ground I had to raise their heads above mine; and their weight was twenty-eight and twenty-nine pounds each. One of them came on the

table baked, but the meat was dry and lacked flavor.
This must have been the one that Audubon referred to
when he said, the flesh "of an old bird is dry and
tough." The General put his own hand to some steaks
cut from the breast of the other, and they were excellent. The grain was coarser than the coarsest beef,
and the color a deeper red, and the meat itself full as
juicy.

When in the water during the day, they keep a re-
markable lookout with their long sentinel neck, and a
shot is impossible, except with a rifle at very long
range. The tradition that one mourns itself to death,
if its mate be killed, can hardly be true of them in a
wild state; for they are gregarious, and sometimes in
the early spring flocks of them are so large as to whiten
whole acres of flowed prairie, or lagoon.

When domesticated they may thus pine away and
die of loneliness; and hence the old English law, as
seen in Coke's Reports, case of swans : "He who steal-
eth a swan in an open and common river, lawfully
marked, the same swan shall be hung in a house by the
beak, and he who stole it shall, in recompense therefor,
give to the owner so much wheat as may cover all the
swan, by putting and turning the wheat upon the head
of the swan, until the head of the swan be covered
with wheat."

There are two varieties of the swan in American
waters, the *Americanus* and the *Buccinator*, or trumpeter. The former is the one usually found on the
Atlantic slope, and in great quantities from the Chesa-
peake downward, sometimes flocks of three and even
five hundred. It is about one fourth smaller than the

trumpeter. Going westward, the trumpeter is met in the waters of the Lower Ohio, and so down to the Gulf, west to the Pacific, and north to the Arctic. It breeds mostly within the Arctic, and as the ice begins to form there in September, it comes south, flying, like the Canada goose, in baseless triangles, and speed one half greater, that is, at the rate of one hundred and more miles an hour. When one and two years old it has a brownish color, but whitens out as it comes to its full growth, at the end of five years. Then it is our noblest fowl in color, form, motion, and size. Audubon had one that measured ten feet from tip to tip of wings, and weighed thirty-eight pounds. A flock of these royal birds, riding at ease, and frolicking out on the bosom of a lake, as they will sometimes for hours, is an exciting scene. The sportsman and naturalist will enter fully into the spirit of the remark of Audubon: "Imagine, reader, that a flock of fifty swans are thus sporting before you, as they have more than once been in my sight, and you will feel, as I have felt, more happy and void of care than I can describe."

I have no means of estimating the age to which the swan may attain; but judging from the toughness of the one Dock baked, I make no doubt the fellow was ancient and honorable when Lewis and Clarke made their exploring tour of the Rocky Mountains in 1803. The teal and mallard, and geese even, that we hung up to-night beside those two snowy Arctic voyageurs, looked diminutive and worthless.

But with fowls as men, we soon learn that height and bulk are no criterion of real worth. The tall bittern and crane yield the palm of excellence at once,

on the table, to those of shorter legs. The children of
Anak were of no account, and had to give way before
the short and stocky Jews; little David, with his sling,
was too much for Goliath, and the giants generally
have disappeared as the race of man has improved.
As the gases and vapors were reduced in bulk to make
the world, and as the huge trees and animals of the
earth before Adam were abandoned for smaller and
more delicate and useful races, so improvements in
the human race run in the line of diminution, and
giants and very tall men are a cumbersome wonder
only. Quinctilian places Thucydides at the head of
Greek historians, and speaks of him as *densus et
brevis.* Some apply these words to his style, as being
" terse and brief." Does not Quinctilian mean to say
that the leader in history was a " short, thick-set " man,
say about five feet four? I hope no offence will be
taken by my tall critics at this implied suggestion
about the proper height for a scholar and gentleman.

But I must not keep The General waiting for listen-
ers.

AMONG THE INDIANS.

"I spent the most of the summer, 1837, at Davenport, and in exploring the country lately purchased of the Indians. The surveys of the public lands west of the Mississippi had been commenced, and I was ready to share in the work. I therefore reported myself to the surveyor general of the north-west, General Robert Lytle, at Cincinnati. I received my contracts and entered on the work October 17. The tract I was to run out lay on the Wabessapinecon River, then but little known or settled, and occupied by returned bands of the Sac and Fox Indians.

" There was an abundance of game in the field of my labor; but supplies of flour, meal, pork, groceries, and clothing must be obtained generally from Cincinnati.

" In order to learn the Indian language I employed one or two Indians to hunt for me, and supply our camp. Often a family of them would make their wigwam beside my tent, and move where we moved. Being in such constant intercourse, I was soon able to talk with them sufficiently to carry on a trade in game, moccasons, skins, and furs for the use of our party.

" Among those who followed our camp was an old Sac chief by the name of Nah-me-naske, who had been in the Black Hawk war. His great anxiety to talk and tell his grievances, and the treachery of pretended friends, like Keokuk, enabled me to make good progress in the acquisition of their tongue, and I often

spent my evenings in the tent of the old chief. Here I
learned much of Indian character, their habits, and
mode of life. Nah-me-naske was intelligent, and
knew well the history of his race. He had ever been
a true follower of Black Hawk, and felt most keenly
the injuries that had been heaped on his people. His
mind was stored with rich historic lore, and the legends
and traditions of his tribe were familiar to him. He
believed that Keokuk had been strongly influenced or
bribed by the whites in the sale of the land, and often-
times he would become so indignant and excited over
the memory of their wrongs, that he would rise from
his mat in a passion, seize his tomahawk, and with dis-
torted features and eyes of bloody vengeance, tell by
his looks and gestures how he would massacre those
who had destroyed him and his people.

"He censured the government, the president, and the
settlers on his lands. He said to me one day, 'Your
great chief paid but little to the Indian for all this
land, and now he sends you to cut it up, and sell a
little piece for a great heap of money.'

"One day in the early part of the survey, and before
our mutual acquaintance had sprung up, I found the
stakes and mounds of my surveys destroyed, my marks
on the bearing trees cut out, and my lines so hacked
and mutilated that I had to do the work over again.
I charged Nah-me-naske with the mischief, but he was
silent, neither confessing nor denying the act. I kindly, but firmly, told him of the consequences that would
follow on the repetition of such a thing. I assured him
that I should send to the fort for troops, and drive him
and all his band from the country in the dead of winter.

I told him that the acts of Keokuk, at which he was angry, were legal, whether just or not, and that the land was no more his; that he lived on it only by permission of the whites, and that I was doing only what I was commanded to do.

"This seemed to pacify him for a brief time, and incline him to submit to his lot; but one could often find him in his lodge sullen and despondent. At such times I would retire. At other times the old chief would order the bear-skin mat to be spread by his side for me, and when seated we would enter into conversation on all topics. He was fond of hearing the news of the white people. Sometimes, when brooding over the past, or unsuccessful in the chase, his countenance would be covered with gloom and sadness. On one of these occasions he said to me, —

"'Nah-me-naske will soon go to the good hunting-grounds of the Great Spirit. No treacherous chief or bad white man will drive him or his people away. Gitche Manitou will be there, and no Sioux or Chippewa can come into the great lodge. My people, that have been slain, will hunt unmolested over the green prairies, and trap the beaver and the otter among the beautiful lakes of Pagunk.'

"The Indian has his creed. He believes in the Great Hereafter, and a heaven where all is pleasure, and no enemies to molest him, and where his feet are never weary in the pursuit of game. He believes in and worships the Great Spirit, because he is great and good, and protects and feeds him. He believes in an Evil Spirit, and makes a feast in his honor, to appease his wrath and keep him quiet. He believes in a place

of punishment, where the bad Indian will suffer in a
deep place, into which all their enemies are thrust,
specially the Sioux.   His acts of devotion are seldom
seen, as they consist of presents and offerings.

" Give to an Indian a pipe of tobacco, and watch him
closely, and you will see him spill some on the ground
and look up.   Give him meat, and his offering will be
found on the ground before him.   In sickness the
prophets, the medicine men of the tribe, cure him by
driving away, with songs and incantations, the evil
spirit that has possessed him.

" The Sacs and Foxes have never been taught by
the missionary.   They have to this day refused to
receive him, or any teachers for their children.   Their
views of a deity, of death, and the future have been
handed down to them from their fathers.   It is not till
they learn the vices of the white man that they offend
the Great Spirit by oaths and imprecations.   There is
no word in their language by which they can swear, and
none to express contempt of God and his attributes.

" When I first went among them I commenced the
formation of an English dictionary of their language,
which assisted me much in learning their tongue, and
was a vast aid to me as long as I had intercourse with
them.   They were always ready to tell me the names
of things, and from the deep interest I took in their
language, history, and general welfare, I became a
favorite among them.   My tent was usually filled with
game, and so I always fed the Indian when he entered,
treated him kindly, never cheated him in trade, or gave
him whiskey, or allowed it in the camp.

" Long after their removal farther west, when they

would visit their old camping-grounds at Davenport and Rock Island, their chiefs and braves visited me at my residence; and many are the feasts I have given them, since the hand of civilization has covered up the ashes of their wigwams.

"On one occasion, when I was on my survey, I had been in my canoe a long distance up the Wabessapin-econ, exploring for my work in future, and became belated in my return. The old chief, Nah-me-naske, was encamped beside my tent, on a small creek, about one mile from the river. The river was very crooked, and full of snags, and when night came on, I found myself a long distance from my camp. But having no blanket, I continued my route with the light of a pale moon, until I thought myself nearly opposite my camp. I had, in the dark, run on a snag, capsized the canoe, sent my rifle to the bottom, and wet my matches as well as myself. As the water was not deep, I recovered my rifle, righted and baled the canoe, and continued my journey.

"I had often shouted, and given the usual Indian whoop, so common among frontier huntsmen, but gained no answer. I landed, and hunted for a trail that led across a point of prairie to my camp, but could find none. It was now midnight, and though not severely cold, it was a frosty November night. I was tired, wet, and hungry. I shouted again, but no answer came. It was usual, in such cases, to discharge a gun, but mine was wet. I could not strike a fire, for my matches were wet also. So I put myself under cover of a log to await daylight.

"My thoughts naturally dwelt on my condition. The

hooting of the owl and the prolonged howling of the distant wolf reminded me that I was quite alone, and far from friends; but I resigned myself for the night. Just at this moment I heard the rustling of leaves, and the soft tread of a moccason; when, turning a little, Nah-me-naske stood near me in dim outline. 'Is Chi-he-maske lost?' said he, as he stepped forward, closely wrapped in his blanket. 'Come with me to your wigwam, where you can be warm, and eat, and sleep.' Taking my wet gun from the canoe, he led the way to the camp, which was nearly two miles distant.

"None but the keen ear of an Indian could have heard my voice so far, and none but a true friend would have come to my relief in that hour and darkness. He knew of my absence, and had probably been listening for hours for the accustomed shout of a bewildered man, well knowing that I could not find my camp alone.

"The Indians had named me Chi-he-maske, which means "strong and swift," because I was short and thick-set, and could travel a great distance in a day. This was no solitary kindness of the chief. Often he would fling down at my door a choice turkey, goose, or coon, for my own special comfort.

"He stood on his dignity and rank. He was a chief, and so was I, in the service of the Great Father at Washington, and so we were equals. When I ate with him by special invitation in his lodge, none others were admitted, except chiefs or braves, and always the choice pieces of the venison or turkey were placed in my bowl. Salt, that is not much used by the Indian, was always kept for the white chief, and was never forgotten.

" He taught me the art of trapping, explained the nature and habits of the animals of the chase, and often entered on some of his hunting and war stories, and related, with much satisfaction, his expeditions against the Sioux, his mortal enemies. He had heard of the great wigwams of the white man towards the rising sun, and of their power and strength. He inquired of me, with great interest, about the white man's Scuti-Nah-ga-tuck-e-sock, or fire-horse, that could outrun the antelope, with a hundred men on his back. I had to make a drawing of it, in charcoal, on the bark in his wigwam; but I could never satisfy him of the principle on which it was propelled, or of the rail on which it ran. He said the white man was very foolish to work hard all his life, and build such large wigwams, with so many rooms in them; and when he made a fire, to make it so big that no one could get near it to warm himself.

"During the whole winter the Indians were constantly at the camp, and always had freedom in and about the premises; but nothing was stolen. They were incessant beggars, but easily put off, when told they did not need the thing, or could not have it. The Indians never steal from white friends, or from one another, in friendly tribes.

"The whole winter of 1837–8 we spent on this survey, living in a canvas tent, and losing but three days on account of rough weather. We returned to Davenport on the 1st of April, having been absent about five months and a half. During all this time I had not slept in a house, or seen scarcely a white man, except those of my company.

"Having arranged for the building of a dwelling-house in a little village a few miles from Davenport, I left for home, by the way of St. Louis and Cincinnati. At the latter place I was detained six weeks in making returns of my surveys and collections for the work at the office of the surveyor general. I then ascended the Ohio to Wheeling, and thence by stage to Washington, where I spent a few days in business at the Land Office, and so on to New Jersey, having been absent from my family more than a year and a half.

"In June following I bade adieu to New Jersey, and, with my wife and two daughters, started back for Wisconsin Territory, then the extreme border of the Far West. We took the route of the Pennsylvania Canal to Pittsburg, down the Ohio to Cairo, and thence up the Mississippi to Davenport, being four weeks on the journey, and leaving Swan Lake on the right!

"It is now little more than a quarter of a century since I saw the land of my adoption. Since that time, mighty changes have come over the scene. The wilderness has become a garden, and barbarism has given place to civilization. The long and tedious journey of four weeks has been reduced to less than three days. The Indian, who lurked around the cabin settlement, has gone on the red man's path, towards the setting sun; the place of his wigwam is covered with the habitations of the pale faces, and the play-grounds of his children have become the fields and gardens of civilization. The home of his fathers, and the sacred resting-places of his dead have been given up to the ploughshare. The canoe that once floated in pride and glory on The Father of Waters is gone, like a shadow by the wigwam, and the Scuti-Chemon — the Fire Canoe of the white man — troubles the great river day and night. Assine-me-nass (Rock Island), the scene of so many councils and conflicts of mighty chieftains, and the home of all that was great and good in Indian life, will become the armory and arsenal of the weapons of war for the white man; and the tattoo of the soldier will take the place of the merry song and the war-cry of the savage. The green prairies, over which he once roamed, chasing the deer and the elk, are now grain fields, and the fur trade of trapper and trader has given place to the broad commerce of a nation.

"A few wandering tribes are followed by a population of more than four millions; and the smoke from their thousands of cities and towns and cabins, from river side and prairie and timber, all through the North-west, goes up like incense from the altars of a great and happy people. The mighty river, where once danced only the light canoe, now bears up a trade greater than ever was tributary to imperial Rome. So empire moves westward.

"The Indian now lingers on the frontier. He must mourn over the graves of his ancestors, and bid farewell to his early home; for he is the child of destiny. The finger of Fate points with unerring certainty to his future. His march is onward, onward, over the mighty midland barriers of a continent, till his weary moccason leave its prints on the sands of the Pacific, there soon to be washed out and forgotten!"

Sadness and gloom, as of a funeral, hung over us as

The General closed his narrative for the night. He spoke with the deep feeling and sorrow of one who mourned for friends, and would embalm their memory. You should have seen our camp fire group after he had done speaking. No one said a word; no one moved. We watched the curling smoke and the light flashing up among the old trees over us; we looked out into the deep and silent outline of dark forest, as if the red men or their ghosts were ·stealing on us. Some of the company felt peculiarly what had been said of the fading out of the race. There was one man, past middle life, who, a boy clerk in the trading-house of his father on Sturgeon Bay just below us, knew these tribes, and their pursuits and habits, and had purchased their furs, and peltries, and feathers; had been in their canoes on these waters, and had seen them disappear. Here was another who had lived and trafficked in the foremost ranks of their emigration as they had gone westward, before the white man, into the Rocky Mountains, and beyond.

A little chit-chat sprang up finally; then we wrapped our blankets about us, and, like true white men, we soon forgot "the poor Indian."

SEVENTH NIGHT.

"There is a pleasure in the pathless woods,
There is a rapture on the lonely shore."

I FOUND it so to-day, as with little Iulus I strolled off through the heavy timber lands two miles to the thickly-wooded bank of the Mississippi. Primitive forest this is, dark with the trees of centuries; some of them strong in their prime, with branches far aloft, that would be counted huge trees elsewhere, and others old and decaying, with limbs rent away, and only naked trunks left standing. The ground is marked by many prostrate trees of immense dimensions, lying where old age or the last tornado left them; some of them only a long ridge of vegetable mould in their decay, and others fresh and solid, the victims of a late gale. You may as well flank them at once, for to go over logs of such diameter, four, five, and sometimes sixfeet, is out of the question.

This bottom land is subject to an annual overflow, and so it is kept quite clear of undergrowth, and you get distant views through long vistas of the tall, smooth trees. Here one feels alone, and there is a charm in the solitude. No evidences lie about you that man has ever been here, and you reflect that yours is the only human foot that has trodden this silent forest for months, possibly years.   The game is less abundant than on the margin of the forests and around the lakes, but the *vastum ubique silentium* makes ample amends.

The gifted and lamented Choate, in whose death the Academy and the Forum lost what it rarely possesses to lose, in one of his letters to Mrs. Eames, written in a little nook of rural seclusion, has this passage : " You see Boston through the trees, and hear now and then the whistle of invisible cars; otherwise you might fancy yourself fifty thousand globes from cities or steam.   These are the places and moments for that discourse in which is so much more of our happiness than in actualities of duty, or even in hope."

If the shade of one little artificial cluster of trees, and that in sight of Boston, could give him such seclusion and sense of distance from man, and such increase of happiness, what would be his solitude and joy in this wild haunt of nature?   He would need the latest editions of both the rival dictionaries to express his emotions; and his "fifty thousand globes" would be only a range of hillocks for the measuring line of his prolific fancy.

As we wandered about, I said to Iulus, " Why not go over to the Mississippi, and have a dinner on its banks?"   So, guided by a pocket compass, we made for the river, bagging three or four fox squirrels as we went along.   We struck the bank on a little swell of land, and above, below, and in front our king of rivers was working his way to the Gulf.   Here and there it lingered around sand-bars, covered to blackness with wild geese; and in the coves fleets of ducks were riding at anchor.   The haze of an October sky hung over the

water, dropping a dimness on the islands, and a veil
on the opposite shore. A poet, or painter, or naturalist, any lover of the beautiful in out-doors, would have
been enchanted with the scene. It was wild, vast,
grand, primitive. Talk of dining-halls at splendid
hotels; the late congress of kings had not its equal
to the one where our table was spread. But perhaps
you never ate an extempore forest dinner. Poor man,
you have our compassion! See how we do it.

Drift wood from St. Anthony, left by a high-water
eddy, is dry and waiting for our match. We lay it
sparingly — for it is a warm day — beside the dead log,
and start the fire. Now, out on one of those sanded,
romantic little bars, we dress our game, water enough,
and of the purest. Back again, and there is a good
bed of coals. Three small switches, four feet each,
with a crotch in the end of each, set in the ground at
an angle of forty degrees over the coals, with a fat and
well-washed squirrel on each crotch; a half-dozen biscuit halved and buttered, and now toasting; a salt-
box and a pepper-box well shaken over the broiling
quarry — boxes as much a fixture to my hunting-coat
as the pockets — is not the prospect good for a dinner?
You turn the switches a few times in the ground, and
how the juices of the meat flash up from the coals!
You gash the ham or shoulder to test the cooking, and
" the gravy from the dish," flowing out of the cut, red and
appetizing, shows you that the time has come. Now set
the switches bearing their smoking loads perpendicular
in the ground in front of a log, and seat yourself on
the same. Your hunter's knife separates into knife and
fork, and you proceed to carve and eat. Your little

Ganymede, who was Iulus, brings your hunter's cup full of the best of water, direct from Lake Itasca. Did you ever enjoy a dinner more? Look on the walls of your dining-hall, the paintings are true to nature. Look out of the Gothic windows, and admire the landscape views, river, forest, islands — now as steamer shooting between two — and the whole canopied by one of the softest October skies. An apple or two from the game-bag for dessert, and then you pick your teeth as complacently as if standing on the steps of the Astor just after dinner.

So we dined that day in the oldest human hotel — the First Adam's House — and it was a table to be remembered. Such a dinner is worth ten dollars a plate to an over-worked, jaded business man. An incident impressed the memory of it for a long time on my — right shoulder. In the warmth of the day and service I had thrown off my coat, and while doing thus the honors of our dining-hall, a flock of geese came flying most directly and impertinently over our very table, just scaling the tree-tops. It was the work of haste and a moment, and, with my gun at a perpendicular, and loose about the shoulder, I fired. One goose at least was winged, but at the wrong end of the gun, and I carried a lame arm for weeks.

This was a favorite ramble with me afterwards, and I often took it alone, not so much for the game as for the wild, solitary nature of the route.

A single settler lived in this belt of timber between our camp and the river. His cabin seemed carelessly thrown in there, where there was no remotest evidence of a clearing. The only sign of breaking ground

was where he had dug a slough well, that is, a hole in
a dry slough, with clay steps cut down to the puddle
of muddy water at the bottom, where frogs, and leaves,
and crickets, and all other little things, creeping, jump-
ing, or flying, could be dipped up, dead or alive.   I had
a curiosity to see the inside of his log shanty, and so
called one day, and asked for a drink of water.   The
man of the house invited me in, and sent a girl to the
well.   The cabin had one room, like a hen-coop ; the
ground was the floor ; in one corner a stove ; one chair,
without a back, which he gave me ; a board against the
rough logs of the wall was the table ; a pile of bedding
lay pitched into one corner, being an old feather bed,
and two or three tattered and dingy spreads.   On this
pile lounged his wife and a daughter of fifteen, while a
squad of smaller children crawled about, through, and
over the heap — I cannot tell how many.   On a shelf
lay a long, thin strip of smoked middlings, the end
hanging over, and, as it showed, within convenient
reach of a knife.   Pieces of corn bread and this mis-
erable pork were the only signs of food.   Two or three
old plates and broken tea-cups, not " wisely kept for
show," were all the table furniture in sight, and nothing
was covered up in that house unless it was under the
bedding.   The cabin had not a cupboard, box, chest,
or trunk in it.   The girl came with the water, bare-
headed, barefoot, and otherwise and generally almost
so.   One of the broken tea-cups came in use ; I put it
to my lips, drank all I wished, and left.   The man of
the house, who stood all the while I was there (I had
his chair) with his hands thrust into ragged breeches,
and the smoke of a stub pipe curling up under a

slouched hat, followed me to the door, examined my fowling-piece with great interest, asked whether "she" was good, and bade me good by. Yet this family was cheerful and contented, and did not seem to know but that it was well off.

Our tents looked more inviting than ever as we rounded the shore and went in at sunset. Supper came earlier, as we all were in sooner, and so The General made an earlier beginning.

Foundations of Iowa.

"In 1839 I was employed in the survey of the public lands in Iowa, on what was called The Black Hawk Purchase. This new acquisition was then being settled up with great rapidity.

"In 1840 I undertook for government the survey of the islands in the Mississippi, between the mouth of Rock River and Quincy. It was a work of great difficulty and hardship. These islands had been surveyed several times by other parties, but their work was so incorrect that the government rejected it. Mine was the last one made. It was commenced early in the spring, amid floating ice and high water, and in rough weather. It was necessary to extend the section lines from the main land to the islands, and then meander the islands. Of course the party were compelled to be much in the water, and, as a consequence, there was much sickness among them, as well as delay in the work. But I completed it that season, and in a manner satisfactory to the government.

"Falling readily into the custom of frontier men, I joined a party of seven, in the fall of this year, to go on a hunting expedition into the Indian country. The outfit consisted of horse and ox teams, with tents, blankets, provision, and, in this case, with barrels, as we intended to take wild honey. It was not usual for hunters to go far beyond the settlements at that early day; but our company was made up of men not only fond of the chase, but anxious to explore a region so much talked of, and not unwilling to have exciting adventures.

" The company set forth about the first of September, and, following the dividing ridge between the Cedar and Wabessapineeon Rivers, were some seven days in reaching the grounds on which they intended to hunt, a tract between the head-waters of these two rivers.

"The constant broils between the Sacs and Foxes and the Sioux, whose lands adjoined, induced the government in 1828 to cut off a strip of land twenty miles wide on each side of the dividing line between the tribes, making forty miles of territory in width, running from the Mississippi River above Prairie du Chien, to the Des Moines, a distance of about one hundred and fifty miles. This strip of land neither party could use for hunting purposes, and was called The Neutral Grounds.

" When the Winnebagoes sold their lands in Wisconsin, they were removed to these Neutral Grounds, being at peace with the Indians on both sides. The Winnebagoes were in possession of these lands at the time our party went on this hunt.

" When we arrived near the boundary line of the Indians, we encamped, and for many days enjoyed the sports of the chase, and took some honey. Here we waited till the Indians should start on their journey to Prairie du Chien to receive their annuity from government, which we knew was to be paid about this time. We also knew that their absence was the only time when we could hunt and gather honey on these Neutral Grounds with any safety.

" We were accordingly ready to remove to the scene of operations as soon as the Indians left. We did so at the earliest opportunity, and camped on what we called Honey Creek, a small stream within the Neutral Grounds. Not far from the camp was a white oak grove, on a rise of land. The trees were large and old, and many of them hollow, and on a half mile square of this grove we found sixteen bee trees. Other game was plenty, and we enjoyed ourselves during one of those delightful Indian summers, so much admired in the West.

" We felt secure so long as the Winnebagoes were away. We had no right on their lands without their permission, or that of the Indian agent; and when whites were caught hunting or fishing there, their property was considered by the Indians as lawful prize.

" We had completed our hunt, having strained the honey and put it in casks, jerked the meat, and got it ready to pack, and prepared everything for a homeward move, except the trying out of a large quantity of beeswax. It was late in the afternoon when some of the party, who had been out hunting, came into camp and reported Indians in the vicinity. Scouts being sent out, several were seen, and one even came into camp, and viewed the rich store of meat and honey that we had taken. He was grave and severe, and refused food, which fact we all understood painfully well. He left, and we sent a spy to watch him. When some distance from camp, he put spurs to his horse, and went at full speed across the prairie.

" It was now well understood that the Indians had

returned from the agency, and that we might expect a
visit from them about daylight the next morning, the
time when all tribes are wont to open their attacks on
an enemy. The hunting party put their arms in order,
and determined on defence, if the enemy should not
prove to be too numerous. All hands were now engaged in packing and loading the wagons preparatory
to a retreat. The barrels of honey were loaded in, the
oxen and horses gathered and tied near by in the bush,
for fear that the intentions of the party to depart might
be discovered by some Indian spy. The company had
taken eight barrels of strained honey, besides much elk
and deer meat.

"Waiting for the rising of the moon, and then building a large camp fire, we hitched up our teams, and
placing a rear guard and pilot, we started for home.
After much trouble and a few miles' travel, we struck
the trail where we entered, and about daylight we
passed safely the boundary line. About the same time,
probably, the Indians were visiting our old camping-
ground to rob us of our booty. These same Indians
had robbed trappers and explorers the fall preceding,
and they were disposed, on all safe occasions, to appro-
priate the effects of the white man to their own use.
But they gave us no difficulty, and we arrived home in
safety, and well laden with game and honey.

"In 1841–2, the public surveys being suspended, I
turned my attention to a more full exploration of the
territory that had been cut off from Wisconsin, and
called Iowa. At this time there had not been any
maps or sketches of the country lying north of the
State of Missouri, and between the Mississippi and

Missouri Rivers.   Major Lee, of the United States
army, had made a tour, with dragoons, up the Des
Moines, and Nicholat had traversed the north-west on
both sides of the Mississippi, by order of Congress,
and made some outlines and topography of the country.   But there was nothing reliable, or what could
give one a tolerable idea of the region between the
two rivers.   The vague and romantic story of the
trapper was all that the people of the frontier knew of
the region.

"These wild adventurers gave the most glowing
accounts of its beautiful groves of timber, its swift-
flowing rivers, and its broad-rolling prairies, its glassy
lakes, with pebbled shores, and abundance of fish, and
its immense herds of buffalo, elk, and deer, that roamed
at will over the delightful wilds.   But they could give
no great landmarks, or inland seas, by which the traveller could direct his course.

"At the instance of Governor Chambers, of the then
new Territory of Iowa, and the solicitation of the surveyor general of the North-west, I undertook the ex-
ploration of the territory, and at my own charges.
With two men and a proper outfit, I set forth, in the
autumn of 1841, to sketch the country and make a
map of the same, as far north as the forty-third degree,
the present southern boundary of Minnesota.   In this
work I was engaged a portion of the time for three
years, making annual excursions, tracing the rivers to
their sources, and marking the timber lands, living the
while mostly on game.

"The Indian title at this time was extinguished to
only a small part lying along the Mississippi River.

9

The rest was inhabited by the Sacs and Foxes, the Potawatamies, and the Winnebagoes. In my first trip I followed up the ridge between the Cedar and the Wabessapineeon Rivers to the boundary line of the Neutral Grounds, on which the Winnebagoes resided. Here I established my headquarters for the winter, and built a depot for my supplies. It was located on a small creek, in a deep and densely-wooded glen, a few miles from the Wabessapineeon, and just within the line between the Indians and the whites. This was about the first of September, and the chief of the band who lived on this portion of the Neutral Grounds, and whose village was only about six miles away, had gone with the most of his braves and great men to Prairie du Chien. No communication, therefore, could be had with him till his return, which would be a month or more. Portions of his people were encamped near by, on their fall hunt, and came often to my camp. In this band were some young men and boys who had attended the Mission School at Fort Atkinson, on Turkey River, established and maintained by the government.

"It is a characteristic of the Indian never to speak English, even if he can, unless sheer necessity compels him, or when he is sure his people will not know it. It is considered a kind of disgrace, as if he were tinctured with civilization, and were apostatizing from the dignity of his fathers, and becoming a white man.

"I had learned some Winnebago words from the Sacs and Foxes, some of whom spoke it, though the two languages are quite unlike. As I could not proceed across the Indian country till Chas-chun-ka (Big Wave) returned, I set my men to hunting and storing away provisions for the winter, while I attempted to gain a sufficient knowledge of the language to enable me to travel intelligently among them. It was always necessary for one to remain in camp to prevent Indian depredations, and to keep the horses from straying. This duty I now took on myself, and encouraged the Indian boys, who frequently visited the camp, to be familiar, giving them presents of red cloth and ribbons, bread and pork, of which they are very fond, and other trifles of civilization.

" They soon became familiar, answering promptly the questions I put them, as to the names of things. One day, what were my surprise and delight, when I inquired of a sprightly lad, about twelve years of age, and who had come into the cabin alone, what he called the victuals that were then cooking in the kettle, to hear him answer in plain, unbroken English, ' Why, it is pork and beans, and I shall want some bread and potatoes to eat with them when they are done.' His dark, keen eye twinkled with the answer, and he burst into a fit of laughter, half hiding his face through shame that he knew so much of the white man's language.

" He saw my delight at discovering his knowledge, and yielded freely to the questions, where, and how, and when he obtained the English so perfectly. He had been a pupil in the Mission School of the Rev. David Lowry for five or six years, and could read as well as speak English quite fluently. When I applied to him to teach me, nothing could exceed his unwilling-ness, even to interpret. But my close familiarity and gentleness, and presents for himself and mother, whose lodge was about a mile distant, won him over, and he proved of great value, not only in teaching me, but in shielding me from dangers afterwards.

"The return of Chas-chun-ka, about the first of November, was speedily heralded through the Indian camps, and I was notified by my friendly and faithful little mission boy, who, by this time, knew all my desires and plans.

"The chief was, like the most of his race, vain and conceited, puffed up with self-importance, but susceptible of flattery, and fond of presents. He was not an hereditary chief, but a Fox by birth, and having joined the Winnebagoes at an early age, he had risen to his present position by the force of native talent. He was worth some property in horses and presents, given him by the agents and officers of the government. He had two wives, and was about to take a third; but as the winter was near, and provisions scarce, he had concluded to wait till spring.

"He was duly notified of my presence in the country, and my wish to hold a conference with him at my tent whenever his chieftainship would please to signify his willingness. Early one morning, a few days after his return, a cavalcade was seen coming across the prairie towards my camp. In due time, and in long Indian file, they drew up around my cabin. I remained inside to receive the distinguished guests, while his officials motioned to the Indians, as they dismounted, to enter the council.

"There were twelve or more under-chiefs and braves who accompanied Chas-chun-ka. He entered first, bowing and shaking hands with me. This salutation was repeated by the whole troop. They then seated themselves around the cabin, on the ground, but their chief on a bench. The appearance of the chief was very surprising to me, for I had expected to see a profusion of paint and feathers, and wampum of costly texture. Instead of that, he was clothed in a buffalo overcoat, a stove-pipe hat, and wore a pair of green spectacles. His belt was probably the gift of a soldier, as it bore the U. S. in front. His outfit had all probably been given to him by some traders at the fort.

"I addressed him politely as he entered, but I did not at first regard him as the chief. On pronouncing his name, he bowed, and, as I supposed by his dress that he must be a half-breed, and could speak English, I addressed him in that tongue, but he would make no response. Still believing that it was only Indian policy and custom not to know English, I pressed the point in broken Indian; but a persistent protest of silence in Chas-chun-ka compelled me to send for my little teacher and mission boy, Wabessa-wawa (White Goose). He came trembling and abashed before the sachem and his warriors, and, as he passed the chief, the latter patted him on the head, and said some approving word, that caused the boy to smile.

"The council was opened as usual with the pipe and the shaking of hands. Then all were seated again, and looked to me to make known my business. I arose, and after telling them of my long residence at Assinni-Manness, with their friends, the Sacs and Foxes, and of my labors for their Great Father, the President, in surveying the lands he bought of them, I told them I had come to see their country by the request of their Father. Then I showed them the passport given me

by General Chambers, and told the chief that I wanted
to go across his country and make a picture of it for the
president.

"After hearing me and examining my maps and
sketches taken on the way up, some of which he cor-
rected—for the Indian is a topographical draughtsman
by nature—he handed the papers back and shook his
head. Looking around on his warriors with an air of
kingly importance, he directed the interpreter to tell me
that he could not let me go over his lands for any such
purpose. He said he well knew the object of his Great
Father in sending me there to make a picture of his
country; that if it was good for the white he would buy
it, but if not the Indian could keep it. No, I could
not go. After many entreaties and presents to induce
him to yield, I found it of no use, and the council
broke up. This was a difficulty that I had not anticipated, and all my plans seemed liable to fail.

"The next day I visited him with one of my men in
his lodge at the village. He was affable and polite,
but rather cool, and when the subject of explorations
was introduced he became silent and morose. I therefore left him, determined to visit Fort Atkinson and
see the Winnebago agent.

"It had now become late in the season, and there
was great danger in traversing an unknown country
at such an inclement season without a guide or trail.
Moreover, I should be subject to the watchful eye of the
Indians, and if the chief found I had left, he would send
his warriors and bring me back. But I was not to be
baffled in my plans, and give up my project without a
struggle. I was not afraid of the Indian, for I knew

that. I was regarded as an agent of the government, and so no harm must come to me in his territory. I would not ask the chief for a guide, or even let him know of my intentions of visiting the agency, as it was on Indian territory, to which I had already been refused access.

"I therefore set out early one morning, with one man and two horses, across the country one hundred and twenty-five miles, for Fort Atkinson, with no map or trail, and with the assurance, almost, that I should be arrested and brought back by the Indians. I knew the course to be about north-west, and expecting to find trails, or see some Indians, when near there, who would direct me to the fort, I entered on the journey. At first I avoided the prairie to escape the vigilance of the Indians. On the second day out a dense fog covered the open country, while it rained in torrents. The streams were so swollen that we were obliged to swim them with our horses. When three days out, and near night, it cleared up, the fog rolled off, and it turned cold. We steered for a grove in sight, which we reached just at dark, and to our surprise found there the ashes of our morning camp fire. We had wandered in the fog all day at good speed to come back there for the night.

"The next morning we put out again, and after a journey of five days more, over wet prairie and swollen streams, we reached the fort. The first night we were entertained within its walls to our full comfort. The agent then provided for us during the ten days that we remained.

"While here I visited the Mission School of Mr.

Lowry. It contained about sixty scholars of both sexes, many of whom had made good advances in reading and writing English. There was a farm of twelve hundred acres, broken up and fenced, with suitable buildings, all belonging to the agency, and intended to teach the Indians agriculture and the arts of civilized life. But they could not be made to work. Government paid for the labor of eight men; but few Indians would go into the fields to work.

"Mr. Lowry gave me a passport to go over the lands of the Winnebagoes: and he also wrote a letter to Chas-chun-ka, telling him what a great and good chief he was, and that he had always been friendly to the white man, and that now he must permit me to cross his lands whenever I pleased, and that by so doing he would not only please him, but his Great Father.

"I returned, and, taking Wabessa-wawa to read the letter, I rode over to the lodge of the chief and presented him the papers given me by the agent. When the letter was read, it flattered his vanity so much that he sent for the chiefs and braves, and had the same read to them. When it spoke of his greatness and goodness he would look around on his men with a proud and haughty air, as if to say, 'Behold your chief, and hear what the white man says of him.' His whole being seemed at once changed, and he told me that I might go all about over his country, and that he would send men with me.

"The next day he came over to see me, and of course to get some presents. He wanted me to wait for him two weeks or so, when he would go with me. I did so, but seeing no preparation by him for such a trip, I

started without him. My route lay up the Wabessapinecon to its head and down the Cedar.

"During my absence the Indians, many of them,
had removed, and among them, greatly to my regret,
had gone the lodge of my little interpreter, Wabessa-
wawa. I could get no information which way he had
gone, only that he left with his people for a hunt.

"After recruiting myself and horses, I again started
towards the head-waters of the Des Moines. I had not
passed the Neutral Grounds, when one day we came on
an encampment of Winnebagoes, who seemed boister-
ous and much disposed to plunder, pulling the packs
from the horses, and demanding bread and meat. Their
rudeness was observed by the old men of the tribe, but
they said nothing, till I went to one of them, and, addressing him in his own tongue, I told him I was the
friend of Chas-chun-ka, and the agent of the government, and that I had a pass from Mr. Lowry, and that
they must not allow their young braves to do such
things. In a moment he spoke to the rude fellows,
telling them who I was, when they left the stores,
but with evident reluctance and disappointment. On
making inquiry for the trail that led to an old trading
post on the river, four or five young Indians stepped
forward and offered to show me the way. We took
their lead, and pursued it for more than a mile, when,
on looking back, I saw an Indian boy coming up in
great haste. The party came to a halt, and the boy
came up, wrapped in his blanket, his face half averted,
but with his keen eye fixed on me.

"Speaking in a low tone, he said, 'You are on the
wrong trail. The Indians who sent you here are bad

Indians, and they mean to follow and rob you.' I pulled the blanket aside, and discovered the pretty face of my Wabessa-wawa. He seemed in much excitement and haste. Requesting me to follow him, he struck off through the woods at a rapid rate, and where there was no path ; and after travelling about a mile, he came out into a beaten track. 'This,' said he, 'is your path. I heard you ask for the trail to the old trading-house, and saw those bad Indians put you in the wrong way, and I came to tell you.' He would not allow me time to inquire where his lodge was, or where I should see him, if ever, again, nor hardly to untie the pack and give him some biscuit and pork. I did, however, adding some pieces of silver coin. Shaking the little fellow by the hand, I let go of him, and in a few moments he was lost in the thick wood, on his way to the lodge.

"Here, thought I, are the fruits of Christianity and the germs of civilization in a savage. This boy had been taught at the Mission School, and, aside from seeing his friend robbed, he knew the wickedness of the deed, and his duty to prevent it. He had the native cunning of his race, and knew how to avoid detection for thwarting the designs of bad men.

"We returned in safety from this trip, and once more recruited at our supply camp, or headquarters. Then we made a short excursion towards the Missouri River, but snows had become so deep that travelling was almost impossible. We were three weeks in snow from two to four feet deep. Our usual method in camping was to find a large log, tramp down the snow beside it, pitch the tent, spread down the green hides of elk or deer, and build a good fire. No dampness could penetrate these fresh skins, and so, wrapping ourselves in blankets and buffaloes, we slept soundly.

"An Indian trader had come to the same place where we had made our depot, late in the fall, and, among other things, he, as usual, brought whiskey. He had built himself a small trading-house near to us. This served to gather about him large numbers of Indians, and though he managed to deal out his poison with some degree of caution, as a thing forbidden by the government, yet at times a few drunken Indians would be found about the camp. On such occasions I never allowed them in my camp.

"On my return from the Missouri River trip I found the trading-house closed, the Indians drunk, the barrel of whiskey, all that was left of the trader's stock, moved up to my camp, and the clerk there in attendance on it. The trader himself had gone to Dubuque for goods, and left his clerk, a cowardly and effeminate fellow, in charge. The Indians demanded liquor, and to prevent their getting it, he had rolled the barrel to my premises, and left it with my tent-keeper.

"It was late in the night when I arrived, and being indignant that it had been placed in my depot, I ordered it out, and it was set outside. But it was too late in the stage of affairs to quell the disturbance. The Indians were already maddened by the beginnings of intoxication, and no persuasion or refusal of the trader's clerk could quiet their demands. I had peremptorily forbidden the sale of any more to them, and the clerk, now finding the trading-house too warm a place for him, closed the doors and took refuge in my tent.

"The Indians had threatened to scalp him if he did not produce the liquor, and followed him to my quarters. Here they found the barrel of whiskey outside the door. I spoke to them with firmness, refusing them any more. A portion of them, Chas-chun-ka, and some of his braves, had come inside, and sat in silence around my fire. Some of the chiefs, who knew me well, had come to me in behalf of the whole, pleading for more whiskey. I firmly refused. Being weary from the long and hard march of the day, I lay down for some rest, ordering my men to keep their arms in readiness, while I placed the heavy hickory fire-poker near me. The Indians were without arms, having deposited them, as usual, with their knives and tomahawks, on the top of the trading-house, and the most of them were too drunk to get them again readily, even if the sober ones would let them. As I lay on my lounge, a large crowd was outside, and ten or fifteen inside.

"An old squaw, in order to bring me to terms, had commenced pounding on the head of the whiskey barrel, as it stood near my camp. Big Wave came to me in great pretended alarm, and told me that unless I permitted them to have whiskey, he feared they would break in the head of the barrel, and then all would be drunk, and great trouble would follow. I told him that if he allowed that liquor to be broken open I would kill every Indian within my reach. In the mean time the old squaw kept up her drumming, and as the chief himself disappeared from the door-way, the head of the cask went in !

"In a moment I sprang from my bed, caught my

walnut poker, a stick five feet long, and cried out to my men, in the Indian language, to kill all in the cabin first. With one stroke I split the table to pieces with a great noise, it being made of the lids of a dry goods box, and continued striking right and left, whooping loud and sharp to my men to kill the chiefs first. The cabin was soon emptied of Indians, and, with those outside, they all took to their heels like a herd of deer. I had the barrel of whiskey moved inside again, the door barricaded, and quiet restored. Of course no Indian was hurt by us, as my men were under secret instructions to injure no one. The next morning a few came back, and were shown a large place in the snow where the whiskey was deposited, with the barrel bottom up over it. The liquor was confiscated and gone, only an odor remaining in the snow.

"An Indian cannot fight with a club, but to him it is a most formidable weapon in the hands of an angry white man. Take from them the gun, tomahawk, and knife, and a resolute man can drive a host of them. When once the Indian has tasted liquor, he does not leave it till drunk, or the liquor gives out. He knows no other use for it, except to produce intoxication. It is not a pleasant beverage to him; he does not like the taste of it; it is only for the effect that he drinks it. His palate is as little vitiated as that of a child. He uses no salt, nor seasoned food, and has a very keen and sensitive taste. I have seen an Indian in apparent agony by the use of whiskey; for the article prepared for their market is often well spiced with red pepper and gums to keep up its strength. And I have seen the young Indian and squaw held by main strength, while whiskey has been administered to them, that they might be taught to drink it.

"I returned to Davenport with my party, having accomplished a good work for the season, on my survey for a territorial map. This I finished the next year. The result of my explorations at this early day were important themselves, though small. My 'Map and Notes of Iowa' were published by Doolittle & Munson, of Cincinnati, in the spring of 1845, and 'did more,' says a late writer, 'to disseminate a knowledge of the Territory of Iowa than anything ever before published.' The legislature of the territory complimented the work by ordering copies for each member of both houses, and for all the heads of departments. 'Many works,' says one writer, 'since written, have been largely indebted to this little work for valuable information. And many a settler from the old world dates his ideas of emigration from reading those Notes on Iowa.'"

This section of The General's narrative, more than any one of the preceding, set the Western members of the party to talking about early times on the Upper Mississippi. The reader will see it was going back to their own cabin days, when red men were compelled by Generals Scott and Atkinson to talk by the council fires of the pale faces, and when the towns of civilization were crowding farther west the wigwam, and when the birch canoe glided away from the danger of being swamped in the wake of the Scuti-Chemon — the Fire Canoe. Some of them had to tell of the days they remembered when there were no white settlements

back of Davenport, beyond Duck Creek, four miles
out, while now it is solid with farms and cities, railroads, and the institutions and improvements, commerce and comforts, of civilization four hundred miles
to Omaha. Since that Seventh Night a railroad has
been opened nine hundred and sixty miles west beyond
Omaha. Then little settlements dotted the western
bank of the Mississippi on the Iowa line, like scattered and lonely beacon lights, heralding the coming
of a great population. Then Iowa had less than
fifty thousand inhabitants; now a million and a half
are gathered in her rural districts, thriving cities,
and, to many of them, palace homes. They talked
of those masses of emigration that had swept on
under their own eyes beyond Missouri and Kansas
Territory to the Rocky Mountains, and over them,
building an empire on the Pacific. It was thrilling to
hear those men of commerce, and of manufactures, and
of the Rocky Mountain trade tell what their own eyes
had seen of the growth of states — a sight and growth
such as no nation or kingdom ever saw before.

I am afraid we sat up that night longer than our
Puritan ancestors would approve, but there was no
nine o'clock bell within scores of miles of us.

EIGHTH NIGHT.

WHEN I arose the next morning I found quite a number ahead of me at the camp fire, and all discussing with lively interest the incidents related the evening before by The General. The frontier and Western spirit of all the older members of our encampment was well stirred, and they were living old times over again. When The General joined the group at the fire, they hailed him as a kind of Christopher Columbus, who had opened that part of the new world to them; and when he assured them of still more thrilling incidents, enacted in regions now well settled and familiar, they were impatient for the evening. But as nothing spoils the hunter's appetite, neither impatience nor delay, tramping or resting, we proceeded to do justice to African labors in the culinary line, and had our usual success.

The hunt for the day had many stirring events, mixed in of game captured and missed, that I will not pause to mention in details. Suffice to say, that after long ranges, and with evening shadows, we garnished the saplings and limbs around the camp with their usual hangings of fur and feathers, and could have filled large orders for a game supper at the Fifth Avenue, without endangering our own table.

It is a marvel to the inexperienced that we hunting

and fishing men can walk so far, and carry so much weight, without great fatigue, and endure heat, and cold, and rain, and sleet, without injury. The fact is, the nature of the sport is strengthening, and legitimately gives one a good physique.

And this helps towards a full manhood. For the intellectual and the moral are not wont to develop well through a feeble body. The greatness of many of our great men stands closely allied to a strong body. Legends of enormous power cluster about Brougham as they did about Hercules. Professor Wilson was as famous for casting the hammer as for throwing his own thoughts at you. Burns led the youth of his day in wrestling, pulling, and other Scotch sports of the athlete. Isaac Barrow, that prince of preachers, was noted at the Charter House School for the muscle he carried, and was strikingly impressive in pugilistic argument. Andrew Fuller was splendid at boxing, and Adam Clarke was famous for rolling huge stones about. It is of little use to try to work a powerful engine in a weak frame. You, a preacher, feel poorly on Monday, and about adequate to the effort of seeing the cream rise on a pan of new milk. A part of this feeling is professionally imaginary, and suggestive that you performed a wonderful and exhausting work the day before. Some clergymen are so very able that they can preach but one sermon a day, and have no evening meetings or pastoral work, and so must have vacations lengthy and often; and if very feeble, and in a wealthy society, they absolutely need a trip to foreign lands.

Others are really weary on Monday. Dear Sirs, you should go to Dr. Nimrod's Water Cure — a leaky tent

— and take his prescriptions, to wit: The Walton fish-
hook every other day, alternating with number six shot.
This is precisely what the fable means about Antæus
and Hercules. Antæus was the son of Terra and Neptune — land and water. He came of good stock, one
of the "first families." Like Brougham, and Barrow,
and others, he was famed for wrestling, and was more
than a match for Hercules, because as often as he
touched the earth — his mother — she renewed his
strength. Then Hercules, discovering the secret, lifted
him up in the air, and squeezed him to death. That
is, the Rev. Mr. Antæus became very averse to the
ground. He disliked a cane, and a spade, and a fishing-rod, and gun, and a prairie hay bed, and birch
canoe. He allowed himself to be lifted up into a carriage, and an easy-chair in his study, and into the
seventh story of a fashionable hotel, and so his life
was squeezed out of him. If he would have kept his
toes on the ground through vacation!

I meet the Rev. Mr. Antæus frequently in the last
stages of his wrestling. He has a thin girl's hand, a
sallow, flabby cheek, a stooping gait, and a Chinese
foot, and the latest issue of the prolific press. Poor
man! There is just one chance for you, dyspeptic and
dying. Come down to the ground, and let your parents, Neptune and Terra, nurse you. Cook your own
trout on the Parmachene, eat moose beef and venison
by your own camp fire in New Brunswick, bear's meat
in the Adirondacks, and grouse on the Iowa prairies.
Then, in the next match, I will bet on you against Hercules.

But you think it undignified in scholarly men to

come down to the earth in this way. Better so than
to come under the earth with semi-suicidal dignity.
Anything, almost, that will enable you to throw Hercules. Perhaps you have religious scruples. Then
read Robert Boyle's Angling Improved to Spiritual
Uses, forty-two pages, royal quarto. But such amuse-
ment and recreation you regard as unministerial. You
should study carefully A Discourse uttered in Part at
Ammauskeeg-Falls, in the Fishing Season, 1739. By
Joseph Seccombe. John xxi. 3. The topic of the
worthy divine, drawn from the words of St. Peter, "I
go a-fishing," and the reply of the apostles, "We also
go with thee," is this: Business and Diversion inof-
fensive to God, and necessary for the Comfort and Support of Human Society. For certain ones, so devout
they cannot smile nearer to the Sabbath than Wednes-
day, he remarks, "Some so muffle up Christianity, and
make it look so melancholy, sickly, and sour, that in-
considerate people are apt to dread its commands."

If you are shy of diversion, and a good, natural, jolly
time, and plead the demands of business, beware of
coming within reach of the sarcasm of Locke: "Some
men may be said never to divert themselves; they cannot turn aside from business, for they never do any."

We were all waiting by the huge fires, in the gray
dusk of the evening, for The General, who always had
ways and times of his own, when he came leisurely up
to the group. He opened on us with a merry remark
that sent a volume of laughter to the other shore of
Swan Lake.

It is a privilege that we hunters enjoy of laughing
to the full compass and volume of civilized life, and

that, too, without disturbing any neighbors. Mr. Smith, across our street, is not annoyed, and Mrs. Bryant's baby, on the next square, is not waked up, by these audible expressions of our cheerfulness. It will be a sad day for this country when the population is so dense that one cannot laugh comfortably without disturbing some neighbor.

Taking his seat on the largest log, he set his compass and laid his chain, like an old surveyor, by the last stake, and so renewed the narrative of his wanderings.

TERRIBLE TIMES IN THE WOODS.

"In 1843 the public surveys, that had been suspended for some time, again commenced. I was sent by the surveyor-general into the country lying north of the Wisconsin River, and on the Kickapoo. This was a rough, broken, wilderness land. It was formerly owned by the Winnebagoes, and obtained from them by treaty, through Governor Dodge, in 1834. It is extensively known as The Sugar Loaves of Wisconsin, from its abrupt and rounded peaks and inaccessible points, separated by deep ravines and impenetrable thickets. It was through this region that Black Hawk warily led his trusty followers when pursued by Colonel Atkinson. His command became entangled among the precipices and gorges, and he was obliged to abandon his wagons, baggage, and all, with the loss of many of his horses, and some men.

"I undertook my work here in May, and though my progress was slow, the weather warm, and mosquitos almost beyond endurance, the health of the company kept good, and the work went forward. Provisions of all kinds had to be obtained from Prairie du Chien, about fifty miles distant, as this was the nearest trading point to my work, and thence they were brought into camp on pack animals.

"About the middle of July our provisions grew scanty, and, as there was very little game to be had, I started for Prairie du Chien for supplies. During my

absence of several days, there passed across this Kickapoo region the most terrific hurricane that the West
ever experienced. From Prairie du Chien to the
Kickapoo River, a distance of forty miles and more,
the country is prairie, but beyond that, inward to my
field of labor, heavily timbered, and mostly with sugar
maple.

"At the point where my trail entered this timber, the
tornado seemed to expend the strength of its fury. Its
effects were almost utter destruction for miles in extent. The forest was uprooted, and trees of immense
size were twisted and broken into all shapes, and then
left piled up in unlimited confusion.

"I arrived at the crossing of the Kickapoo with my
supplies just at night, and saw the utter desolation and
destruction. Even the river was full of broken trees
and limbs, afloat and fast, and my way appeared to be
shut up beyond my power to open it. With much
anxious thought for the morrow, I encamped for the
night. My only hopes were, that the extent of the tornado had not reached my camp, and that their supplies
would hold out while I worked my tedious way to
them through these forest ruins. My detention at
Prairie du Chien had been unexpectedly long, and I
knew their provisions could not last many days. The
exigencies demanded prompt and vigorous action, and
I summoned all my energy to meet them.

"There was a Winnebago camp near the crossing,
and I soon found my way there, amid the barking of
dogs and crying of pappooses. I at once made known
to the chief my condition, and the situation of my men,
shut off from me by the tornado. From him I learned

the course of the tornado, and the width of its track of destruction. I hired several Indians, and early the next morning crossed with them the river, and commenced cutting a bridle-path through the confused and tangled mass. The progress was slow and discouraging. We spent hours in trying to find a zigzag course around the impenetrable piles and windfalls, often only to come at last to some confused mass that I could not pass, much less my pack-horses. Tired and distressed, I recrossed the river at night, and encamped with my Indians. The next morning I was again at work, hoping to find the range of the tornado such that I could turn to one side from its debris, but in vain. The second night found me back in my old camp, totally baffled.

"I then had canoes prepared, and the next morning I started the Indians up the river in them with the supplies, while I followed on the land. I took but one pack-horse with me, and ascending the Kickapoo till I had passed across the range of the hurricane, I swam my horse over, landed my provisions, and discharged the Indians. The sun was setting as I stood alone on the bank. The canoes of the faithful Indians were receding from my view, and my never-tiring horse, that had been with me for years in my explorations west of the Mississippi, alone was left as my companion, while no habitation of a white man was within forty miles of me.

"Increasing excitement for the safety of my men nerved me for struggle with any difficulties. That night I carried my supplies half a mile, and spreading sticks and grass on the wet ground, I placed them there carefully, and covered them over with bark and brush. I slept but little that night, and as soon as it was light enough to travel, I made fast a sack of flour and some pork to my horse, and then laid my course in such a direction as I thought would intersect, beyond the sweep of the tornado, the trail by which I had originally entered the forest. Unfortunately, I had no compass, or any other guide below the sun, except the Indian's north star, the moss on the tree. The country was broken into ravines and precipitous peaks, of which I have spoken. With my hatchet in one hand, and the bridle-rein in the other, I plunged into the dark forest in my perilous journey, hurried and strengthened by painful anxieties for the fate of my men.

"Though I avoided the confused path of the tornado, I found difficulties in the way, and my progress was very slow through thickets, and around sloughs, and mountains, and ravines. By shunning the trail of the whirlwind, I had nearly doubled my distance to the camp, and my physical energies were taxed to the utmost, while the exciting conviction urged me on, that my men must now be entirely destitute of any supplies, and possibly starving and dying before I could reach them. When darkness overtook me again, my little camp fire was lighted, and my faithful Luke was spancelled out to crop such scanty vegetation as he could find in the dark recesses of the wood. I prepared and ate my scanty meal in silence, and then, rolling myself up in my blanket, I slept. Then dreams came, not of home, with its comforts and blessings, nor of its dear ones, but of those who looked to me for protection and food, now shut up among the rocks and dells of the wilderness.

"At early dawn I was again on my route. This day was stormy, and the wilderness was dark, and in my wanderings I lost my course, and much travel and time. The next morning came with a clear sun, and my hopes and strength were renewed. The next night, just as darkness began to remind me of a place for encamping, I came into a beaten track that showed the footprints of horses. Passing along rapidly, I came to a little rivulet, and following it a short distance, I found a spring of pure, cold water, and quickly recognized the place of an old encampment, that I had made when I first entered the country. Now I felt fully relieved of anxiety as to my course, and of any uncertainty as to finding my camp. Again I ate my solitary meal, and wrapped my blanket around me, feeling that one more day would reveal all to me of what I hoped and feared.

"My suspense was agonizing, and I started up with the full purpose to press on till I knew all. But darkness forbade, and my better judgment brought me back to my blanket. But my mental torture that night can never be forgotten. My imagination, in my half-sleeping condition, would picture to me the emaciated features of my men, calling for food, and frowning over my delay. Daylight brought relief, because it allowed me to struggle on again.

"I had gone a little distance, not more than half a mile, when, turning at the foot of an abrupt precipice, I suddenly stood before one of my men! Pale and thin, with matted hair and beard, I hardly knew him. His blanket was drawn loosely around him, and his eyes stared wildly, as if he were bewildered. The recognition was mutual, but so sudden and unexpected, that neither had time to prepare for the meeting. The story was soon told.

"V., the assistant, had left the camp, with one other man, two days before, and on this trail, with the hope either of meeting me or of reaching some place of relief. He left the others in a starving condition. The camp stores had been exhausted, the two bear dogs had been killed and eaten, and the party had been for days with only a young pheasant for food, boiled with a kind of wild nettle, and made into soup.

"One of the party, Fitz P., had refused to eat of the dogs, and was in a very reduced condition. They had not been able to kill any game, and such berries and roots as they dared eat were very scarce. They had a supply of coffee, and used it freely; but, taken without food, the effects of it were unpleasant, and often painful. All had been confident that I was killed by the Indians, or lost in the wilderness. V. informed me that one of the party, who had left camp with him, was but a short distance behind, but too weak to proceed. Giving V. some food, I hastened on, and found the poor fellow lying by his little camp fire. Peeling some bark from the linden, and mixing some flour, and pasting it to the bark, I soon baked for him a little bread. Leaving there a small portion of pork, I hurried on to camp, where I found the remaining four of my scattered band.

"It was a scene I could not look on without tears. On a log near by were stretched the skins of our two bear dogs, and their bones lay scattered about the camp ground. In the tent lay the men, prostrate by weakness, discouraged, and given over to despair. They waited, in the confidence of my return, too long before they made an effort to save themselves by seeking a settlement and food. Yet had they left, the probability is, they would have been driven back by the barrier the tornado had thrown up, or, in forcing their way through it, become entangled, and so perished. When I entered the tent, they wept in surprise and joy.

"I soon had food prepared, and dealt it out to them in small quantities. Such were their gnawings of hunger, after they had once tasted food, that I was obliged to sit on the provisions, and keep them from the men by main force, or they would have eaten to their death. All that night their pleadings for food were heart-rending. Long after the darkness shut us in, the two absent ones, who left two days before, came back.

"The pack-horses had strayed off into the mountains before food was wholly gone, or they would have shared the fate of the dogs. We hunted them up in due time, and as soon as the men were sufficiently recruited, we slowly took the back trail to my depot of supplies, hidden under the brush on the banks of the Kickapoo. After a wearisome march, and when our provisions in hand were nearly gone, we reached the *cache* only to find that it had been plundered of its precious contents by the Indians. A wandering squad, from the Root River band, had been on the Kickapoo, fishing, and, discovering my tracks and signs, they had robbed us of our last hope. We had intended to recruit here, and then resume work in another part of the field;

but now our only chance was to flee to the nearest settlement.

"The river here was not passable without swimming, and our only open way was to ascend to a ford ten miles above. This we did, and in a few days we all reached a place of safety, and of supplies and rest. Many articles of clothing were afterwards found in the liquor shops of Prairie du Chien, that belonged to our plundered camp, but no Indian who sold them could be found. They had gone up the Mississippi to their wigwams on Root River, and we turned our steps homeward.

"In 1844 there was great excitement about mineral lands. The copper regions of Lake Superior had been explored, and marvellous stories were told of the immense wealth hidden there. Large companies were organized in the North and South, and mineral lands were sought after all through the North-west. A kind of mineral 'float' had been issued, similar to a preemption right, and parties organized to find mineral lands and locate 'floats' on them.

"A company was formed in New Orleans, with General B., an old friend of mine, for its head. In June of this year, an expedition in the interests of this company left Davenport for the head-waters of the St. Croix, in Wisconsin Territory, now Minnesota. Of this expedition I was intrusted with the command. It consisted of a surveyor, two geologists, a full set of camp hands and Canadian voyageurs, with bateaux adapted to the swift streams of the mountains.

"We left the head of the St. Croix Lake, about the middle of June, in a Mackinaw boat, and after reaching the Grand Falls of that river and making its portage, the party divided, a portion going on by water, and the rest by land, with the Canadian ponies. We ascended to the mouth of Snake River, one of the principal tributaries of the St. Croix, and then followed it up, past the portage, into Cross Lake, where the missionary station for the Chippewas was located, and to the head of Pokegoma Lake. Here we remained a few days to recruit, and then started for the Porcupine Mountains, the destination of the expedition.

"There was much in this trip to interest and please me, specially as I had the control of my own time, and was general director of the camp and the movements of the party. The season of the year was delightful above all others, and the country was uninhabited, except by the Chippewas, who were friendly. This was their fishing season, and as they were very successful, our camp was abundantly supplied.

"The scenery in this wild region is most sublime. There are no precipitous mountains, but a high range of table-lands, interspersed with lakes, the most beautiful and romantic that one can imagine. Little streams of the purest water run at your feet, alive with the speckled trout, while the lakes, bays, and inlets, shaded by the sweeping boughs of the pine, spruce, and birch, invite you to their cool retreats, and sing their lullaby over your camp. Sometimes the little waterfall, or the more mighty cataract, would recall one from his reverie, and draw him to its side, where he would sit in the spray and admire the never ending, never wearying music of the water.

The stillness and the beauty of such a scene, un-marred by any touch of civilization, could never fail to call forth adoration and praise, and fill the soul with love for Him who made the mountain and the plain and the wilderness without inhabitant.

"The geological survey was made, specimens obtained, and land located. At one time in our exploring we were near to the shores of Lake Superior. The survey being completed, the expedition returned to the mouth of the St. Croix and disbanded.

"Several of us then made up a new and smaller party, and visited St. Paul, then consisting of a few cabins, the Falls of St. Anthony and Minnehaha, and Fort Snelling at the mouth of the St. Peter's.

"There the Sioux lived at ease in his native forest. His wigwam stood on the banks of the Minnehaha unmolested, and his children played on the camping-grounds of his fathers. Cities now cover the ashes of his lodge, and where he then chased the deer, elk, and buffalo, the husbandman gathers in the harvest of civilization. The midnight lamentation of the Indian mother, the Rachel of the Red Man, over the grave of her child, is now exchanged for the music of the maidens of the pale faces, and the wild notes of Indian lovers are replaced by the hum and bustle of the settlements. The Laughing Water of his native forest has been immortalized in song, while the footsteps of the Indian have followed in his trail of doom over the prairies of the Far West."

The General closed his story for the night with a touch of sadness in his tones. He pitied, as he always

pitied, the Indian, feeling that he was the victim of a
heathen religion and superior race. Cupidity, more
than Christianity, has prevailed in the earlier dealings
of the whites with the Indians, so that our treatment
has debased rather than elevated them; and what we
called "Indian outrages" were but their natural and
national modes of self-defence, according to their Law
of Nations, which, unfortunately for them, they had
no Vattel to expound and defend. The General had
rarely experienced anything but kindness from their
hands during twenty-five years of intercourse with
them, more or less intimate and exposed. And while
thus detailing the beginnings of imperial success in
the founding of new states, he felt keenly the sacrifice of one race for the elevation and glory of another.
We, the mean while, were considering only the sacri-
fices of our own race in this gigantic march of western
progress.

It costs something of white toil and hardship and
sorrow to turn a wilderness into the fruitful field; and
these continuous narratives of The General were pressing this truth on us nightly and more amply. I felt it the
more, coming from Massachusetts Bay Colony, where
two hundred years stood between my childhood home
and the wigwam of Samoset. To this pioneer work
of the surveyor must succeed the blazed tree, the
emigrant wagon and cabin, the rude trail from settlement to settlement, the ford and bridge, the log school-
house and church, the larger villages, farms, population, wealth, and all the powers of a Christian civilization. Those improvements and forces have followed
up in the wandering and lost steps of the surveyor

among the Sugar Loaves; and a heavy population, with cities and farms, highways, public buildings, and thrift, are now on the ground where his men ate their bear dogs and the soup of the young pheasant. Crawford and Vernon counties, the present Kickapoo country, could then muster only one scattered camp of white men and a pack-horse. The few cabins of St. Paul have grown to a noble city, and the Minne-haha is now the Laughing Water, among spindles and lathes, belts and cogs, huge wheels, millstones, and manufactories.

NINTH NIGHT.

SOMETHING besides story-telling and listening was going on at our camp fire last night. While all ears were attentive to The General, and every hearer floundered along with him, in sympathy, through the windfall and overflow of the Kickapoo, Dock and Rube caught every word, as well as the best of us, while they worked hard in plucking, and roasting, and basting an extra two dozen of ducks. When the story wound up with the plundering of the *cache* by the Root River Indians, the task of the cooks was nearly complete, and before the last of us left the crackling brands for our blankets, the twenty-four ducks, plump, brown, and crisp, lay cooling off in tent number eight. The case was thus : —

Six or eight miles inland from our grounds were some lakes and lagoons, where, in a former hunt of the club, they had found large supplies of geese, coming in from nightfall till midnight. A few of us proposed to make a stand hunt there the following night. This would necessitate our absence from camp two days and one night, and hence the need of the extra cooking.

Bright and early, with rations for two days, and a blanket for a bivouac after our evening shooting, we

11

set forth, our only regret being the suspension for one night of the personal history of The General. Our route, much of the way, lay over bottom prairie. A chicken or duck broke now and then the tedium of our march, as we used a warm October day, sweating under our burden. Indeed, the labor would have had a strong resemblance to work if we had done it under pay. Lucky had it been for us, had we been drawing pay; for when we came to the lakes and lagoons, we found only blank and dry mud bottoms. The drought had been severe in all that section of Illinois, and the shoal bodies of water had dried up. We visited the familiar stands, where, the year previous, they had knocked down so many geese when coming on their night feeding-grounds; but the reeds, and grass, and wild rice were shrivelled and brown, and the water was all gone, leaving a baked and cracked lake bottom. We lunched famously by a shaded spring, and then hunted leisurely back to camp, knowing better than ever before what is meant by "a wild-goose chase."

And why not *we* know, as well as anybody? A wild-goose chase is not the worst a man can make. Some persons follow smaller game for years over the pavements, and fare no better than we did. The hunt itself was royal; what we caught was quite another thing. The chase has always been royal sport. Charles III. of Spain run the stag or wild boar eight hours every day, except the Sabbath and great holidays of the church. Forbidden by his confessor to hunt on those days, he had an aviary carried into his park, and shot the birds as they were let fly one by one. And the melancholic Burton tells us that the kings of Persia were accustomed to hawk butterflies with sparrows and starlings, that they had trained for this petty falconry. How much above kings were we, in chasing geese, even though we failed. Louis XIII., when a boy, had the same small sport with butter-flies. Indeed, I have seen many grown-up people chasing butterflies, though they call them by other names.

After you have turned aside from the great and proper aim of life, to make this world wiser and better by your residence in it, and have dropped away into pursuits of pleasure and selfishness, your game may as well be in lakes as in counting-rooms, country res-idences, ownership of railroads and steam lines. It is all geese, only differing in size and color. A span, a yacht, a month at Saratoga or Newport, the only shawl of the kind this side of Cashmere — it is all a wild-goose affair, and half the adult world are in the chase. If Branch Pierce, the old Plymouth hunter, to whose cabin Webster made his annual pilgrimage, kill in fifty years two hundred and sixty-seven deer with the same gun, why has he not followed a pleasure as honorable for manhood, and as useful for mankind, as he who hunts his pleasure in a "corner" of the corn exchange, where he doubles the price of each kernel for the poor consumer, and bags his two hundred and sixty-seven thousand dollars to make his idle sons fast young men?

We all must hunt geese of some kind, and probably the smaller the better. In the hunt referred to we made a failure; but our camp fellows were well re-

signed to our disappointment, as it brought The
General before us, without the loss of a night. We
came soon and easily into listening attitude, wondering
what new adventures, in an energetic and wonderful
life, were now to be opened up to us. We were not
kept long in suspense.

Over the Plains.

"After the mineral lands expedition, I was engaged for years in surveying the public lands of my own state. The Indian, the buffalo, and the elk had fled before the swarms of immigrants that were filling our new lands. The last canoe had crossed our Missouri boundary westward, and the original owners of the state had found a new home in Kansas Territory.

"California had given hints of her hidden treasures, and a wonderful excitement followed. The more venturesome and enterprising of our western men, flushed with the visions of immense and easy wealth, began to traverse the Plains and American Desert — so called then — and to climb the snow-capped mountains, to reap the golden harvest. Many fancied that the precious metals could be had there with only the labor of scraping them up.

"In 1849 all public surveys were again suspended. Business of all kinds became dull in the West. At this time a favorable opportunity presented itself for me to gratify a long-cherished and ardent desire to visit the Plains, the Desert, the Rocky Mountains, and the shores of the Pacific. This project had been in my mind for some time. I had watched the progress and westward movement of civilization with deep interest, hoping and expecting that in the course of events my foot would follow in the trail of the Indian, and my face be turned, with his, towards the setting sun.

"The Mormons had sought the valley of Salt Lake,
which was their only possible resting-place between
the Mississippi and the Sacramento, and from three to
five months were consumed by them in the trip. Numerous tribes of hostile Indians at that time lived on
the route, and but few of the emigrants had knowledge
or judgment enough to arrange an outfit for such a
journey, or conduct it safely. Wagons were made
too heavy; large quantities of unnecessary provision,
machinery, tools, and trumpery, were loaded in. So
the animals were worn down before they came to the
mountains and feeding-places, and their bones were
left by the way, and the emigrant was doomed to pursue
his journey as best he could on foot.

"In the spring of 1850 the opportunity long desired offered itself to me, and I embraced it. With a
light two-horse wagon, five horses, two men, and such
provision and clothing as good sense suggested for the
trip, I crossed the State of Iowa to Council Bluffs, before the frost had left the ground. We went into
camp at St. Francis, a village of huts six miles below,
on the Missouri.

"At the request of many enterprising men, I promised to make observations on the route, and report on
the feasibility of a railroad to the Pacific — a project
just then starting up. Always ready and willing to
assist in the progress and welfare of the West, I took
with me my surveying instruments, and such other
apparatus as would enable me to make a preliminary
topographical survey. This survey I made, and reported on the same, after my arrival in California, giving the latitude, longitude, and altitude of all the more

prominent landmarks and stopping-places on my line of travel. This report was published at the time in the New York Herald, and extensively copied, as the first one ever made, I think, for a railroad to the Pacific.

"The season was cold and vegetation backward. All who passed over the Plains that year can well remember the trials and hardship endured. Our encampment below Council Bluffs was long and tedious, while we waited for the grass to start.

"During these many days of delay I visited the country up and down the Missouri, Platte, and smaller rivers. I visited Kanesville, then the great Mormon rendezvous, and point of departure for Salt Lake. I formed the acquaintance of the Mormon elders and missionaries, and acquired a good understanding of much of their doctrine. The Boyer River I also traversed, from its mouth to its source in the vast prairies. At this time the Otto and Omaha Indians were living along the Missouri, from the mouth of the Platte to the Big Sioux, and I travelled freely among them. The mission established by the government among them was then an active institution, and at a place since called Bellevue. The Rev. Mr. Kinney had charge of the mission, and school attached. Here I attended church during our delay, and had ample opportunities to see the work of the missionaries in turning the Indians from the darkness of barbarism to the light of the Gospel.

"Long will be remembered the days I spent on the grounds of the old Omaha mission. He who all his life has only read of the trials and hardships of the missionary should have been there with me to see and realize the labors of one who has set apart his life to so good a work. The school contained about seventy-five scholars of both sexes. The only hope of the missionary is in the children. These were taught daily, and in some the progress was astonishing, while others were like the untamed fawn, whose eyes and ears are ever so open and alert that it can scarcely pause to crop the grass and appease its hunger.

"Many of the girls boarded at the mission, and were there taught the various branches of female employment. On the Sabbath all were gathered in the log chapel, together with any stray whites who chose to come in. On these occasions you would see the father and mother of the scholars, seated around the sides of the room, evidently feeling that it was the place of the Great Spirit. As the service was about to commence, the aged warrior would come in, bowing in solemn silence, as if he knew it to be the place where the God of the white man was worshipped.

"The time drew on, though very tardily, when we must take up our line of march. The organization of our company had taken place by choosing me as The General."

Here one of the lads interposed to inquire if that was where he got his title as General, and he was informed that his commission bore that date, and place, and authority. The General resumed : —

"We passed by-laws and resolutions to regulate our camping and marching, feeling that nothing but order, authority, and due subordination to the will of the whole, deliberately expressed, could insure us a safe trip over so long a route, and through so many dangers, as we knew would beset us. For the company consisted of sixty men, one hundred and eighty-five horses, and twenty-seven wagons.

" On the 20th of April we broke up camp and began the crossing of the Missouri. This we completed the next day, and went into camp on the Nebraska side, preparatory to a final departure. This was our last camping in sight of a settlement. There was no grass as yet, but the great uneasiness of the company to move carried the vote for a start.

"It was Saturday night, and all had their tents pitched, and horses and mules cared for. The moon in its splendor seemed to vie with the bright and blazing camp-fires, as I took my official round to see that all was in trim for a start. At nine o'clock the bugle sounded from the tent of The General, and all were soon gathered there to hear of plans and regulations for our travelling. In a few words I reminded the company of their readiness to depart, of the poor prospects for forage, and of the constant care required to keep up the strength of their animals in the first stages of the expedition. I also very feelingly reminded them of our departure now from home, and friends, and settlements, and that we were about to strike out on unknown prairies, and to encounter trials and difficulties of which as yet we were totally ignorant. I also called attention to the fact that the next day would be the Sabbath, a day of rest for man and beast, and that while I had the honor to command, the expedition would not move on that day.

"Monday morning, April 22, the announced day for the departure of the train, came at last, bright and beautiful. It was one of those April mornings when the bluebird sings, and the early robin is seen, returned from the sunny South — a day well calculated to call up sweet recollections of home, and all its endearments. The camp was in motion at an early hour, and at six o'clock the bugle sounded for the train to move off according to their assigned number. Long will that beautiful morning be remembered by the survivors of the company, as the train wound around the point of bluff that overlooks the valley of the Platte.

"As the train rose on the high prairie, from which could be seen the beautiful land of Iowa, that lovely spot, which contained to many in the expedition all that was dear to them on earth, and as its rich and undulating plains receded from view, many a silent prayer went up, and many a tear was brushed away. So we bade farewell to the 'States' and entered the Indian country.

"Great was the undertaking, and difficult the overland route that day to California. None knew the dangers and destinies of those who undertook it. The parting from home was a sad farewell, and this was renewed as the wanderer passed the border of the settlements.

"Forage had become scarce on the Missouri, and, though the grass had not grown sufficiently to sustain the animals, it seemed almost imperative to move on. For more than two weeks after starting we fed the stock on flour wet up with chopped dry grass gathered from the prairie, and on browse, when we could find it.

Along the Platte and Loup Fork Rivers we obtained for this purpose limbs of the linwood, mulberry, and elm. The cavalcade moved slowly to the Elkhorn River, and thence to the Loup Fork, a distance of one hundred miles, to a crossing about five miles above its mouth. Some enterprising emigrants had made a flat-boat here, and were keeping a kind of ferry, the river being high, and not fordable, except in July and August. There were one or two companies, waiting to be set over when we arrived. Some days the winds were so high that not one team could be passed over. We went into camp to await our turn for the flat-boat, there being timber and browse in abundance, and old grass that we could prepare for our teams.

"While encamped here, I started out with my old and tried friend C., who had been my companion on many of my Iowa expeditions, for a hunting tour up the Loup Fork. There had been a recent battle between the Sioux and Pawnees, who fought each other, on every occasion, somewhere on this river, and we were very desirous of finding the ground. After travelling one day till nearly night, we came to the bloody field in a willow thicket near the bank of the river.

"The attack had been made by the Sioux. The Pawnees were out on a hunt, and, as usual, encamped in a thicket to hide themselves from their enemies. But the keen eye of the Sioux discovered their retreat, and fell on them in the night, killing six. As we approached the battle-field, we found on the edge of the prairie, about a hundred yards from the site of their camp, a number of small holes dug, not more than a foot in diameter, and an equal number of small poles,

or sticks, placed by them, pointing in different directions, showing whence the enemy came, and which way
they retreated.

"Along the side of these holes lay twelve small
sticks of willow, about a foot long, and of the size of a
pipe-stem, each end being finely splintered, like a broom.
These we could not interpret, though both of us were
acquainted with the dumb language of Indian signs.
But at the place of battle in the willows, and where
the dead fell, the signs were more intelligible.

"In front of the lodge, or rather of the place where
it was — for the poles were still standing there stood — a
straight willow pole, about five feet high, and painted
red, bent over a little at the top, from which was
suspended an Indian effigy, cut from undressed elk
hide, painted and hanging by the scalp lock. On each
arm were cut six notches, representing the six Pawnees
killed in the engagement. On the top of this pole was
placed a brass finger-ring, broken, to show that the
enemy had professed friendship, but broken it. This
was an allusion to a treaty of friendship made between
these two tribes not more than six months before.
About four inches apart from the top of the pole downward were tied six pipes full of tobacco, each in a rag,
with a lock of the hair of the deceased Indian attached
to it. This was an offering to the Great Spirit, that he
might supply the departed with tobacco to smoke forever
in the hunting-grounds of the Gitche Manitou. On each
side of this pole, and not far distant, two others of
smaller dimensions were placed, from the top of each
of which swung, like an old tavern sign, a piece of
grained elk skin about eighteen inches square. On one

of these were painted a large number of horse and mule feet, signifying the number of such animals the enemy had. On the other side the number of the enemy was represented by so many Indian heads, painted with scalp locks. On the other parchment was represented the number killed by each party, and the number of horses taken. From this spot commenced a line of poles, with small flags or bits of rags on the top of each, pointing in the direction in which the enemy went.

"In addition to all this, and the most interesting of all, were the rude hieroglyphics on the ashes and sand around the camp, where their religious ceremonies took place, and the offerings were made to appease the Evil Spirit. The dead of both parties were carried off — six Pawnees and three Sioux — after this manner: Long poles were cut and attached by one end, two for each horse, to either side of the saddle. The other ends dragged on the ground. In this way a kind of litter was made, and to it the dead were lashed and drawn away to their village. It is their custom to remove the wounded in the same way.

"The funeral obsequies differ among the different tribes, as do also their customs of courtship and marriage; and while we are waiting, as it were, for the ferryman at the crossing of the Loup Fork, I may as well tell you something of the latter.

"With the Sacs and Foxes, a young man selects his future wife at some feast or dance, and then informs his mother, who calls on the mother of the girl. If an arrangement for the match is made by the mothers, a time is fixed, and the lover goes to the lodge of the

girl's parents in the night, when all are asleep, or are
supposed to be. He finds the matches, which have
been provided for the occasion from the pitch of the
pine tree, and lighting these, he soon discovers where
his intended sleeps. He awakes her, holds the light
to his own face, that she may know him, and then
places it close to her face. If she blows it out, the
ceremony is over, and he appears in the lodge the
next morning as one of the family. If she does not
blow it out, he leaves the lodge, and the light is left
to burn till it expires.

"But the next day he will place himself in full view
of her wigwam, and play his flute. The young women
there assembled will then go out, one by one, to see
whom he desires. As they approach singly he changes
the tune, for each successive one, to discord and confusion, till his intended appears. When she shows herself
in the door of the lodge, he plays the soft, sweet notes
of a lover, until she retires. She does not approach
him. Her appearance while he plays encourages him;
and so at night he goes again to her lodge, and this
second time he is generally successful.

"During the first year of the marriage, they ascer-
tain whether they can live together in peace and
happiness. If 'incompatibility' appear, they separate, and try again for new partners.

"The courtship of the Chippewa is still more simple. The lover appears at the door of the wigwam
of his desired bride with a bundle of furs, peltries,
beads, and wampum. He enters and lays the gifts at her
feet, and then retires a short distance from the lodge
to await her decision. If he is accepted, she soon

appears at the door, and holds aside the curtain that he may enter. If he is rejected, his furs and other presents are suddenly thrown out of the lodge, and he picks them up and retires, as if they were 'the mitten.'

"It is not to be supposed, however, that these lovers are strangers to each other. Long years of acquaintance and courtship may have passed between them; but the ceremony of the offered hand and acceptance must be carefully regarded.

"With some tribes the negotiations are made by the parents, when a certain number of horses and blankets is given for the bride, and she is driven or forced off, like a slave to the market, which the Indian wives so generally become, after marriage. For they plant and harvest the corn, cut and pack in the wood to the lodge, move the wigwam in summer and winter, rain and snow, without any aid from husband, father, brother, or son. They skin the game, dress the furs, cure the meat, dry the fish, gather the rice, and cook the victuals, while the lazy Indian lies on the mat and enjoys the fruit of the wife's labors.

"As to the burial customs, the Sacs and Foxes, Winnebagoes and Potawatamies, bury their dead in a sitting position, with the body left above ground as high as the ribs. The blanket is thrown loosely over the shoulders; the paint is in one hand, and the pipe and tobacco in the other. The grave is enclosed with high pales, set closely together in the ground, so that no animal can enter. The Sioux and Chippewas bury above ground, if I may so speak, on a scaffolding. This is built with poles and bark, often ten feet high, and sometimes in the branches of the trees. The body is prepared for the funeral rite by closely wrapping it in blankets, and the clothing of the deceased. When placed on the scaffold it is covered with bark to prevent the birds from devouring it.

"It is no uncommon thing for the traveller in the Sioux country to find, a short distance from the lodge, the dead body of a child, wrapped in its cradle of bark, swinging from the limbs in full view of the mother's watchful eye. She guards it sacredly from the rude touch of man or beast. She listens to the sighing wind, as it rocks the precious burden, and adds her wild lullaby for the spirit of the departed.

"Some tribes lay their dead on the top of the ground, and cover them over with stones and earth; but very few of them bury, like the white man. It is the custom of all the tribes to visit the graves of their dead often, and for years. A noted chieftain's grave will often be surrounded by his warriors and braves, and the most bitter lamentations will be sent forth, awakening hill and dale with their sorrow. So with the mother at the grave of her child, and the maiden at that of her lover. Bitter wailings may be heard at midnight, but none goes near to comfort the sorrowing.

"Of their sports and pastimes the Indian has more than the white man. Besides their feasts and dances, they have, in the most of the tribes, the great game of ball, at which five hundred can play on a side. Horses, guns, blankets, and trinkets are staked, and the winning party takes the stakes.

"The Indian is also an inveterate gambler, and will

lay down his last blanket, or even the wampum of his squaw, to indulge this passion. They play with cards, but it is a game different from any known to white men.

"Well, at last the ferryman is ready to pass us over, and the men are weary of delay. The gold fields of California glisten before them, and they are eager to press on. But ferriage over the Loup Fork by night is a dangerous thing. We must wait now till morning."

With the promise of pleasant rambles up the Platte, through the Pawnee country, and among elk and buffalo, at our next session of the Swan Lake encampment, we broke up for the night.

12

TENTH NIGHT.

A DAY of miscellanies. The keen edge of hunting has been wearing off, and we have gradually come into it as a routine of business. No new specimens of game are expected. We have ranged from the jack-snipe to the lordly turkey and royal swan, and from squirrel to coon. No new localities are to be hunted up. We have trailed to the outer edge of our saucer. of bottom land, and know every creek, lagoon, and puddle. Incidents to the game or ourselves, by land or water, are no longer extraordinary among twenty men daily seeking them; the exciting, and the marvellous, and the hair-breadths, have come by their abundance to be ordinary, expected, and commonplace. In the generous natural supply of game on our grounds, we are not driven to hunt to live; we merely live here to hunt.

So to-day there has been no great enthusiasm for the sport, and no wide ranges were planned. It has rather been a day of all works. We made short excursions, or shot what came in near on the lake shore, and down the outlet. A little municipal or philosophical phenomenon engrossed the attention of our canvas village early in the day, and thus : —

After leaving The General and his expedition at the Loup Fork Ferry last night, and betaking ourselves in an orderly way, as good hunters will, to our lodges, one of the tents was warmed up by a little pocket stove, with a three-inch pipe, for a supplement to the evening cheer. The inmates, a little invited company, sang, and told stories, and laughed, and did a dozen other merry and innocent things, till the wee bit of a stove became suddenly asthmatic and wheezy, and could not catch its breath. Dryer wood was of no account; the lifting of the tent curtain brought no relief by draughts of fresh air. After all the coaxing and forcing, the smoke refused to go up the legitimate way, and socially filled the tent instead; at which many tears were shed. So the fire was put out; singing and joking, and stories and laughing, came to an end after a short half hour. The men wondered, and the boys too, what the matter could be, and then all went to sleep. This morning, in attempting to solve the mystery, masses of leaves and grass, much like an old squirrel's nest, were found in the upper end of the pipe, where it was made steady against a tree. The men wondered, and the boys too, that squirrels should build in a stove-pipe at night, and while the fire was burning. The men had never heard of the like before, and the boys said they had not. Strange things do sometimes occur in camp, specially where there are boys.

Some time was spent to-day in packing off game to friends up and down the river, as we had an opportunity to forward it to a landing. The plump ducks settled in cosily in the boxes between geese and turkeys, and the fox squirrels filled up the chinks, while partridges and snipe took the place of honor on the top.

A gentleman hunter came into camp during the day,

amusing us more than he disturbed the game.   He was
dressed in good black broadcloth, and his boots had a
splendid polish, while his hunting apparatus was of the
most approved pattern, and military finish, for he ranked
high in the army. His movements on the game were bold
and soldier-like. When he returned from his first and
last attack on the ducks down the creek, his broadcloth
and boots looked otherwise than so as they did look
when he marched forth; and he did not say so much
of game when he put off his armor as when he put
it on.

To one experienced in camp, angle, and gun life, it
is vastly entertaining to see your fastidious and exquisite book sportsman enter the field. His outfit is ex-
travagantly expensive, as well as unfitting; he has more
luggage than a belle at Cape May, yet learns at last that
a very small bag and boy can carry all his game. The
rain and the sunshine, the flies and the mosquitos, the
brush and the open land, the bog and the rocks, all
trouble him, and he, in return, troubles all his companions; and the universal prayer is, that he may be taken
home tenderly and speedily to a dressing-gown, slip-
pers, and an ottoman.

I well remember fishing for mackerel, during a college holiday, from a wharf in Dorchester, when a gentleman was driven down pompously in a splendid open
buggy, to try his chance. The driver so placed the carriage that his eminence could sit in it and fish. With
much ado he rigged a beautiful jointed pole and reel,
and made a beginning. If there had been one aristocratic or snobbish mackerel in Boston Bay, that establishment wanted him, and ought to have taken him.

But, as it turned out, the first fish was an impudent and vulgar sculpin. We laughed, the gentleman was disgusted, and the carriage left. Our military friend came down the river, and then — he went up the river.

During this same day the skin of a swan was carefully removed from the original owner, and packed for the East by The General, and threescore and ten squirrel tails were removed to make eminent bashaw boys at home. A solitary turkey called us a half mile into the forest, and there left us quietly to our own meditations on the deceitfulness of hope.

To relieve the tedium of that idle Indian summer day, so soft in its haze, and lying so lazily all abroad on the tinted forest, and lake shores, and laps of prairie, we made sundry empty pickle jars serve as targets for our revolvers and rifles. It was a good study and practice for the culture of exactness.

The man who would give precision and a clear cut to his thought, and send the idea accurately home, should practise rifle shooting. In this he learns to depend on a single ball, and on his skill in putting it in the right place. It is practical mathematics, conic sections applied, in a very demonstrative way. A good sharpshooter must be an accurate reasoner. Distance, refraction of the atmosphere, and currents of air, as well as the most vulnerable point in the game, and its speed, if it be moving, must be estimated.

I well remember my first lesson on the deceptiveness of a dense and refracting atmosphere. It was a prairie chicken on the marshes below Davenport, clean burnt bottom, and loaded down with the heavy vapors

of an approaching April evening. My vision of the bird
was, of necessity, in an upward curve. My first ball
made a good perpendicular, but three inches above the
bird's head, as its strike beyond showed; the second
was lower, and the third lower still. The bird, true to
habit, kept itself motionless, till the fourth ball reduced
its head to a vulgar fraction. Distance, and vapors,
and refraction, and breezes, and the changing positions
of men, not being taken fully into account, many public
speakers make random shots. Some hit the hearer
the second time just where they missed him the first
time.

Specially men who handle canons ecclesiastical
should practise rifle-shooting. Dependence on a single
ball in the right place will give them command of "the
inevitable words," so honorably credited to Robert
South. O, but how many use shot guns, and small
shot at that, and like an old British soldier, they seem
to come no nearer to taking aim than raising the gun
breast high. Some, in their trepidation, and with un-
practised hands, let their pieces off at half cock, which,
perhaps, is just as well, after all.

Moreover, this rifle practice will help the speaker to
know that, after he has fired, his piece is empty. It is
no use to cock and snap till he loads again. How
much snapping of explosive, sensational caps in the
pulpit and on the platform, with an empty rifle, because
the speaker does not know that he has fired, and is
empty, and should be ended of his noise.

Men who use shot can, if able, carry a double barrel,
and so fire twice in close succession. Father Gleason,
the good missionary among the New York Indians,

had a Deacon Two Guns in his church. Probably in his wild state the man was the possessor of a double-barrelled gun, and so came by his name; to which the church affixed the title, as an officer in it. Happy the pastor and the church where Deacon Two Guns is an office-bearer, provided always that he knows how to handle his piece. It was, no doubt, the frequent and ill-timed pop of a single barrel of small shot, and the unskilled use of a double barrel, that led Dr. Todd to make a characteristic reply on a certain occasion.

" Dr. Todd," inquired a friend, " how do you proceed when about to elect a deacon?" " With great reluctance, sir."

I am aware that the Council of Agde forbade hunting and hawking to bishops, presbyters, and deacons, and they were not allowed to keep dogs and falcons for field sports. Also the Council of Trullo restrained the clergy from baiting wild beasts and hunting them with dogs. But this was far back in the darkness of the sixth and seventh centuries, and in the Papal church. Against all such restrictions I am a thorough Protestant, and my Lord Coke rules that I may hunt, as you will soon see.

If all bishops or ministers should keep a fast day, as Laud did, for every awkward shot, their weeks would not be long enough. The story runs thus: The famous Laud had been nominated as Bishop of St. David's, but was not installed. Visiting Lord Touch at Bramshill Park, Hampshire, he is persuaded to join in a hunt, which was very well, before or after induction. But not skilled in the crossbow, as good Hugh Latimer would have had him — and in some other

things, too, he was far from Latimer's model for a
bishop — he unfortunately shot a man instead of a deer.
It was a sad thing, and Laud went penitently into
retirement, while his rivals urged that a man of blood
could not fill a bishopric. The king issued a commission of inquiry on the objection, and they declared
it to be no bar. The opposition also consulted Sir
Edward Coke, whether a bishop might hunt at all.
He wisely declared it to be good canon and civil law
that a bishop may hunt. Sir Edward was learned and
scholarly, as the world knows. Laud was inducted
Bishop of St. David's, November 18, 1621; but he ever
after sorrowfully kept that fatal day as a fast day.

Awkward shots, erring, wounding shots, have kept
many candidates from installation, and disturbed the
settlements of not a few, and their fast days are not
near enough together. Yes, practise rifle-shooting, as
a means to clear ideas, accurate expression, singleness
of aim, and definiteness in result. For, as that most
excellent sermon hath it, "Men shall never shoote well
except they be brought up in it." Study carefully
the archery of the Psalms, and all the arrows of the
Old Testament, and trust to no bow drawn at a
venture, though a careless man did once so kill a
wicked king.

Well, we were shooting rifles at the empty pickle
jars beside Swan Lake. So in doing various nothings
laboriously — for to do nothing in a series, and follow it
well, is hard work — the leisure day waxed and waned in
all the mellow glories of October in the forests. We
were as merry, and jolly, and free from care as Robin
Hood's men in Sherwood, and if we made no shots as

good as Callum Dhu's among the McGregors, it was the fault of our education in degenerate times.

Supper came, and went too.   Then The General set us all over the Loup Fork in one boat load, and we struck out for the Rocky Mountains in bold style, as you will now see.

Indians! Indians!

"I like a good starting-point in a story, and a ferry is such. We crossed over, the next morning, from where I left the expedition last night, and were now fairly in the Pawnee country. Large bands of them would often follow the train from morning till night, begging and stealing according to opportunity. They are a low, filthy tribe, inferior in every respect to the Sioux of the Upper Missouri. They were friendly, but most inveterate thieves, particularly of horses, in which they abounded.

"They had often demanded and received presents from small companies passing through their country. When our train encamped on Wood River these Indians made their appearance in large numbers. The guard was set across the bend of the river within whose curve our camp was, and no Indian was allowed to enter. With previous trains of emigrants they had had the privilege of going within the lines, and even tents, ostensibly to trade, but really to steal. At my un-looked-for check on their custom and plans, they became clamorous and abusive. They had pressed up hard on the line when I ordered the guard to be doubled, and all my men to come inside. At this juncture of affairs two young chiefs came forward, and in broken English demanded to see the captain. I was called from my tent, and met the two chiefs outside. They demanded tribute in tobacco, pipes, blankets, powder

JOHN ANDREW & SON.

THE GENERAL DECLINES TO PAY TRIBUTE. Page 187.

and lead, because my band was passing through their territory, eating their grass, killing their buffalo, and burning their wood, adding that other bands of whites had paid this tribute, and I must. I replied, that they had a large country, and did not need all the grass and wood, and that their Great Father at Washington had given me permission to go through, and that he gave them annually many horses, and guns, and blankets, and provisions,.and money to pay for letting bands of white men go through, and that he expected his children, the red men, would not trouble his other children, the pale faces.

"They then demanded to be let into the camp to trade, and sell moccasons and fancy things for food and ammunition. This I also refused, telling them that their people were thieves, that I could not trust them inside, and that all their demands and threats for presents or trade I should resist with force.

"At this the Indians all retired to a small rise of land at a short distance in front of the camp, and set up a most terrific cry, with fierce gestures of revenge, brandishing their knives and tomahawks. All at once they started for their village, two miles off, yelling as they went, some on horses, and some on foot. This act caused much alarm in camp, and I was censured for my arbitrary course towards the Indians. But I was forced into the measure by their constant thefts from the wagons. All along the route, where a halt was called, at a watering-place or encampment, a crowd of the vagabonds would come about us, and while one Indian engaged the attention of a driver by the sale of some trifle, others would steal whatever came to hand that could be concealed and carried. On an examination the day before, it was ascertained that many of the company, not used to Indian trickery, had not only lost trifling things, like knives and hatchets, but whole hams and large pieces of other meat. An Indian can place two or three hams under his blanket, and walk off without being mistrusted. I well knew the sad consequences of such losses, when, in the progress of the journey, misfortune might come and provisions be scarce. Moreover, if I submitted to these demands, smaller trains of emigrants would be compelled to surrender, and be robbed wholly, and without mercy. I therefore set them at defiance.

"As the Indians went off in great anger, the more timid of our company believed that we should be attacked that night. But as the evening wore away, the little circles grew less and less around the camp fires. One after another disappeared in his tent, so that by ten o'clock all attacks by Indians were forgotten.

"It was a dark night, with no moon and few stars. The prairie was on fire in the distance, lighting up the solitary waste with a lurid glare far along the horizon. It was nearly eleven o'clock, and a few of us, officers, were sitting around the fires of the guard in front of the encampment, when the tramp of horses' feet was heard approaching from up the river. In an instant I laid my ear close to the ground to listen. The sound was distinct, and as I rose up I could see by the light of the prairie fire, and between us and it, horsemen approaching at a gallop. I at once shouted, at the top of my voice, 'Indians! Indians!' Those inside who were awake repeated the alarm, and it spread like flashing lightning through the camp.

"I gave orders for all to form in line in front of the camp. Men rushed from their tents half clothed, bewildered, and without arms. Some brought guns unloaded, and others axes, knives, and hatchets. A few sought refuge in the tents, or under the wagons, and hid themselves away among bags and blankets. One old man, a Methodist exhorter from Iowa City, and who died soon after his arrival in California, was found under his wagon, praying for protection against the Indians! Just as the officers had succeeded in forming a line of so many as had the courage to come out, the enemy was discovered to be a small party of our own horsemen, who had been feeding their stock up the creek — a circumstance of absence forgotten for the time by the wagon-master, and never mentioned to me.

"Intending to profit by the occurrence, so seriously opening, and ending so ludicrously, I ordered the roll called, and all delinquents to be brought forward. This revealed a bad state of things. Some of them could not find their arms in time to fall in; others had no ammunition. Indeed, but few of our entire company were really ready for an Indian surprise. Out of the company of men in camp when the alarm was given, only twenty-four were found in the ranks ready to fight. I at once took measures to have all their arms put in good order, each man to be provided with ammunition; and I passed the regulation that they should keep their pieces loaded, but not capped, and by their sides at night. After a protracted address on watchfulness among the Indians, two rounds were fired, and then all retired to rest, except the guard. To this day many of that company believe that I planned that alarm and played a game on them, to see what kind of material I had to depend on in crossing the Plains.

"There was another company that passed while I was in controversy with the Pawnees, and not only saw their angry manners, but were told by the timid of my train that we should be attacked before morning. This train passed on about two miles, and camped some distance from the road, through fear of the Indians. They were aroused by the report of our guns, and supposing we were attacked, instead of coming to the rescue, they broke up their camp in haste, and at midnight, and commenced their march for the next day. About a mile beyond them, and just before regaining the main road, there was one of those sunken marshes, so often found on the bottom lands of the Platte. In attempting to cross this in the darkness, their teams mired, and many of them remained there till morning. Our company saw them from the thoroughfare, as we passed by, and reminding them of the story of the two friends and the bear, we left them to extricate themselves as best they could.

"The company were now ascending the north fork of the Platte, and were fairly in the buffalo country, and vast herds of this animal were seen in the distance. The valley of the Platte is from three to ten miles wide. In some places, the bluffs or high prairie come near to the banks, while in others they recede. Under the edge of these bluffs the grass springs much earlier than in the more open prairie, and immense herds of buffalo were here quietly grazing. When at a distance, one would see a long, black line of them beneath the bluff, and this line would continue in view from morning till night. This accounts for the oft-repeated and never-explained assertions of travellers, that they had seen thousands of these animals in single herds, and had travelled through them from morning till night, and for days together. They had seen a thin line of these animals on that strip of early and tender grass, and not deep and dense herds.

"In the extreme hot weather the little lakes, creeks, and ponds dry up in the interior, and by instinct these animals approach the Platte for water, in distances of hundreds of miles across the plains, and their movement is marked by vast clouds of dust. When once started they neither stop nor turn out till they reach the water. In these annual migrations they always seek a beaten track, called a 'buffalo trail.' It is composed of five hundred, it may be, or a thousand paths, side by side, like furrows in a field, only that they are deeper and about four feet apart. These are quite uniform in depth and parallel distance, and often make a belt of great width. The trail is begun by a herd starting for water, and travelling side by side through the prairie grass, the platoon, so to speak, being several buffalo deep, and each following in the steps of his predecessor. They return in the same track and order, and as they go back and forth thus, the paths are worn deep, while the grass along the trail is wholly destroyed.

"When the stranger beholds one of these trails, his first thought is, that he has come to a cultivated land,

and that this is a vast field ploughed and furrowed for planting. He looks off right and left on it, and sees each path bearing its regular curve to the other, like the crooked furrow the farmer has followed in plough-ing each succeeding one. When the train comes to one of these trails the men must find a high ridge, where the wind has filled in the paths with sand, or they must level a road with the spade, for, in many places, the paths are too deep for any carriage to pass them.

"If a traveller is once caught in a buffalo trail when they come along, pressing on for water, he has no way of escape. The buffalo could not turn out if he would, for he is pressed on each side, and from behind, by the rushing herd. If an animal falls down, he is trampled to death by those following, who cannot stop. The eyes, nose, and mouths of these creatures are filled with sand and dust; their tongues hang out swollen and parched with thirst, and no obstacle — man or beast — can stop them in their passion and haste for water.

"The Indians and trappers say that the buffalo often came down to the Platte in such wild fury as to rush over the banks into the river, treading on one another, so that thousands are drowned. We found hundreds of them dead and dying on the open plain that had been burned by the annual prairie fires. On the season of our trip, however, the fires had been unusually severe, for the old grass was heavy — perhaps the accumulation of two or three years. Some advanced trains had set the fires during a wind storm, so that the blazing tufts were carried to a great distance, and a wide country fired at once. Not only had the buffalo been overtaken by the flames, but the wolf, and even the fleet antelope, as we found, had perished in the fiery tornado.

"Many blind buffalo lay along the banks of the Platte, and at times, when the road ran near to them, we had to send scouts forward to clear the way, lest they should run into us. Through all this region our camp was well supplied with buffalo and antelope meat. Of the latter animal but little notice is taken, as his fleetness prevents his being captured to any practical extent by the sportsman. They are animals of great curiosity, and no strange object can be shown to them without their approaching to know what it is, depending on their swift foot for safety, if danger arise. The hunter uses this curiosity to kill them. Selecting some log, rock, or cover, he lies flat on the ground, and putting his handkerchief or some showy object on his ramrod, he waves it back and forth till the attention of the animal is arrested. In a few moments it will come towards the hunter with a bound. As it comes quite near it will begin to circle around the object, coming nearer and nearer, till within the range of the fatal rifle, and so is killed.

"Of all the animals that inhabit the Plains, they are the most beautiful and innocent, resembling somewhat the fawn, or yearling deer, except in length of body and neck, which are shorter and more like those of the goat. They have the color of the deer, with white stripes along the sides, a mottled face, with a tender, beautiful eye like that of the gazelle. The antelope is often called the American gazelle.

"We had now travelled three hundred miles from
13

the Loup Fork, and to a region on the Platte where the timber gave out entirely, and nothing but a treeless waste lay before us. Here we spent some days in resting the animals. Two hundred miles lay between us and Fort Laramie with only a single tree in all the distance! A sense of loneliness comes over one as he enters this vast prairie ocean. After a journey of two or three days his eyes are greeted by the sight of the Lone Tree, known to all trappers, traders, and emigrants of the Platte. Whence it came, or how long it has braved the storms of rain and wind, sand and fire, none can tell; but there it stands, a solitary sentinel of the desert, unscathed by the lightnings, while the hand of man has not presumed to mar it. It looks, at a distance, like the first speck of a ship at sea, and is a great landmark, for it counts three hundred and seventy-five miles from Council Bluffs, and one hundred and forty-seven to Fort Laramie.

"Another curiosity met with on these prairies is The Saleratus Beds. These are composed of a white substance that rises from the earth, looking like lime or plaster of Paris, sown all over the land for many miles. It whitens the grass like snow, and persons travelling through it find their pants covered with the white powder to the knees. When pools and other bodies of water impregnated with it dry up, an incrustation is left, like ice, an inch thick, and large flakes or sheets of it can be lifted as ice from under which the water has been drained off.

"These ponds form a curiosity to the traveller, as he beholds their dazzling whiteness in the morning sun, sparkling like acres of diamonds. The substance is often used for baking purposes, but it has a bitter taste, and is a poor substitute in camp for saleratus. When the water impregnated by it is drunk by man or beast in any large quantity, it produces death, while very small quantities act directly on the kidneys, producing weakness and disability. In some portions of the route to California, it is very troublesome, and has produced great disasters, destroying the entire teams of a company, leaving the poor emigrants helpless and destitute on the desert.

" We were at this time passing over immense prairies, and no living being was visible, except the buffalo, the antelope, and the cayote, or prairie wolf. Water was scarce, and at wide distances apart, so that we were often without it at night, except as the men had carried it in their rubber bags and tin cans.

" As soon as a halt was called at night, the cooks of each mess would be seen running in every direction, with sacks and blankets, for buffalo chips, so called politely, for fuel. When dry the article is a good substitute for wood, and produces no unpleasant odor. It makes a mass of coal not unlike peat, and answers all the purposes of fuel.

" The *mirage*, as seen on these endless prairies, is wonderful, and often sublime. At one time the traveller sees before him, and directly in his course, a beautiful lake; but as he approaches, it recedes. Its placid waters, that invited and excited the thirsty wanderer, prove to be a false and fleeing shadow. Again, he will see a city, nigh or far off, with magnificent domes and spires, minarets and towers, lying up in the noonday sun. But as he gazes and approaches, it moves off,

like the aurora, till lost in the distance. The small em-
inences, at times, loom up like mountains, and shrubs
become groves inviting to their cool shades, that fade
out and move off, as one pursues them, under a burning sun.

"The dust we encountered was a great annoyance,
and was often so severe as to bring the train to a halt,
and compel an encampment. After travelling all day,
it happened that we did not recognize each other, or a
man his own team, having put on goggles and a veil,
and being covered with a deep coating of white dust.

"Another curiosity to us was the prairie dog, of
which trappers and travellers of those regions have
told so much. This animal is about as large as the
wharf rat, with head and ears like the woodchuck of
New England. He inhabits only the prairie, and that
the high ground, lives on grass and roots, and burrows
like the gopher, bringing the dirt to the surface. And
so, as they never live solitary, but in villages, one of
their haunts, covering acres, looks like a city of mounds.
The only visitors they admit to their subterranean
houses are the owl and the rattlesnake. Some have
supposed that the prairie dog has instinct, like the
beaver, that leads him to organize a settlement on a
plan and under regulations, and that the owl and snake
are there on invitation, or by consent, as guests and
friends. But I am satisfied, from long observation, that
this is a mistake. This animal has less shrewdness or
wisdom than the common farm rat, and possesses little
power of self-protection. Hence the owl comes in to feed
on their young, and the snake to find a place of comfort and safety. Their reputed bark, as of the dog, is

much a matter of the imagination. It is true that on the approach of danger they sit at the mouths of their holes, and make a chucking noise, but it most resembles that of the squirrel.

"Of the landscape curiosities in ascending the Platte valley there are but few. Chimney Rock and Court House Rock are perpendicular escarpments of sandstone, nearly seventy-five feet high, and they stand out as sentinels, to be seen at a great distance. They are also favorite places of resort in summer for the Dakota Sioux, as there were trading-posts at both these Rocks, and a good range for grazing, and opportunity for laying in the annual supply of fish.

"On the 17th of June we reached Fort Laramie, at the upper forks of the Platte. Here we rested for several days, visiting the fort and vicinity, and in recruiting. This is the country of the Dakota Sioux of the Upper Missouri. They are a fine, athletic specimen of the Indians who inhabit the extreme frontier, and were then reputed to be friendly to the whites. Here, on his own soil, he walks in dignity and self-respect, free from many of the vices of the white man. Bowing to no superior, he asserts his rights and defends them. Those whom I saw were dressed with much taste in the beautifully tanned leather of the antelope and mountain sheep. Their garments were gaudily embroidered with beads and the stained quills of the mountain porcupine. They had splendid horses, and were good riders, both men and women.

"The departure of the train from Laramie was full of perplexity and doubt. Various rumors were afloat of hostile Indians on the line. Then there were other and more certain difficulties to be encountered. The mountains were to be passed, the Great American Desert was to be crossed, the snowy heights of the Nevada climbed, before we could rest on the plains of the Sacramento. Piles of letters were despatched from this place to the loved ones at home; and it seemed like parting anew from all that was hallowed on earth, as the train moved out from its encampment on the banks of the north fork of the Platte, from this the last outpost on the American frontier."

Night and sleep come in a very easy, off-hand way in camp, and it is a pleasing study to watch by the blazes and see the men, one by one, do the last whittling, the last smoking or joking, and then drop off, half awake and half asleep, to the tent. We did it quite promptly this night, wishing to be up bright and early, and see The General lead off his company from Fort Laramie.

ELEVENTH NIGHT.

A NOVELTY to-day, and therefore welcome. We are here to shoot, and flesh and fowl have been the rage with us in the field and on the table. This morning the rumbling of prairie wagons and the loud talking of strange voices up the lake shore attracted our attention. The scattered farmers, far outside, had made up a company to lay in a winter's stock of fish, and they were on hand at early dawn with nets and seines, spears and hooks, and the conveniences for cleaning and salting sundry wagon loads of the finny folk of Swan Lake and waters adjacent.

All day long there has been with us a divided interest between the camps of St. Peter and of Nimrod. The guns and dogs were not idle, and yet some of us have been constantly watching the hauling of the seines. The amount of fish taken is wonderful, but the kinds are more so. Some of them are outlandish enough. · The teams carried off on the second day several wagons full, dressed and somewhat salted.

The varieties of the fishes in the western waters is not yet fully known, though in some localities the discoveries and classification have been quite thoroughly made. About seventy-five species have been tabled scientifically, as belonging to the waters of Ohio. Of these many are common throughout the West. The

fishes taken here for family use were the white perch,
rock bass, pike, black bass, buffalo, and catfish. The
perch is a fish of sometimes sixteen or twenty inches
in length, and, when taken from running water, a good
table fish. The rock and black bass are among the
best, specially the latter, a fish of two or three pounds
sometimes, and of a flavor much like the tautog or
black fish, such a favorite in the eastern markets.

The pike is substantially, if not identically, the pick-
erel of New England. The structure, color, habits, and
flavor are the same, allowing for some local influences
and the greater size of many of those taken. They
are not uncommon in the West of twenty or thirty
pounds' weight, and sometimes are taken much larger.

The General, in his early days in Iowa, took one with
a spear that weighed thirty-one pounds and a fraction.
I well remember the jaws, as they were sent East, and
the teeth were as long as the longest of a cat. As the
fellow was lying some distance off, he threw the spear,
and being thus made fast, like a harpoon, the pike carried it across the creek, where he was captured by an
associate. How large some may grow is unknown.

In the Notes on the Pike, in Walton's Angler, the
London papers of January 25, 1715, are cited as mentioning one taken near Newport that weighed one hundred and seventy pounds. This may well be, if another
statement in the same Notes, and quoted from Hake-
will's Apologie of the Power and Providence of God,
is to be taken. He says that a pike was caught in Swe-
den, in 1497, carrying a metal tag with a Greek inscription, to the purport that Frederick II. put this
fish into those waters in 1230, two hundred and sixty-

seven years before. Such age might well give great weight.

The pike is a savage, voracious, sharky fish, and your more gentle feelings are never tried in landing him, as when taking trout or salmon. St. Izaak calls him "a· solitary, melancholy, and a bold fish," and you are ready to treat him as you do the other bachelors or solitaries of nature, as the lion, eagle, hawk, and the like, that spurn social and neighborly life.

The buffalo is one of the sucker family, and the largest of the kind — a coarse fish, often three and four feet long, and would commonly be regarded as very poor eating.

The catfish is well known through the States by its family name. The cat of the Mississippi is among their best articles of fish in the market, if not too large. They often attain to the weight of a hundred pounds. A friend of mine once took from four night hooks, hung in the mouths of Rock River, four catfish, whose united weight was about three hundred pounds.

Among the worthless fish hauled to shore by these countrymen there were two that would attract a stranger — the gar and the spoonbill. The former is a long, lank, arrow-shaped creature, whose main feature is a piratical and rascally-looking head, one fourth his whole length. This is all jaw, and teeth, and eye, like an out-and-out politician living on spoils. In character it is the shark of the river, and grows large. In Sturgeon Bay and Swan Lake they were five feet long; and in the Lower Mississippi, taking the name of the alligator gar, as another species, they grow to the fearful size of eight and even twelve feet, and are said to be a match for the alligator. They would be a most uncomfortable bathing companion.

The most marked fish, however, is the spoonbill. The body is not unlike the cat or cod in general appearance, but it has a huge head, with coarse and stout jaws of equal length, and in the Swan Lake variety, toothless. But on the upper jaw is an elongation of cartilage, equal almost to bone in firmness, which is one third of the entire length of the fish. This runs tapering till near the end, where it expands like the bowl of a spoon. This snout is used for rooting or digging on the muddy bottom for food, much after the manner of the hog; and as this fish sometimes gains the weight of a hundred pounds, one can conceive what a monstrous sight it must be with such a head and nose.

Of course we had fish for supper, baked, boiled, and fried, dishes good enough for the old Romans, who expended so many tens of thousands of dollars on their fish ponds; and then, better still, came The General.

But as "finally" sometimes comes midway in a sermon, so now, though through my Prelude to the Eleventh Night, certain extended "concluding remarks" remain to be made on this matter of fish and fishing.

It is angling, and among game fish, to which I refer, and can best commend it, generally, in the words of Sir Henry Wotton, the intimate of St. Izaak. He says that it was to him, "after tedious study, a rest to the mind, a cheerer of his spirits, a calmer of unquiet thoughts, a moderator of passions, a procurer of contentedness; and begat habits of peace and patience."

The Scriptures recognize this art, and in a very honorable way. Job, the most patient man, speaks of drawing out leviathan with a hook, which, were he to do it, would make him "high line" among all fishermen. The prophet Amos talks of fish-hooks in a clerical way; and in the catalogue of the apostles, four are fishermen, and stand first on the roll. The meditative quietness of the exercise favors a serious turn of mind, though I think the Hon. Robert Boyle, in his tract entitled "Angling Improved to Spiritual Uses," has but poorly presented a good theme.

It is to be noted that some of the worthiest and noblest of men have been men of the angle. Not only did Antony and Cleopatra enjoy it, as Plutarch informs us, but excellent divines. Most worthy Dr. Nowel, Dean of St. Paul's, London, in the reign of Elizabeth, who wrote a Latin Catechism, long bound up and used with the service-book of the English Church, and that was also published in English and in Greek, was accustomed to spend a tenth of his time in angling. He gave all his fish and a tenth of his income to the poor, and "at his return to his house would praise God he had spent that day free from worldly trouble, both harmlessly and in a recreation that became a churchman." A picture of him, long seen, and I hope yet, in Brazen Nose College, Oxford, he left to tell posterity who was the Dean of St. Paul's for forty-four years. He stands in it clerical, with the Bible before him; the top of the picture is surmounted with a fishing-rod and several fishes, and the fish-lines intertwine the sides and loop around the inscription underneath — "PISCATOR HOMINUM" — a worthy ornament for college halls, and suggestive in these days, when we are straining wits and consciences to devise Christian amusements.

Sir Walter Scott, though puny and lame, and at the University at Edinburgh called the Great Blockhead, could strike a salmon equal to the best fishers on the Tweed. His feeble and unpromising boyhood developed into vigor with field sports. At that early day the Harp of the North and the pen of Waverley hung delicately and doubtfully hooked on his fly-rod. Fortunately for the world, he was able to reel them in.

The world knows how Daniel Webster handled the Constitution of the United States, Hayne, and Nullification, and international questions. Born fortunately among trout brooks, he handled huge trout in the same ardent, easy way. Webster was a prince among fishermen, as elsewhere. He loved deep-sea fishing, and made long casts, in more senses than one. While steadying the ship of state, he often rocked in a yawl on the Potomac. Says one who frequently took him out on these excursions, —

"When Secretary of State he used to come here, always early in the morning, and accompanied by his private secretary. He liked the fresh morning air as much as any man I ever saw, and when he talked to me freely about fish and fishing, I could believe that he had been in the business all his days. I remember well the day that he caught his biggest rockfish. I had taken him in one of my boats to the 'Catting Rock,' and as we swung across the roaring waters, the great man clapped his hands like a child. The fish weighed sixteen pounds, and gave him much trouble; and when I gaffed the prize, and we knew it was safe, he dropped his rod in the bottom of the boat, jumped to his feet, and gave a yell, a regular Indian yell, which might have been heard in Georgetown." His voice was wont to be heard afar at other times, when heavy prizes were made safe for the country.

Walton, in his Complete Angler, expresses quite clearly my own views on this interesting subject: —

"No life, my honest scholar, no life so happy and so pleasant, as the life of a well-governed Angler. For when the lawyer is swallowed up with business, and the statesman is preventing or contriving plots, there we sit on cowslip banks, hear the birds sing, and possess our souls in as much quietness as these silver streams, which we now see glide so quietly by us. Indeed, my good scholar, we may say of Angling as Dr. Boteler said of strawberries, 'Doubtless God could have made a better berry, but doubtless God never did.' And so, if I might be judge, God never did make a more calm, quiet, innocent recreation than Angling." "Let me tell you, there be many that have forty times our estates, that would give the greatest part of it, to be healthful and cheerful like us, who, with the expense of a little money, have eat and drank, and laughed and angled, and sung and slept securely; and rose next day, and cast away care, and sung and laughed and angled again; which are blessings rich men cannot purchase with all their money."

That was a happy conceit — so Fuller understands it — of Dr. John Colet, when he founded St. Paul's School, London, in 1512. He made the free scholarships there "a hundred and fifty and three," the number of St.

Peter's "great fishes" when he "cast the net on the right side." Good fishermen are wont to make good endowments, as well as to remember and record the exact number of "great fishes." I am not advised on the point, but think the doctor must have been fond of the angle. If so, the world of letters may thank this successor of St. Peter for Milton, and Halley, the great astronomer, for they were educated in this school of fishes, and went on swimmingly over that hard bottom into the deeper waters of Cambridge and Oxford.

It should be added that these manly sports on land and water have much to do with the stalwart energy and free spirit of a people. The man who ranges the wilds of nature, and exercises "dominion over the fish of the sea, and over the fowl of the air, and over every living thing that moveth upon the earth," according to the divine commission, is not the man to part readily with his freedom of thought and of conscience and of person. It was New England fishermen largely who manned victoriously our navy in three wars. Lord Wilton well says, in his book on natural sports, that no nation devoted to manly sports can fail to flourish, or enjoy political freedom.

This familiarity with land and water in their natural and unsubdued state, as they are seen in the higher grades of sporting, has much to do in promoting a manly independence. So there was deep truth, as well as the deeper humor, in Webster's social, depot kind of speech at Rochester, after they had shown him Niagara Falls: "Men of Rochester, go on. No people ever lost their liberties who had a waterfall one hundred and fifty feet high."

I hope these supplementary remarks to my Eleventh
Prelude will prove conclusive as to the virtues of the
goodly art of angling. It only remains to say that,
steadily and temperately indulged, it promotes length
of days. Its quiet contrasts strangely with the fric-
tion and chafing of other sports and indulgences that
so soon wear one's life out. Walton died at the
advanced age of ninety, "in the great forest at Win-
chester." Jenkins, who lived till he was a hundred
and sixty-nine years old, was a Yorkshire fisherman;
and the parish record of Llanmaes, Glamorgan county,
Wales, has the following original entry: "Ivan Yorath,
buried a Saturdaye the xiiii day of july, 1621, aged
about 180. He was a sowdier in the fighte of Bos-
worthe, and lived at Lantwitt Major, and hee lived
much by fishing."

But The General is anxious to leave Fort Laramie.

There at Last.

"There are always hanging about these outposts of the frontier, Indians, trappers, and half-breeds of both the French and Spanish mixture, who are ready to serve as guides for the travellers over the mountains and plains. We had so far had an old mountain ranger, who joined us at Council Bluffs; but he knew little of the regions beyond Laramie. We felt, therefore, the need of another guide, specially as several routes were talked of, and no one of them was very well known. As we had concluded to go by the South Pass, and Humboldt and Carson Rivers, we wished an experienced guide, who would take us over that route.

"After due consultation Gaspero was taken for our new guide and interpreter. He was one of those inevitable loungers I just now mentioned. This class of people are very fond of adventure and excitement, and love to tell of their hair-breadth escapes among Indians and wild animals. Gaspero was about forty years old, had been in the mountains eighteen years, and was familiar not only with the passes through the wild country and plains, but was well versed in Indian tricks and the habits of the wild game which he had so long hunted. His tangled locks and matted beard, innocent of a razor for years, presented the appearance of anything but a pleasant companion, while his keen, piercing black eye indicated hate, revenge, and deadly strife, if need be. He rode a small Spanish mule, a tough, hard-looking animal, of mottled colors, called by the trappers the Cricket mule. Quarters were assigned to him in my tent, as the place most convenient for consultation. He spoke broken English very well when calm; but when excited, Spanish, Indian, and English all came at once, a perfect jargon, that himself could hardly interpret. He was very fond of telling his hard stories by the camp fire, and spent many long evenings in this way, to the vast entertainment of the crowd. But he knew the country well from Laramie to the Nevadas.

"With such a guide we left Fort Laramie. Following up the North Platte through the Black Hills for a hundred and twenty-five miles, we left on our south a river that we had learned to admire and love while we kept it company for more than six hundred miles. It was like parting from an old friend. We had camped on its banks, drank its pure waters for weeks, and now turned our backs on it. Soon, however, we made the acquaintance of the Sweet Water, a river flowing from mountains of the same name, but not till we had known the discomforts and perils of being without water. Here we encamped for recruiting, and the hunters feasted us on the antelope, the mountain sheep, and the black-tailed deer.

"One evening, as a large company of us were gathered around my tent fire, Gaspero, who had been moody and sullen for some days, began one of his mountain yarns. 'Here,' said he, 'is the very place we were in twelve years ago. We were in camp yonder on the other side of the grove, under the cliff, and we had a desperate fight with a band of Blackfeet.' Then

14

knocking the ashes from his pipe — a signal for a story — he began. 'There were about twenty of the rascals, and only six of us. We had been up to the canon yonder after a wounded grizzly that the boys had shot the day before. We had killed and dressed the old gentleman, and after cutting off as much as we could pack in, we hung up the balance. Feeling a little hungry, we roasted some before our fire, and, after eating, started for camp with the rest lashed to our backs. It was near sundown and the distance ten miles. Now to you, boys, it don't look half as far; but I tell you, if any of you get lost about here, you'll know the full length of the roads. You see the air is so pure in this mountain range, a fellow don't know distances by looking. Why, you can see an antelope five miles, and tell him from a deer; and when the sun shines right you can see even the white stripes along his sides. A buffalo shows his hump that distance just as plain as a Blackfoot does his teeth when a bullet disturbs his in'ards. You need not follow antelope in this region; you will never come up with them.

"'Well, as I was saying, we had strapped on our meat, and gone about a mile down the timber, when, crossing a little run, one of the boys saw a moccason track in the mud. It was fresh, and the little bits of sand and mud left on the grass were not dry; and we knew by the shape of the foot and point of the toes that it was a Blackfoot. We had seen no Indians since our encampment. We were just leaving a gorge in the mountains, and following a skirt of timber along the open prairie, when we came on the track again. We then came to a halt, examined our rifles, and took each to a tree, while old Pamaska, a Dakota chief, who was with us, examined the trail and pronounced it Blackfoot, and not far off. The Blackfeet were Pamaska's mortal enemies. He had often fell in with them in the mountain, and many were the conflicts the old fellow had had with the rascals. Now his savage nature was aroused by the prospect of a fight and a scalp. He was a brave, and showed no fear. Ordering us "to tree," he followed the trail, with true Indian instinct and caution, into a gorge among the cliffs. There he found traces of their recent encampment, and from appearances he judged their band to contain about twenty persons. The ashes of their fire was still warm, and we presumed they were then acting as spies on our movements.

"'Our trail lay along the timber another mile, when it emerged into open prairie that we must cross before reaching camp. It had now become quite dark, and a consultation was held as to our future operations. Our Dakota taking the lead, we followed cautiously in single file, with rifles all ready, and packs so that we could slip them on the instant. As we arrived at the point where the trail left the timber, and were bending our course into the prairie, an arrow whizzed past the ear of old Pamaska; but no Indian could be seen or heard. In an instant we dropped our packs, and fell flat on the ground, awaiting the attack. Not a leaf stirred nor twig cracked. No motion of the enemy told their place or number. Both parties lay low, awaiting an onslaught. The Blackfeet wanted us to attack and be drawn into the timber, while we were determined to draw them into the prairie, as no Indian can fight

well in the open.   If the dog cannot tree, he will
run.

"'Well, the moon had just begun to light up the
mountains, and we could distinguish objects at a little
distance. Gathering our packs, we crawled off a distance from the timbers. It was too dark for the red-
skins to use their arrows, and we could get no clear sight
of them among the trees and underbrush. In case of
attack, therefore, you see, it must be at close quarters,
with tomahawk and knife. We lay for an hour or
more in the grass, awaiting events, and then cautiously
started on our way for camp without a trail. About
two miles ahead we had a deep ravine to cross, through
which, in the wet season, a creek run ; but now it was
dry. The Indians, when they found we had with-
drawn to the prairie, run down the timber to this
ravine, to cut off our approach to camp. We drew
near to this crossing with great care, fearing an ambush.
We had nearly reached the bed of the creek when the
whole band of Blackfeet sprung on us with a fearful
yell, tomahawk in hand.

"'Pamaska discharged his rifle first, and we next, in
quick succession, but mostly at random, as we could
only hear the Indians climbing up the banks of the
creek. Our packs were again dropped, and our rifles
clubbed; and as the Indians came up the bank, we
tumbled them back again with heavy blows, killing
some and wounding others. Enraged at defeat, they
fought like demons in a renewed attack, and at this
time drove us from the ravine into the prairie. Here
they well nigh surrounded us, and our fate seemed inevitable, when Pamaska singled out their leader, and

closed with him in a deadly struggle. This renewed the conflict on our part with desperation, and knife to knife. Their number grew less. The long rifle was evidently too much in its wide sweep for their short-handled tomahawk, and so many of them fell wounded and dead that victory seemed certain for us.

" 'The fight had lasted about half an hour, when a yell of anguish came up from the ravine. We rushed down the bank, and found the two chiefs locked in mortal combat, the Blackfoot underneath. Old Pamaska had his knee planted on the breast of the chief; with his left hand in the scalp lock, he fastened his head to the ground, and in his right glittered the fatal knife. The other Indians hastened up, but we kept them at bay till their leader had his last grief from Pamaska's knife.

" 'This ended the struggle. The Indians who survived made good their escape, carrying off what they could of their dead and wounded; but Pamaska secured the scalp of the chief, and one or two more. Two of our number were wounded severely, one by a toma-hawk cut on the shoulder, and the other by a bad gash on the arm; but both recovered in a few weeks. I broke the stock of my rifle, which caused me much trouble till I came round to the fort. But we carried home our bear's meat, though we came near losing our topknots.'

" 'Silence was broken as our hero interpreter closed his narrative, and the men scattered to their tents for the night.'

" Our course now lay up the Sweet Water, a beautiful mountain stream, flowing forever in solitude, and

singing its own music to the shadows of the Rocky
Mountains. The valley of this river is very beautiful
and fertile, and furnishes pasturage to vast herds of
buffalo that gather here in the summer months. The
current is swift, and generally fordable, and we followed it far up, till we came to gorges where it leaps
from the mountain in a number of little silvery
cascades.

"At the base of the mountains, just where one begins
to climb, is that great landmark of travellers, Independence Rock, a giant bowlder, probably the largest on
the American continent. This rock is nearly two hundred feet high, with an area of nearly two thousand
square yards. It is wholly separate from any mountain
range, and stands isolated, evidently brought there in
the glacier period, in one of those immense ice-floes of
higher latitudes. It has a smooth surface, with all the
appearance of having been ground and grooved in the
glacier process. Here caravans rest and recruit, and
the southern front is covered with names to the height
of ten feet and more, put on with paint, tar, and the
like.

"A party was made up among us to dine on the top
of it. We made the ascent by Indian ladders, and the
aid of little projections, till we reached a graded
crevice, and by it the summit. It was a dangerous
undertaking, but we achieved it without accident, and
the splendid view from the top well repaid us. Choice
stores were taken up, such as canned oysters, sardines,
buffalo and antelope steaks, together with fuel and the
inevitable coffee-pot. Here half a dozen of us dined
sumptuously on a granite table eight thousand feet

above the level of the sea, drank toasts with the pure water of the mountain, made speeches, and remembered the dear ones at home. Long will the memories linger of that gathering on an isolated rock in the valley of the Sweet Water.

" Five miles from this, on our line to the South Pass, this river goes through what is called the Devil's Gate. The cut is through limestone, two hundred feet deep and one hundred broad, and about one thousand long, The walls are perpendicular and smooth, having the finish apparently of mason work. The whole body of the Sweet Water rushes through this natural canal in the rocks, bounding and foaming, and throwing up spray like the Falls of St. Anthony, or Minnehaha. The ascent is quite difficult and dangerous, owing to huge seams and chasms; but we accomplished it, and viewed from the giddy top the wild scene.

We were now fast approaching the summit level of the mountains, and the scenery in many places was most enchanting. As we pressed on up the great dividing ridge between the two oceans, the noble streams that we had been following so long dwindled into little rivulets. Sometimes we were compelled to work our way through narrow and winding defiles, and as often came out into beautiful and luxuriant valleys.

The train had now come within fifty miles of the highest elevation, and was following the winding trail among the escarpments of sandstone, looking for a place of encampment, when we opened on one of those most beautiful and enchanting valleys, blushing and fragrant with flowers. It showed no human habitation

or trace of man, but was as silent and highly adorned
as the abode of pure spirits. The guide dismounted,
and all, as by instinct, began to pitch their tents and
light their fires. The animals were spancelled and
turned loose, the guard set, wood and water provided,
the daily inspection of man, beast, and wagon gone
through, and the several messes took their evening
meal, and retired for the night.

"The morning came with a brightness and glory
peculiar to the climate. It was the morning of the
holy Sabbath, a day that we had uniformly observed,
from the first, for rest and for sacred purposes, so far as
the men were inclined. While the camp was yet
sleeping, I arose and strolled off. The stillness of the
scene was very impressive, as the sun began to light
up the horizon, and touch with mellow light the rugged
hill-tops that shut in our valley. Not a sound disturbed
the quiet of the place, not even the note of a bird. The
region seemed hallowed, and thoughts of God and of
his greatness and glory went up like incense in silence
from a Jewish altar. My feelings led my steps, and
following the little trail of the mountain sheep, I at
length gained the very top of the encircling heights,
and had a full survey of the sublime and majestic
scene.

"The snowy peaks could barely be recognized in the
distance, the plains we had passed were almost lost to
view, and the South Pass, as a narrow chop in the
mountian range, just showed its outline on the open
sky beyond. Here, if anywhere, the diviner part of
man will lift him up, and purified and humbled by the
surroundings and the influence of the holy day, his

thoughts will go up reverently and devoutly to the Creator. At least, such was the effect on me as I returned to camp.

"And here another scene, in perfect keeping with the day and place, awaited me. A young man by the name of Jones, from one of the interior counties of Iowa, had joined our company after its organization, with the hope that the expedition would benefit his feeble health. He had been in a decline so long that he was incurable. His brother was with him, and the two had a good outfit, and were not dependent on the company for anything but protection and sympathy. The invalid won the good will and tender regard of all, specially as he had left behind a wife and child and an indulgent, loving mother.

"His days were numbered and hastening, and he seemed fully aware of it, yet had no fears of the great change. He often rode reclining, and in such a way that he could view the beauties of the country as we passed through. As we entered this valley the evening before, he caught a glance of its loveliness, and with a sad yet sweet smile he expressed the wish, that if he must die in the mountains, and no more see the loved ones at home, he might find his final rest in that valley, trusting in God that in the morning of the resurrection he should not be forgotten. His wish was gratified, and he died that morning, while I was rambling on the mountains.

"Just as the last sunbeams were burnishing the tops of the surrounding hills, we moved, in solemn procession, to a knoll at the head of the valley, and there, beneath the spreading boughs of a pine tree, we laid the young husband and father in his rest. It was a mournful and instructive scene, as the twilight fell on us around his grave. All was still save the sobs of a fond brother, when I broke the silence by reading the burial service of a Christian funeral, only adding, 'The separation will be short. The reunion with the loved ones will soon come. Here it is earth to earth, ashes to ashes, dust to dust; but there it will be heart to heart, and face to face.'

"The next day we moved on, one less, towards the unchangeable landmark, the South Pass. At the distance of fifty miles or more, it has the appearance of a small gap, just wide enough for a team to pass through. But as one draws near, it widens into a beautiful prairie, quite level and covered with grass. Nearer and nearer we came, till the last brook running towards the Atlantic had disappeared, and we were on an elevated plateau, where the waters were in a quandary which way to run. This space, where Fremont made his summit level, is not more than a fourth of a mile in extent; and as the traveller passes along to its western border, he finds the first little rivulet that runs towards the Pacific. Here an encampment was ordered, and we entered fully into the enjoyment of the scene and of our circumstances, giving up the day to our eyes.

"Knowing that we could have but this day on this ridge or water-shed of the continent, I set myself at once to the fullest indulgence of the opportunity. It was an occasion to which I had long looked forward; indeed, it was one of the ends of very many of my most ardent wishes and hopes from childhood. My intimate companion, S., and myself strolled off immediately, and were soon on the highest point of rocks that over-looked the vast panorama. The great basin of the Rocky Mountains, five hundred miles in extent, was before us, destitute of wood, water, herbage, or tree, or any object to obstruct the sight. On one side of us, far up the north, were the snow-capped peaks, though now midsummer, in full view.

"From my earliest youth, as I well remember, my feelings thrilled me when I read or heard of the mysteries locked up in this region. Its outlines on my little school atlas, with the inscription, Unknown Interior, created an intense desire to know about it by personal examination. This desire grew and strengthened with my years, till it became a passion with me; and I had been for a long time approaching this spot, as the sailor in beating and tacking against a head wind. First it was Central New York, then Virginia; then I stood again on the same tack to the Mississippi; then Wisconsin Territory; then the Kansas borders, where I laid my course for these headlands, midway between the two oceans. And now the vision of my youth was a reality, the hopes and wishes of my childhood had become fact.

"I also remember my feelings, when, as a lad, I read of the covered mysteries of this wild region. How I longed to go over the plains, now behind me and before me, to hunt the buffalo on them, and to climb, till the rivers became gurgling brooks and springs on these heights! Long years I labored for it, and now I was repaid.

"To the north lay the everlasting snows, and above us the rocky peaks towering into the clouds. There the intrepid Fremont threw our Stars and Stripes to the breeze. Westward is the Great American Basin, or bowl, of five hundred miles diameter. Far to our left, and southerly, like a half-coiled serpent, lies Bear River, in dim line, emptying far away into Salt Lake, but finding no outlet from it, except by evaporation. We note in the far distance rolling piles of smoke and steam, reminding one of Atlantic cities. They arise from burning coal mines and hot springs, whose fires, Indian tradition says, have been smouldering from the day of creation.

" We are on the land-crest between the oceans. Here, on the narrow belt where we are standing, the waters divide for the Atlantic and Pacific. I said to my friend S., 'Let us change the destiny of two cupfuls.' So we walked to the nearest rivulet, that had begun its tiny course for the Pacific, and dipping from its crystal waters, we carried a hunter's cup of them across the dividing ridge, and poured them into a babbling brook, that had just started for the Atlantic.

"Then we followed, in thought and conversation, the water that would have been but a swallow for the buffalo, down into the Sweet Water, then six hundred and fifty miles on our back track in the Platte, then eight hundred down the muddy Missouri, and thirteen hundred more down the Mississippi, whose tributaries drain a valley in which scores of the kingdoms of Europe and the old world could be hidden away. We left the solitary cupful to its changed destiny, and long, silent wanderings, to Atlantic tide waters, and then balanced the exchange by carrying a similar portion from the

Atlantic slope of our high plateau, and starting it in the head springs of the Columbia for the Pacific.

"We wandered among the ridges and peaks till we clambered the highest in the immediate region, and, there seating ourselves, we had a full feast of the eyes. My friend had been in foreign lands, seen the old cities of Europe, bathed in the Sea of Galilee, and threaded the narrow streets of Jerusalem; but never before had he seen antiquities, vastness, and glories like what now surrounded us.

"It must be delightful to follow where patriarchs pitched their tents, to ride over the hills of Judea, to enter the Holy City over the way where the triumphal procession followed our Saviour with palms and hosannas. But it must be mortifying to say to the wandering Jew, or any other foreigner in those stinted ancient lands, that you have not seen Niagara Falls or Minnehaha, the mouths of the Missouri or a prairie. To 'travel,' as some affect and delight to say, when they have seen nothing of the vastness and richness, the glorious rivers and lakes, mountains and forests, and prairies of their own country, is not my passion. My own, my native land first for travel, as it is in rank, and other countries afterwards."

The General thought the summit of the Rocky Mountains the best place to end an evening story, and so stopped suddenly, to the surprise and regret of all. We felt this the more as but one night now remained for us in camp, and we could not see how he could take us the rest of the way to the Pacific in one evening. But we were obliged to content ourselves with what

we had of the story of his eventful life, and leave him
to hurry us down the western slope of that ridge of
the continent in his own time and way.   A half hour
was given to questioning him about the mountains;
our fur trade companions talked with him of scenes and
trails there known to both parties; and the changes in
that wild region since the summer of 1850 were noted.
By and by the conversation fell to the lot of two or
three who knew the route; the others dropped off one
by one, and at length all retired to their tents, and the
sentinel owls went on picket for the rest of our Eleventh Night.

TWELFTH NIGHT.

THE last day in camp! That has an unwelcome
sound to the sportsman's ear. It suggests the last
beat down the creek, around the cove, up the lagoon;
the last evening stand for geese and swan; the last calls
on the duck family, from the comic and juicy little teal
to the portly alderman mallard with his aristocratic
green head. The frosty morning wash at log, stump,
and camp stove, around the crackling fire, is more cosy
and chatty than usual; the jokes are more practical,
and the laughs louder. You see, reader, our lungs are
better than when we entered the forest, and there is no
danger of "disturbing neighbors" by throwing our
feelings quite energetically into our voices. The washing does not give our faces the pale, clean look we had
when we left our counter, desk, or study, though Swan
Lake water is of the very best for ablutions, if used on its
shores. What a breakfast one eats the last morning in
camp! Our appetites have gone on increasing in a
cumulative ratio now for fourteen days, and Dock has
kept his table temptingly in advance of us in variety
and abundance. I never realized before into how many
eatable conditions a cook could put a webfoot or small
quadruped.

The change in one's physique by camping out is a
marvel. The first day the nervous man, the dyspeptic,

the feeble clerk, who has not strength enough to work his molars on a cracker, fingers the food very delicately, and for Dock, very provokingly. The second day fair rations are drawn and disposed of legitimately. The third day these same men take up eating as a business, and as the days go by it increases on their hands. Mark another fact keeping pace with this, and helping to explain it. The first day they hung about camp, and whittled, and read, and grew very tired. It was a kind of sidewalk life. The second day they strolled out of sight, with gun or fishing-rod, and lost their way, and found an appetite. Before the week was gone they cared not whether they lost themselves or not, but to have lost one meal they would have regarded as a calamity.

The air in that wild region is an independent fortune to the man feebly creeping out there from the city. At home, in his office, shop, counting-room, study, or bay-window even, he does not get one cubic inch of atmosphere that has not been meddled with by somebody. If he is not enjoying a stiff north-easter, his city air has a touch of Erin, or Holland, or both in it. He can tell which way the wind is by the odors of the different back alleys that he knows so well.

But throw back the fly of your tent in the early morning, step out, and fill your lungs, and you feel that there is more nourishment in such air than in boarding-house soup. No mortal ever snuffed that air before. It is not second-hand. You have it pure from the manufactory. You have been breathing it all night, charged with the exquisite aroma of your hemlock or prairie-grass bed.

A jaded, worried man, you felt poorly; entered Nature's hospital on Swan Lake, under the superintendence of Dr. Nimrod; took fish-hooks every other day, alternating with number six shot; shouldered Edward Winslow's Puritan "fowling peece, fearing not the waight of it;" and now, just breaking camp for home, you are a new man, after the short treatment of fourteen days. The marvel has been wrought by a combination of causes, centring in "a lodge in some vast wilderness."

What we shall do for relief and recuperation I know not, when every Umbagog has a steamer on it, and every White Mountain has a railroad to its top, and every charming nook of wilderness has a first-class hotel and dress dinners. For the joys and profits of the camp lie in its difficulties, physical exertions, denials, and glorious distances from anybody. I am, I think, profoundly grateful for the architecture of our domain, in that it has some mountains, and morasses, and river gorges, that railroads, and Saratoga trunks, and bills of fare, can never annoy.

Yes, on this last hunting morning in Swan Lake camp, we are a brown, hungry, healthy-looking group of fellows. Our muscle is not flabby; there is nothing weak about our lungs, and no "melancholy crack" in our laugh.

Now for a careful hunt for the rarest bits and the best of game, for other hands must grace other tables with the spoils of to-day. We are making up parcels to go home with us. The seven dogs and the seven boats must do their best. All the ground is thoroughly known, each cover and range of flight, and minimum

15

bay, and jam of drift wood, wild rice patch, and scanty
puddle far out in the tall bottom prairie grass.

Early evening brings us all in, and no one ashamed.
The record, or journal rather, of the encampment reads
well. Evidently some of the best of the queen's wild
fowl had come over the border for our special benefit
and honor at home. The saplings, that have now seen
service, bend under the trophies. We are not timid
about seeing a steamer, or a city where we are well
known. Our credentials are ample and of the best
authority. They are from the first families of the first
settlers of the country.

But we are to make an important movement to-
night. Last night The General gave us all free lodging
on the summit of the Rocky Mountains. To-night we
hope to sleep in San Francisco. So, supper being over,
we hurry to our blazing camp fire to take an early start,
and all together for the Pacific.

The General is not hard to start off on a story of
personal adventures, and he got under way as soon as
Dock had started a roaring camp fire, and hushed up
with a supply of bones three or four growling dogs.

THE PACIFIC OCEAN.

" I believe I left you all sleeping, in my life-narrative, last night, in the upper story, the very attic of North America. I hope you had pure air and a good view of sunrise. I also hope that you are well refreshed by your mountain sleep, for it is a long trail I shall lead you before you make camp to-night. I mean you shall hear the breakers of the Pacific before you strike our next camp fire. Fortunately our course is now down, rather than up, the continental slope, and we shall make easy speed.

" Our company bade adieu to the delightful spot and panorama, of which I told you last eve, and at early morn we commenced our descent of the mountains. Three miles from the summit we made a brief halt at Pacific Springs, noted for their pure water and rich grass. Here we took a lingering and last look. In our rear, and a little to the left, was Pike's Peak, with its white cap of winter still on. A little farther along was Spanish Peak, and to the north Fremont's and other noted landmarks. Forty miles away on the right were the Wind River Mountains, full of wild and glorious nooks of scenery.

" But we took our farewell, and passed on over the Dry Sandy, then the Little Sandy, and then the Big Sandy Rivers, from the last of which we found neither water nor grass for twenty miles. After a weary plodding of sixty-five miles we came to Green River, one of the most beautiful streams, with the most charming valley of all the mountains. And I know not which enjoyed it most, we or our animals. Here we found encamped some Snake Indians and half-breed Spaniards, from whom we obtained a supply of jerked buffalo meat. Since we left the South Pass we had been in the Snake Indian territory. They are a fine specimen of the mountain tribes, being well built, and well dressed, and athletic, as well as friendly.

" The river here was a hundred yards wide, and generally fordable. Like many other mountain streams, its mouth was not then known. Strange stories were told by the Indians, and traders, too, of the wonderful appearance of some of its valleys. They say that one of them is in a state of petrifaction, the trees in full leaf, flowers in bloom, birds on the limbs in natural colors, and deer feeding on the green and glassy fields, and all done into stone, as if the vast work of an artist. They called it the land of the Great Spirit, said their fathers had visited it, and offered to take me to see it, if I would go.

" We bore away westward, leaving the Bear River Mountains and Salt Lake more than a hundred miles to the south, passing hot and cold springs, as well as copperas and soda, and over a country intolerably rocky, reaching the head-waters of the Humboldt on the 6th of June.

" Here, for the first time, our animals showed serious signs of weakness and breaking down. They had had a good supply of grass, and been carefully driven, but had drank water affected more or less by alkali, while the juices of the grass probably carried the same poison. The high waters of the Humboldt drove us to the moun-

tains, and into difficult passes. We were now in the
Ute Indian country, and entering that of the Root
Diggers. Our progress was slow and wearying, and we
left our evening camp fire for our tents and blankets at
an early hour, usually, and some of the men began to
feel that California gold would cost them a hundred
cents to the dollar. The heavy snows of 1849–50 had
swelled all the streams, and so we were often detained
in crossing. Frequently the horses were detached from
the wagons to swim over, while the goods were ferried
over in such wagon-bodies as were water-tight, while
the running gear and other carriages were hauled over
by ropes. This had more work than romance in it, and
it is much prettier to read of it in a book than to do it
in the Rocky Mountains. Fuel was scarce, the only
growth of this barren region being the wild sage, a
dwarf bush three feet high.

" We started Gaspero's memory of a promise of that
other story about a 'fight with the Utes;' but the toils
of the journey had made him, like the rest of us, quite
willing to take all the sleep that our camping would
allow. For now our animals were so reduced that we
were all obliged to walk, relieving them of every article
of luggage that could possibly be thrown away or
packed by ourselves.

" We were now among the Root Digger Indians, the
most extensive tribe on the western slope, and extend-
ing from the head of the Humboldt to California and
Oregon. They are, emphatically, the wild Indian of
the mountains, and the most ignorant, degraded, and
filthy of all the tribes of North America. With a low,
flat forehead, they have no intellect, little clothing, and

no wigwams, living, like wild animals, in caves and
burrows. They have no horses or mules, and seem to
know of no use for a domestic animal except for food.
They have no fire-arms, but use the bow with great
skill. Of course I am speaking of them as they then
were, thirteen years ago. They live on roots, seeds,
acorns, lizards, snakes, frogs, and grasshoppers. They
may be seen in the early morning, on the sunny slopes,
gathering the seeds, wild oats, and grasshoppers into a
huge conical basket suspended from the forehead and
hanging on the back. It will hold a bushel or more,
and comes to a point at the bottom. The squaw takes
the cover of the basket in one hand, and while the
grasshopper climbs to the top of the grass or wild oats
to get the rays of the warm sun, she scoops or mows
it off, with the motion of one cradling grain, at each
swoop emptying the contents of the lid into the
basket at her back. When the grasshoppers become
warm enough to fly, she puts on the cover of the
basket and returns to the wigwam. Here a fire is
kindled in the pot made in the sand and lined with
fire clay. When this is hot the fire is taken out, and
the grasshoppers put in and baked. The seeds, oats,
and acorns are dried and parched in the same way;
and then they, with the insects, are pulverized together and baked into bread.

"Fish is a great article of food with them, and they
are very expert in spearing the salmon. They often
follow the emigrant trains down the Humboldt for days,
picking up cast-off clothing, scraps of iron, buffalo
robes, now burdensome in that latitude, and also for
the purpose of shooting any stray ox or horse, that
they may have it for food.

"One night, while we were encamped in a little valley, surrounded by hills and sand plains, the scarcity of feed had compelled us to turn the animals loose, and give them a wide range, though still keeping guard on them. The midnight watchman, when he came in, failed to rrouse fully his successor before he turned in, and so the animals were without guard for perhaps half an hour. The Diggers, who had been lying in watch and wait for any such chance, suddenly encircled five of them, and started them off for the mountains. We roused the camp, but no trace or trail could be found till morning. We then followed them eleven miles into the mountains, where, among the gorges, we discovered two of the animals skinned and ready for cutting up and drying, and a third dead. They had all been shot with arrows. The last one killed showed that the arrow had made a clean passage through the heart, and entered a sand bank beyond, where we found it still sticking. But no Indians could be found. The other two horses came into camp afterwards with arrows hanging in their flesh, which we drew out, healing the wounds.

"At the Sink of the St. Mary we made a long halt, to recruit and prepare grass for the passage of the Desert. This Sink is where the Humboldt spreads out and loses itself in the sands of the barrens. Whether it reappears after a subterranean passage, or there ends in absorption and evaporation, we could not learn.

"Great need we had for rest at this place, for we were much exhausted, both men and animals, and the great Sahara of North America was before us. We found it necessary not only to rest and recruit, but also to reconstruct our entire train. We had become reduced to a few teams. Some had found it difficult to travel as fast as others, and so had fallen behind into other parties. Some had lost a part of their horses, and were compelled to linger and unite with others following us, who were in a similar condition. We were all reduced to foot travel and short rations. The Desert before us was eighty-five miles wide, without wood, water, or grass, with the thermometer at one hundred, often, in the shade. Of course hay must be made and packed to take the animals over. To do this we waded in the overflow, cut the grass under water with our belt knives, backed it to shore, and dried it on the burning sand. The water cans and kegs were filled, enough for man and beast, and all surplus baggage, and every article of weight or bulk that could possibly be spared, were thrown aside, to make our perilous trip as expeditious as possible.

"We struck out on the barren waste at four in the afternoon, and did not stop, except for feeding and rest of an hour or two at a time, till we reached the Salmon Trout River. But it was too much for many of the already exhausted animals. Some died on the way, and others after we were across.

"Now our real troubles began. Up to the time of crossing the Desert provisions had been plenty, and no particular disasters had occurred to hinder our progress. But now our animals were worn out, through want of feed and by use of the alkali waters. Having lost two of my own beasts, I abandoned my wagon at Salmon Trout River, threw away nearly all my camp furniture, tent, axes, and spades, and reduced my baggage to the smallest possible compass. We made pack-saddles from the spokes of an abandoned wagon, of which there were many along the road, and so carried the little we kept. Our entire party was now reduced to five men, four mules, and three horses. The rest of our original train were scattered along the route behind us.

"Though now over the Great Desert, we frequently found ourselves on smaller ones of twenty and thirty miles, destitute of all vegetation or water. A party just in advance of us showed the straits and perils of the California emigrant of those days. As we came on their nightly camping grounds, we invariably found the skeleton of a mule that they had slaughtered for meat. These sights much discouraged my men when they counted the long and weary miles before them, and estimated their scanty supply of buffalo meat and hard biscuit, now reduced to one per man a day.

"At length one of my horses gave out for want of feed. Then we were two days without food on the small sand deserts, leading our pack animals under the burning sun. On the third morning I shot two sage hens, and in the evening a mountain hare, all of which we devoured at a meal, in our encampment on Carson River. Here another horse failed us, and was left; but the mules kept up, though very weak.

"Again we made a reduction of our luggage, casting off all but our guns, a small supply of ammunition, a few articles of extra clothing, and my surveying instruments. We had now travelled about four hundred miles on foot, and were near to the end of our hard journey, though we did not know it. For our guide, Gaspero, had long since deserted us, and at that early day no one was returning from California, whom we could meet and question of our position.

"It was now the 6th of July, and we were encamped on a rivulet, but without food of any kind. Many were the plans and suggestions, at that gloomy camp fire, for the safety of the party.

"To kill a mule that was so poor he could hardly stand alone was revolting, and our last horse was not more tempting flesh. Our ignorance of our position and distances was distressing, and the desponding, hopeless feelings of the party shook not a little my own usual determination. I appealed to the love they bore for those left behind and at home to keep up courage and renew their energies. One of my men was a Frenchman by birth, and his terrors at the thought of starvation were intense. We were all lame from travel, but no one felt that he had a right to think of starvation while the horse or a mule yet lived. Our great anxiety and most oppressing thoughts were as to our location. We knew not where we were, and the Desert seemed endless.

"It was finally agreed that I should push on ahead in the morning, since the animals could not travel as rapidly as I could walk, and find relief and send it back. So, at early dawn I started, following the Carson River over a rough and barren country. At noon the oppressive heat and my own weak condition compelled me to take shelter under an oak for an hour by the trail. As I started on again, descending a hill, I met a man with a double team and wagon, loaded with supplies. Some humane Mormons, living at the base of the Nevada, on the Carson River, were expecting friends over the plains, and, fearing they might be in a starving condition, had sent out this man to meet them with supplies. His provisions consisted of salt pork and flour. He informed me that I was not more than one day from the Mormon settlement, where I could obtain all I wished to take my party through. He gave me a pound of pork and a cup of flour, and promising to relieve my men, we parted. I took the pork in my hand, and poured the flour into my hunter's pouch. Under the terrible gnawings of hunger I ate both uncooked, dipping the pork into the flour and eating as I went. The next day at noon I entered the Mormon station, and my wants were amply met. In a few days the rest of my advance party came in, and, after recruiting, we crossed together the Nevada between the 12th and 15th of July. On those heights we passed chasms yet filled with snow, probably a hundred feet deep. No further incidents of special interest occurred, and in due time we, the jaded five, slept in San Francisco."

The last night in Swan Lake camp, and the last of the Twelve Stories of The General! I think I had best not pause to tell how late our fires burned that night, and what shorter stories were told of fowl, and fish, and animals of the chase, and cosy camps nearer home than the Rocky Mountains. If we had a second supper, and every one took from the larder what game he pleased, and cooked it in his own way, it does not concern my reader so much as it did Dock in the morning, when he suggested that some of Mosby's guerrillas had made a raid on our commissary tent while we slept. Perhaps I need not speak of midnight guns mysteriously rousing our encampment, and the sound of dipping paddles and war-whoops out on the lake, as if some of the ghosts of Black Hawk's braves were back from the hunting-grounds of the blessed to be revenged on the pale faces. I think our camp was not as quiet and orderly that night in the small hours as a young ladies' boarding-school, where they all sleep to order and sneeze by rule.

The morning at length came, as it is apt to do, whatever the night may have been, and with it the teams to haul us out; and also a powerful rain storm came, I know not for what purpose. Whether for us or not I cannot tell, but we had the principal advantages of it while we packed and loaded, in its drenching and pelting. We kept the fires going and the tents standing to the last. When finally we struck them, and stepped out into the cold world, we found ourselves on equal footing, literally, with the webfeet and squatter sovereigns of the region. We came out from our camping-grounds as we went in, by land and water, though, technically speaking, we made our exit on wheels. Sleet, snow, and slosh greeted us, with the evening, at New Boston, and we greeted a supper, and in a very friendly way. The hot viands, good fires, and dry clothes made a merry company of us, and we lost no time in moody melancholy, while waiting for an up-ward-bound steamer. Late in the evening her whistle broke in on our story-telling and laughing, and again we crowded her with men and dogs, boats, tents, luggage, and game. The spoils of our raid on Swan Lake were the general centre of observation and admiration. Who can look on a large collection, variety, and fine specimens of game from prairie, woodland, and river, and not linger to inquire, and be pleased, and surprised?

As we passed the opening to Sturgeon Bay on the right, and, some time after, the low, flat belt of timber lying between us and our favorite lake, we turned wishful eyes towards the dark shore, and the grove of our encampment by the outlet of that beautiful water. It had been a kind of paradise to us, and our tent had stood by that stream somewhat as Adam and Eve's in their forest life. For we are told that "a river went out of Eden," and I suppose our first parents had their bough-house on its banks. Nor is it strange that "some natural tears they dropped" when they left it. We could sympathize with them.

A night and a morning and we were home.

Our camp life at Swan Lake was too short by at least ten days. Not that this amount of added time would have satisfied us in concluding the hunt. I know not what number of days would have served for that. At least I never saw enough at one time in any one camp. The true sportsman always wants one more shot and bite. Our time was short for The General, as he was only midway in his life stories. He had come down only to 1851, and the opening of California. The ten years following to him, some of us knew, had been full of incident and romance in frontier excursions and pioneer life.

Iowa had become a state only five years before
(1846), and he had had much to do in unfolding her
resources, and making them known at home and abroad.
The first map of Iowa Territory he published, from
personal surveys and observation, about 1845, the result
of labor, at intervals, of three years. A new edition
of this, with notes, was published in 1854, and many
were led to settle and invest in the new state from the
information it gave them; and works more recent on
Iowa have been much indebted to it for valuable facts.

From his being in the Public Surveys for so many
years, and from his personal knowledge of the state
and general land interest, he was able to do much in
settling Iowa; and he probably did more than any one
man, first and last, to bring in immigrants and locate
them.

With Scott county, his adopted home, he was inti-
mately familiar, and had written out its full and de-
tailed history, drawn from its few records, old settlers,
and his own personal knowledge. This has been published in the Historical Annals of Iowa.

Ten years of such frontier life, while the Territory
is passing into the noble State, must be full of thrilling
incidents with a man of stirring and moulding energies,
such as The General had. We greatly regretted, therefore, that we had not a few nights more, in which he could
bring us down in his narrative nearer to our own time.
He had so much to tell of the first log cabins and frame
houses, the first bridge, and church, and school-house,
the first wedding and funeral, the first corporate meetings of the people, and struggles for the county seat by
imported voters and citizens of a day. He was full of

reminiscences, too, of the ruder and rougher social life, that must accompany the pioneer's axe and breaking-up plough. There had been their early rollicking, and junketing, and merry-makings, where now are cities, and palace homes, and a graded society.

There were many incidents, too, in Indian life with which he was familiar in Iowa and its borders, in those twilight times, when the gloomy shadows of the wig-wam were giving way before the rising light of the settlement and village. His business had taken him, with the Congressional Commission, over the grounds and among the survivors of the terrible Minnesota Massacre, in which fifteen hundred whites were killed by the savages in all strange and barbarous methods. He had given to the public the most accurate and graphic account of this tragedy that has been published, and we wished much to have it from his own lips. It was just the place to tell and hear it, by that camp fire, under those grand old hickories, and on grounds where many an Indian romance had been acted out.

But our camp and narrative were broken up together, for business men made up the company, and office calls were too imperious to allow longer sporting and story-telling.

Even then The General was planning a tour of ex-ploration and trade to Idaho and Montana. For about one year before, in July, 1862, the two brothers Fair-weather had discovered gold where now stands Vir-ginia City, Montana; and by December over two thousand persons were there digging it. With his characteristic love of adventure, travel, and business,

The General headed a company for this region in the spring of 1864, the season following our Swan Lake encampment.

I can here travel out of and ahead of my sketching only to say, that this trip to Virginia City, full of novelty, peril, and enterprise, was performed by the overland route, with a private outfit of four persons, four horses, and ten mules, in one hundred and six days, the distance being sixteen hundred and fifty miles. The return was made late in the same year by stage. In 1865 he made another excursion to Idaho and Montana, by the Missouri River, a distance of over three thousand miles, on one boat, from St. Louis to Fort Benton. Of both these excursions The General took full notes — a habit with him from early life — which were published in The Boston Review for 1865 and 1866. These published Notes will interest any one who wishes to see wild life on the prairies and mountains, the Indian on his good and bad side, the buffaloes on a promenade, the grizzly without a cage, and the man who means to get a fortune, without work, by pick and spade in the Rocky Mountains.

I have made this wandering from Swan Lake to Montana, and gone two years forward from our breaking camp there, to introduce the last story of The General. While starting on his last western trip, he promised my four children A Christmas Story, written out, since he could not come on to tell it to them. The material of the promised story came to hand on this wise : —

In this excursion up the Missouri, The General, on the steamer Roanoke, passed the mouth of the Yellowstone on Bunker Hill day, 1865, and afterwards rounded to at Fort Union, five miles above. This point is twenty-two hundred and seventy-five miles above St. Louis. This is the land of the Assiniboins, a branch of the great Sioux nation. Strolling among their lodges while the boat was lying to at the levee, he gathered the incidents and details of the thrilling narrative. If my boy-readers wish to make it more like the stories of Swan Lake, and more befitting the wild scenes it describes, they had best read it some dark autumn evening by a camp fire in the back of the garden, or over the hill.

16

CHIN-CHA-PEE, THE MAID OF THE ASSINIBOINS.

"As we were strolling among the lodges of the
Assiniboins with the interpreter, a half-breed French,
whose home has always been among them, and who
very well knew the individual history of almost the
whole tribe, we tarried a moment before a more than
usually neat and tasty wigwam, varying a little in its
structure from others, and having a slight enclosure
upon one side protecting some beautiful mountain flowers in full bloom. Our guide seemed to have a little
pride in lingering, while we examined the rude but neat
little flower garden. The mountain lily, with its long
tapering leaves and slender stems, loaded with its crim-
son blossoms, seemed the most prominent of the group;
although the pine-apple cactus, with its many-tinted
colors, was beautiful, and seemed to acknowledge a care
and attention not common in savage life.

"When we turned to pursue our way, we found our
guide had strayed inside the lodge, and was engaged
in conversation with some one whose sweet, silvery
voice attracted our attention at once. We stood for a
moment at the entrance, when he invited us in, and
waving his hand towards an Indian woman, in a kind
of French salute, simply said, Chin-cha-pee.

"She was dressed in the fine, soft skins of the mountain sheep, richly embroidered with beads and the
quills of the porcupine. A double row of elk teeth,
neatly fastened to a strip of blue cloth, surrounded the

bottom of her dress, while her beautiful neck was loaded with strings of beads of many colors. In her hand she held a curiously carved stick, or paddle, the usual implement for digging the 'kamas root' or the 'pomme blanche,' a kind of prairie turnip, that grows here in great abundance, and is very nutritious for food.

" She was evidently about leaving the lodge for the purpose of procuring her vegetables for dinner. Her features were far from those common to her race; and although a tinge of sadness could be traced upon her face, yet none that beheld her could help but acknowledge that she had once been beautiful. A kind of melancholy seemed settled upon her countenance; and as we scanned her genteel form, and the neat apartment she occupied, we longed to know her history, feeling that some hidden sorrow was slowly, but surely, wasting a life at once romantic and interesting. As we bade her adieu, and were passing out, she raised her dark, piercing eyes, and fixing them fully upon us, seemed to inquire our business there, but never spoke.

" We passed on through the village, and, with the excuse of weariness, seated ourselves upon a log, under the shade of a wide-spreading cottonwood, asking the interpreter for the past history of Chin-cha-pee, the Firefly.

" The Assiniboins and Blackfeet have ever been the most bitter enemies. War parties are formed on both sides, and scarcely a year passes now that does not find them engaged in deadly strife.

" The former chief of the Assiniboins, Tchetka, the most noted leader that ever governed that tribe, was an unscrupulous, ambitious man, another Blackbird in atrocity and crime, and often resorted to poison to rid himself of his political enemies. He died by his own hand.

"His successor to the chieftainship, We-non-ga, was brave, fond of war, and ever seeking an opportunity to go against the Blackfeet, their most implacable enemy. In their annual hunt for the buffalo they often approached the hunting-grounds of the Blackfeet, at the base of the Rocky Mountains, always taking with them, on such occasions, the squaws, to cure and dress the meat and skins; as an Indian never does anything, as a hunter, but kill the game.

"It was early in September, many years ago, that We-non-ga summoned his warriors and hunters to assemble at their village at the mouth of the Yellowstone, preparatory to the fall hunt.

"One beautiful, sunny morning, after the buffalo feast had been duly celebrated by dancing and feasting, he set forth with four hundred of his choicest hunters and warriors, taking with him his only daughter, Chin-cha-pee, the Firefly, whom we saw this morning, then about eighteen years of age, the first time she had ever been permitted to leave the paternal roof, as was the custom for maidens of her age to do. The mother was left at home, and it was with many fears that she parted with her only child, well knowing the dangers to which she was exposed. She was attended by her cousin, Vi-oli-noti, Mountain Lily. She was mounted on a most beautiful cream-colored charger, her favorite steed in all her rambles over hill and prairie around her native village.

"Her boon companion was ever by her side, for she

was like a sister, and the only one she ever knew. She rode a no less spirited pony than that of Firefly, although not as beautiful, nor so richly caparisoned.

"These two maidens did not attend the expedition as laborers, nor were they expected to fill any particular position, but as daughters of the chief, beloved by all, and having due respect shown them by the whole camp. Their apartment was in the chief's lodge, which was ever guarded with double care.

"It was one of those Indian summer evenings, when the soft, hazy atmosphere settles down in sweet silence, and all nature seems sinking to rest, that the first camp was made up the valley of the Yellowstone. For long hours, by the light of the moon, did old warriors, expert hunters, young maidens, and wooing lovers, sit around their camp fires, or wander upon the banks of that sweet-flowing river, talking of the past, enjoying the present, or speculating upon the future. They were upon their own lands, and felt secure.

"Firefly and Mountain Lily sauntered arm in arm around the camp, accompanied at times by some young braves, companions of their early youth. All was glee and mirth. Unalloyed pleasure seemed to reign supreme throughout the camp of this free and happy people.

"The morning came, and with it the usual routine of camp life, to gather the vast herd of ponies, strike the encampment, pack the train, and take up the line of march. Thus, day after day, the expedition passed on, killing by the way the smaller game, the deer, the antelope, and fishing from the stream.

"After many days they reached the mouth of the

Big Horn River, intending to hunt between the Judith and the Big Horn Mountains.

"Their main camp was fixed on a little creek near the Yellowstone, in a gorge of the mountains, opening out on the broad prairie, facing the east. There was a high point of bluff in the rear of the camp, from whence could be seen the loose stock, the buffalo, or an enemy approaching, and a watch was constantly kept there during the day, as a kind of sentinel. A few days after the encampment was made, late in the evening, buffalo were seen off in the distance some two miles. All necessary preparations were made that night. The ponies were corralled, the quivers of the hunters were filled up, and the bow new strung. The sentinel descended from his lookout, and reported the probable number, the course they were travelling, and the looks of the ground over which the chase might extend.

"The chief of the hunters then assigned to each squad the position they were to occupy, the manner of attack, and to what distance the chase might extend, that parties might not get separated, and captured by the Blackfeet. The buffalo song was chanted, the Good Spirit invoked by the incantations of the prophet of the tribe, who always attends these armed hunts, then all retired, to be ready to start by the early dawn.

"Long before the clouds began to brighten in the east, the camp was full of life and activity.

"The warrior and hunter laid off his wampum, and his paint was washed from his face. Every unnecessary encumbrance was laid aside, and nothing but the knife and belt, the quiver and the bow, was to be seen about him. The simple trappings of the hunter's horse and his saddle, his bridle, and his lasso, fastened to the bow of his saddle, with his short whip hanging from his wrist by a buckskin string.

"The squaws were no less busy in preparing their pack-saddles, ropes and lariats, knives, hatchets, and sacks, to follow in the hunters' track, and commence the work of butchering as soon as game was killed.

"The party moved at daylight, separating into small bands as soon as the position of the herd was ascertained. When the attack was made from the farthest point of the drove, in order to force them towards the camp, all lay in ambush, until they should rush upon the hunter, receive a discharge of arrows, and wheel in another direction. Then all the bands met them, when in dismay the poor animals run in every direction, being enclosed in a circle by the hunters, from whom there was but little chance to escape.

"Personal combats are often entered into between a wounded bull and an unsaddled hunter.

"The rage of the wounded animal becomes terrific, and nothing but the cool courage of the Indian and his trusty bow can save him from a horrible death.

"The chase lasted some three hours, when the excited hunters, with their panting steeds, drew up in the centre of the field of action, upon a high piece of prairie, overlooking the slaughter-pen of the chase.

"A long string of pack animals was seen wending their way back to camp, loaded with meat and skins, while the prairie was spotted with slain and wounded buffalo.

"One hundred and seventy were killed this day, and their meat and skins taken to camp.

" The scene presented in camp was now all life and animation. The choice bits of the buffalo were laid aside for the feast and dance, which always follows a successful hunt. Then are all made happy.

" The old warriors and hunters preside, and their children and friends carry their precious morsels. The chief of the hunters is toasted, and he who has slain many is loaded with presents. The feast ends by setting aside an offering to the Great Spirit, which is laid upon poles outside of the lodge.

" And now follows, day after day, the dressing of hides, and drying of meat which is to furnish food for the winter months when no game can be found.

" The skins are stretched first upon the ground, with the flesh side up, and with a paddle, the end of which is full of notches, like saw teeth, the squaw cleans off all flesh and grease; and when sufficiently dried, they are strained on bars and poles, like cloth on the frames of a dyer.

" The meat is cut into thin slices, and dried in the sun; and strange as it may seem, thousands of pounds are annually preserved in this manner without the loss of a pound, and without salt.

" But to return to the story of Chin-cha-pee. While the various tribes were at the trading-post at the mouth of the Yellowstone, as was their usual custom, both friend and foe, to dispose of their furs; and before the setting out of this expedition, a party of Blackfeet, headed by a young chieftain, had determined on following the trail of We-non-ga, and, watching the opportunity, not only to steal horses and take scalps, but to capture Firefly and Mountain Lily, and bear them in triumph to the village of the Blackfeet. No opportunity, however, was presented on the route.

"They had seen the maidens often at their town, in their gay plumage, riding about the fort upon their matchless steeds, or sauntering at twilight along the banks of the river, but never so far from the protection of the fort as to allow them the attempt of capture. They therefore followed the camp of We-non-ga until near the mouth of the Big Horn, and then secreted themselves.

"At the hunting camp the maidens were cautious, and ever on the alert, well knowing the danger; but in the excitement of success, the pleasure of a life so new and full of romance, they became careless, and often forgot themselves, riding beyond reach of succor from the camp, and sometimes out of sight, unprotected and alone. Several times they followed the chase, but the sport soon became uninteresting to them.

"One day, when near the close of the hunt, and the meat sufficiently dry to pack in bundles, the skins all dressed to snowy whiteness, and the ponies fat for their return trip, the two girls were riding, as usual, up the little creek upon which they were encamped, which was skirted with timber, and without any attendant, when, seeing some uncommonly brilliant flowers upon the opposite bank, they dismounted. Tying one of their ponies, and leaving the other to graze, they crossed over upon a fallen log, and were busily engaged in gathering flowers, when five Indians rushed in between them and their horses, rendering their escape impossible. To their horror they soon discovered them to be Blackfeet.

" Lily, who was the more timid of the two, sent forth a most heart-rending scream, while Firefly stood the very image of Indian defiance and revenge. Her noble bearing for a moment riveted the intruders to the spot with awe and admiration, as she stood with arms folded, holding in one hand her gathered flowers resting on her heaving bosom.

" In a moment she recognized in the leader of the party the young Blackfoot chieftain, whom she had often seen at her home, in her rides and walks around her village. Firefly now comprehended all.

" The young chief had followed her, with a few trusty men, and she was a prisoner among the hated Blackfeet, the bitter enemy of her father and of his tribe.

" Slowly and gently the young chieftain approached her, and calling her by name, asked her to accompany him to his country and his wigwam, telling her that, although their tribes were enemies, yet peace and happiness might reign in their lodge in the mountains, in the land of the Blackfeet. He told her of his family distinctions, of their prowess in war, of the scalps his own brave hand had taken; he told of his admiration, his long pent-up love, of the days and weeks he had followed her trail to make her his own.

" Chin-cha-pee stood like a statue of marble, immovable, and not a word escaped from her half-parted lips.

" The chief motioned to his attendants, the ponies of Firefly and Lily were crossed over the creek to them, and they were mounted, an Indian leading each by the bridle up the creek, about a quarter of a mile, to where the ponies of the Indians were concealed in the bushes. All were now soon on the way. Following up the creek

THE CAPTURE OF FIREFLY AND MOUNTAIN LILY. Page 250.

to its source, and striking a dividing ridge upon the broad prairie, they followed it in a northern direction all that day. Night coming on, they encamped in a deep ravine, where the ponies could find grazing. No fires were made, as they might aid the pursuers in their course. A sort of bower was built for the girls out of some blankets, and the horses were tethered and guarded. The night passed quickly away, for it was late when the encampment was made. The chief and one of the Indians stood sentry for the night. They left with the light of day. They followed all day along this same ridge until near night, when they struck the head-waters of a creek that emptied into the Mussel-shell River, down which they travelled till late in the evening. All efforts to induce Chin-cha-pee to enter into conversation were in vain. She would not even speak to her captors. With true Indian stoicism she maintained her self-possession, and never for even once did the sound of her voice escape her lips. Once during the sleepless night did she whisper words of solace to the weeping Lily, who so keenly felt her horrible condition.

"Thus did the wearisome days and nights wear away. No hope of escape offered, although the girls were allowed to ride their own ponies, the fleetest in the party; but they were led by two Indians.

"Every day added to the distance of separation from all they loved on earth. Awful and bitter were the reflections that continually crowded in their minds; but all was covered in their own bosom. Firefly never allowed her emotions to betray the agony of her soul to her captors.

"On the tenth day, in the evening, the party arrived at the village of the Blackfeet, on Musselshell River, and the prisoners were conducted to the lodge of an aged squaw, and given into her keeping.

"The young warrior chieftain had never yet succeeded in extracting a single word from the lips of Chin-cha-pee. Lily had answered some questions for the young Blackfoot; for he could speak with fluency the language of the Assiniboins.

"But to return to the hunting camp on the Yellowstone. Deep was the sorrow and loud were the lamentations of that camp when night came and the two maidens came not with it. All night long did the agonized father and chief walk up and down the camp, heaping imprecations on the Blackfeet, and beseeching his warriors to go upon the trail with the light of the day, and as it dawned, twenty picked men, with the fleetest steeds, were in pursuit; but missing the trail at first, they had to return to the place of capture, and it was long before they were fairly on the way.

"They followed for several days, often finding signs left upon the bushes by Firefly and Lily, where they had staid over night, such as twigs broken and bark peeled from little limbs by the teeth of the girls. The sign was well understood; but to overtake them was impossible, and they returned to the camp with blackened faces, indicative of the frowns of the Great Spirit, and the deep sorrow and misfortune that had come over them.

"We-non-ga ordered an immediate return home of the whole party to the mouth of the Yellowstone, which place they reached after a march of some fifteen days.

"Quickly the news spread over the village of the capture of Chin-cha-pee and Vi-oli-noti.

"A grand council of the tribe was summoned, and all the warriors ordered upon the war-path against the Blackfeet. 'For,' said We-non-ga to his tried and faithful men, as he addressed them in council assembled, 'I have often led you to the battle-field, and lifted the scalp from the Blackfoot. We-non-ga is no coward; he never fears the foe. You see, my brave warriors, my face is painted like the burnt prairie, and my eyes are red with blood [vermilion]; but I cannot go upon the war-path now. I am overwhelmed with grief. I am broken down like a woman, and must weep; for my child, my lost Chin-cha-pee, and her whom I love next, are prisoners in the village of the Blackfeet. The light of my wigwam has gone out. I sit in darkness. The Great Spirit turns away his face. O, my brave warriors, bring to my deserted lodge Chin-cha-pee and the Lily of the Mountain, and make my heart glad, before I go to the good hunting-ground, to the island of the blest. The Great Spirit will guide you on the trail, and the war-song of my people shall be sung each night as the sun goes down behind the dark hills beyond the prairie. I have spoken.'

"It is customary, on every occasion of a grand council, for all young braves, and others who may be entitled, to present themselves for service in the war-party. Some brave act is necessary to insure admittance, unless it be by some special permission of council.

"Among the youths that were candidates for admission was a young brave by the name of Ta-to-kah-nan, The Antelope. He was the companion of Firefly and

Lily in all their juvenile sports in earlier days; was in
the expedition when the girls were captured, and felt
most keenly the sad event, particularly as he had a
special interest in the safe return of Firefly.

"He had never distinguished himself sufficiently to
entitle him to the war-path; but being the son of a
brave, active, energetic, and a good marksman, his ap-
plication was received, and he was placed upon the list
to give him a chance to show his bravery. And he
longed for some opportunity to carry trophies of victory,
and lay them at the feet of Firefly, the chieftain's
daughter.

"The feast and the war dance were celebrated. The
prophet and medicine men of the tribe had consulted
the tutelary spirits, and early one morning, late in
October, the war-whoop was sounded, and five hundred Assiniboin warriors, mounted on their best
horses, left the village for the home of the Blackfeet,
on Musselshell River, more than five hundred miles
distant. The command of the expedition, in the absence of We-non-ga, was intrusted to the second
chieftain of the tribe, Wa-to-me-ka, He that runs fast.
Striking up the dividing ridge between the waters of
the Yellowstone and the Missouri, they travelled late
and early, until they reached the land of the Blackfeet,
when, by slow and cautious marches at night, they
came within about thirty miles of their village. Here
they secreted themselves in a little valley, surrounded
by hills, and sent forth spies to the camp of the enemy.
Among this number was young Ta-to-kah-nan. They
travelled in the darkness of the night, and secreted
themselves by day. The village of the Blackfeet was

situated on the banks of the river, having a kind of amphitheatre of prairie hills on the north and east, some of which ranged near to the village. Over one of these hills was a ravine with a cluster of trees and thick underbrush, a kind of an oblong grove, running to a point as it came up towards the summit.

"In this point of timber, Ta-to-kah-nan secreted himself, from which he could at all times crawl to the brow of the hill unobserved, and get a complete view of the village.

"The spies had met with but one small camp of the Blackfeet, and this was but a few miles from their village. In the dead of night, they crawled upon them, and each to his man; they slew them all, five in number. Ta-to-kah-nan in triumph slung his scalp in his girdle, and the next morning found him in the point of timber above described, with his war-horse by him screened from view, in a dense thicket of bushes.

"As the sun rose he crawled from his hiding-place to the top of the bluff, and in the course of a few hours he saw the well-known ponies of Firefly and Lily led round to the door of a lodge, standing on one side of the town, by a tall young Indian, who held another horse by the bridle line. Soon came forth the two maidens, and, stepping upon a log, bounded into the saddle for their morning ride, attended by only one Indian.

"They took their course at first up the banks of the river, stopping at times to watch the wild goose or the duck, as they sailed upon the placid waters, or view the chattering squirrel (ad-je-do-mo) as he sat upon the limbs of his native forest; but with a bend of the river into the dense forest, they turned their course towards the hill where the young spy lay. In a moment he withdrew to his hiding-place, and awaited events with a beating heart.

"On gaining the summit of the ridge the party halted, as if to enjoy the autumnal breeze and view the seared leaves of approaching winter, as well as to select their course to pursue still farther their ride.

"The first thought of Antelope was to send an arrow through the heart of the attendant, and flee with the maidens to the camp; but the other spies were not in, and would be taken. They were all to meet that night at a spot agreed upon, and report their discoveries.

"They all started down the hill towards the point of timber, Firefly being behind, as she had stopped to look at some flowers of rare beauty. The first two passed the point. In a moment Ta-to-kah-nan advanced from the bush and discovered himself to Firefly, unseen by the others, making the sign of silence, and pronouncing her name in a loud whisper. Firefly started, while a half-smothered shriek escaped her lips. Her quick perception and keen Indian cunning told her all. Assuming to see something interesting, she advanced to the edge of the thicket, and the young brave, crouched in the brush, told her of the warriors sent by her father, the course of their camp, and the plans laid for her escape. She advised him to call in the scouts, and return to the camp of the warriors; and the next morning, at the same hour, she and Lily would be there prepared for escape, while he so disposed of the troops as to cut off pursuit from the village.

"Firefly soon joined her party, and, although excited, managed to escape the notice of the attendant.

She changed her course, and by a circuitous route soon returned to the village, to give Antelope an opportunity for arranging things for the morrow.

"O, how did the heart of Firefly bound within her, and leap for joy at the prospect of deliverance. She longed for a secret moment to tell Lily all, the sweet prospects of home and friends, and as soon as they arrived, and the attendant was discharged, they sought the little bower that had been built for them in front of the lodge. Here, in an excited state of mind, did Chin-cha-pee unfold the plan to Vi-oli-noti, telling her of the hurried interview with Ta-to-kah-nan, of his true devotedness to their cause, of his daring and bravery in venturing almost into the very camp of the enemy, of the scalp that hung from his belt, and of her love for him. Lily seemed ready to scream for joy. They wept in silence, and thanked the Great Spirit for his goodness to them. Soon the bright eyes were dried, and the all-absorbing thoughts of escape, of home, father, mother, friends, were uppermost in their minds. The two maidens lay locked in each other's arms that night. Sleep forsook them, and with the dawn they rose, full of hope and fear.

"The young warrior chieftain, as was his custom, passed round their lodge, tarried a moment, and, with winning smiles, tried to engage them in some conversation; but Firefly, as yet, had never spoken to him. She could but admire his magnanimity, his nobleness of heart, his kind indulgence during all their imprisonment; for not the slightest indignity had ever been offered them, and every facility for enjoyment granted that they desired. They walked, they rode, and rambled,

17

and were never separated. At night the old sentinel fastened the door of their lodge, and slept at its threshold.

"What would not the warrior chieftain have given to gain fully the affections of one so lovely, so pure, so noble in character, and exalted in birth, so beautiful in form and feature! He loved to see her, the admired of all, mounted on her splendid charger. He was as fleet as the deer, and never did woman sit upon a horse with more grace and beauty. No horse in the whole Blackfoot camp could outrun him, or that of Lily, who also was a good rider, having been long taught by Firefly.

"Ta-to-kah-nan was soon joined by the other spies, and all returned to the camp of the warriors. Antelope was now entitled to rank. He had slain an enemy. The scalp of a Blackfoot hung from his belt, dripping with blood, and he was no longer to follow, but to lead, upon the trail of an enemy.

"The camp was aroused; the report of the spies heard in council, and that night Ta-to-kah-nan led the armed warriors to the field of battle.

"It was arranged so that a protecting force should be in readiness to cover the flying retreat of the maidens, but in such a manner as to draw the enemy into a pitched battle.

"The several squads of braves were placed around the hills, while the main body was posted in a valley surrounded with hills, in such a manner as not to be seen until fairly entrapped for battle.

"Ta-to-kah-nan alone awaited the arrival of the girls at the place appointed. Hours, and even minutes, seemed days to him, as he sat concealed, watching with eager eye the summit of that little hill over which the maidens were to come.   How did he watch the waving of each bush and twig that obscured his sight! and with what breathless anxiety did he long for the moment when Firefly should give the signal for flight!

"At last they came, Lily in the lead, the attendant by her side, and Firefly lingering in the rear.   She saw Antelope for a moment, and received from him a token of assurance.   In another moment a wild scream burst from her lips, and her bounding steed flew past Lily, whose animal had now caught the alarm, and seemed to skim the ground like a bird.   The attendant, dumb-founded and speechless, seeing an Assiniboin warrior in close pursuit, turned, and fled to the top of the hill, gave the alarm, and soon the whole village was in wild commotion.   Warriors were at once mounted, and in full pursuit.

"Ta-to-kah-nan, with the captives, had rested upon the top of a hill, as if in defiance of their enemy, but in reality to draw them into the camp of the Assini-boin warriors.

"The war-whoop of the Blackfeet now rang through the village, and little squads of horsemen were seen leaving in all directions.

"While Antelope and the maidens sat watching the scene with anxiety, a company of twelve Indians rushed upon them from behind a knoll — a point they had gained unobserved by the captives — and now began the chase for life and death.   The young warrior chief-tain led the band, and with the most deafening whoops and yells, on they came, but without gaining an inch upon their prey.

"The race now became wild as the wind. Over hill and dale, across ravine and prairie, did Firefly lead the yelling enemy, with Lily close behind her, and Antelope by her side. All pressed their noble steeds to their greatest capacity.

"The Blackfeet, in desperation, strained every nerve, until, rising a sharp ridge, the Assiniboin camp lies before them! A yell of triumph arose from the assembled warriors, all mounted, and 'Chin-cha-pee! Chin-cha-pee! Vi-oli-noti!' is sounded through the camp. But on came the pursued and the pursuers. Firefly, with hands lifted, imploring the aid of the Great Spirit, half raised in her saddle, her long, glossy hair floating in the breeze, and the lines of her horse flung across his neck, looked more the picture of an unearthly being than the mute and silent Firefly! She gave an anxious, imploring look behind for the safety of those she loved, and patting her faithful horse, a few more bounds brought her into camp, and she sprang from her cream-colored pony into the arms of her friends.

"The pursuing Blackfeet saw the stratagem, and turned to flee; but it was too late. They were surrounded, led to the centre of the camp, and a strong guard placed over them.

"Short was the rejoicing over the lost maidens now, for on came the Blackfeet with most desperate fury, shouting their terrific war-cry, the *sassiskivi* of the tribe. Burning to avenge so daring an outrage upon their village, they rushed forward with great impetuosity from every hill, and from behind every nook. But the Assiniboins were ready for them. They had formed in a circle, having the captured maidens and the Blackfeet prisoners in the centre.   The scouts had now all come in, and the battle became general.   Chin-cha-pee, mounted on her foaming steed, with the 'to-tem' of her tribe floating over her head, rode round the circle with Vi-oli-noti by her side, shouting the war-cry of her people, and in the thickest of the fight urging the warriors to desperate conflict.   The repeat-ed and fearful charges of the Blackfeet drove the Ansiniboins into closer quarters.

"Chieftain and brave alike fought with desperation, all lashing themselves to their horses, that in case of death their bodies would be carried from the battle-field, and their scalps saved from their enemies.   At every charge they were repulsed, and the enemy fell like buffalo before the arrows of the Sioux.

"The battle continued for more than two hours. Many a Blackfoot had bit the dust, and many of the Assiniboins had also gone upon the trail to the good hunting-grounds.

"Night came on; the battle began to wane.   The Blackfeet seemed determined on one more desperate charge, before giving up the contest; and, rallying in solid column, they came down with almost resistless fury, striving to break the ranks of the Assiniboins, first discharging their arrows, and then with knife and tomahawk seeking a hand-to-hand conflict.   The carnage was dreadful.   Horse and rider rolled alike in the dust, while many a steed bore away the bleeding, lifeless corpse of his master from the field of battle.

"The Blackfeet now turned and fled in dismay, with the Assiniboins close in pursuit, following them even to the outskirts of their village.   Eighty-five of their number were slain, and upwards of twenty of the Assiniboins. Among the latter was the young, the brave, and noble Ta-to-kah-nan, the protector, preserver, and lover of the beautiful Chin-cha-pee, the Firefly. Her grief was inconsolable. She wept in bitter anguish as she remembered the self-sacrificing spirit of the noble youth, in his recent success, for he had slain many in the action, and was in the thickest fight. With him were buried all her future hopes, and from that day a settled melancholy fixed its indelible stamp upon her dusky brow.

"All that long night there was mourning in the camp of the Assiniboins for the brave dead.

"Morning came, and after burying their dead and securing the scalps of the enemy, they started on their return home, taking with them the prisoners, whom it was usual to put to death on the evening after the battle, when the scalp-dance is performed; but this was deferred for the night of the first encampment, when four were tortured to death, and on the arrival of the party upon their own lands, four more were led to execution. The other four, among whom was the warrior chieftain, were to be kept until the arrival of the party at their village, when all could join in the sacrifice and dance.

"Chin-cha-pee had watched with earnest care the victims brought forth for sacrifice, intending to interfere in behalf of her captor, the young chieftain, when his turn came for the torture.

"The last camping-place was at length reached, on the banks of the Yellowstone; and on the morrow the grand entry was to be made into the village of the Assiniboins, with the trophies of victory borne by the victors.

"A halt was called a mile from the town, and the procession formed. First came the chief appointed by We-non-ga to lead the expedition, and by his side rode the prophet and medicine men of the tribe. Then came Chin-cha-pee and Vi-oli-noti, upon the same ponies they rode away weeks before, bearing the totem of the tribe, as the daughter of the chieftain. Then came the warriors in great triumph, followed by the scalps taken in the expedition, closed up by a long train of pack animals, the poor, lame, and wounded of the party.

"When the procession reached the chief's lodge, there was a halt, and one wild cry of joy went up from the gathered multitude, and 'Chin-cha-pee! Chin-cha-pee! Vi-oli-noti! Vi-oli-noti!' rang throughout the vast assembly, as the aged chieftain clasped his long-lost daughter to his bosom.

"Long and silently did he weep over her whom he thought lost. No word was spoken, nor was there any wild outburst of affection, but that still and silent joy for her return, and deep sorrow for the loss of him whom she loved, for Chin-cha-pee had whispered her lover's death in her father's ear.

"There was another scene for Firefly to go through. Her mother was absent from the village at the time of the arrival, and hearing of the return of the war party, she hastened to her lodge, and with deep emotion, forcing her way through the dense crowd, found Firefly leaning upon the bosom of We-non-ga. A moment, and the mother and daughter were locked in each other's arms, amid the cries and shouts of the tribe, and with sobbing and tears sank to the earth.

"While this scene was going on at the lodge of the chief, the village crier had summoned the grand council, and the prisoners were before them. The closing scenes of the great drama were fast coming to an end. The grand scalp-dance was already begun, and one of the prisoners had been chopped in pieces, when Chin-cha-pee and Vi-oli-noti came in and stood before them. Their wild joy for a moment ceased. The young Blackfoot stood bound, chanting his death song, when, on raising his eyes for the last time on his enemies, his mild but piercing eye rested on Firefly, who had taken her place beside her father, near to the stake of execution.

"No pleading look from him seemed to ask for mercy. For a moment his haughty nature seemed to scan the pitying look of Chin-cha-pee, but her piercing glance sank like an arrow deep into his heart, and he felt the wrong he had done her, the bitter anguish he had caused her.

"Firefly now stood forth, and, addressing her father, said, 'This is the young chieftain of the Blackfeet. He was my captor. He is the son of a great chief, although our enemy. His hand has taken the scalps of our people. But his heart is big, noble, and good. He ever guarded with honorable and jealous care Chin-cha-pee and Vi-oli-noti, while prisoners in his camp. His good heart ever fed us with the choicest morsels of the deer and the antelope, and all our wishes were granted when in his lodge. To his kind indulgence are we indebted for our escape and restoration to your arms. Pardon him, my father! The Good Spirit whispers me for his return to his tribe, that he may tell how honor, and principle, and justice can be rewarded, even by an enemy.'

"The aged chieftain, We-non-ga, ordered the thongs cut from his arms and legs, his pouch filled with buffalo meat, and set upon his own horse with a safe guide until he reached the land of the Blackfeet. But Chin-cha-pee never spoke to the young warrior chieftain of the Blackfeet.

"We-non-ga, and the aged Wah-to-mee-ka, his wife, have long been laid away in the 'Village of the Dead,' at Fort Union.

"Firefly and Mountain Lily, at the death of the Chief, took the neat little lodge where we saw Firefly this morning, but Vi-oli-noti was no more. She had fallen a victim to that scourge of the Indian, the small-pox, with thousands of others, and her spirit had been wafted to the banks of that river where the flowers bloom forever and the Blackfeet never come.

"Chin-cha-pee could never forget Ta-to-kah-nan. His memory fastened strongly and closely to her heart, and although many a noble chieftain had sought her hand, she ever refused, since she had no heart to give with it. Her beauty has faded; sorrow has tinged her once fair brow, but the light of her eye is yet undimmed."

In Memoriam.

IT was on the opening Sabbath of 1868 that this life
of honorable labor and varied incidents ended, and
the weary feet of The General rested from their travels.
He had indulged his youthful wish in seeing the wild
nature of his native land in her wildest dress. He had
laid out ample fields for agriculture, surveyed the channels and thoroughfares for the wealthiest inland commerce, run the boundaries for new states, and aided to
found their cities. Educational, humane, and religious
organizations shared in their beginnings in the energies
of his mind, and the warmth of his heart, and the lib-
erality of his hand. Society felt the sunshine and the
glow of his private life. So was the great purpose of
his boyhood realized in the achievement of a truly
noble life, in which the mental, and social, and Christian
honorably obscured the mercenary.

His grave overlooks the land he loved so well, and
led so many others to know and adorn. "Oak Dale"
looks down on the beautiful city of his adoption and
nurture, and over the broad river that was his pride
and glory, and out upon the vast, billowy prairies,
where his were the first compass and chain, and corner

bounds for the immigrant. This region he selected for a home, as the crowning beauty of all the wide lands he had traversed; and fitting it was that his final resting-place should have an outlook over the beautiful panorama. Native oaks stand sentinel about his monument, and the delicate prairie flowers spring at his feet, as in tender memory of an early friend who found them in their wild homes.

IIis final rest is where he prepared for it by enclosure and monument, and in the manner of being laid in it his wish was gratified. For at the first festival of The Pioneer Settlers' Association of Scott County, Iowa, in 1858, he said, in closing an address, "Thy people shall be my people, and thy God my God; where thou diest will I die, and there will I be buried. And when I shall have gone to

> ' The undiscovered country, from whose bourn
> No traveller returns,'

the greatest boon I can ask is, that my grave may be surrounded by the Pioneer Settlers' Association of Scott County."

His desire was sacredly regarded, and they sorrowfully gathered about his grave, and tenderly placed in it all the mortal that remained of

WILLARD BARROWS.

www.ingramcontent.com/pod-product-compliance
Lightning Source LLC
Chambersburg PA
CBHW031334070726
47496CB00018B/1857